VALENSHEK

FORGERY

TATE JAMES

Tate James

Forgery: Valenshek Legacy #2

Copyright © Tate James 2023
All rights reserved
First published in 2023
James, Tate
Forgery: Valenshek Legacy #2

No part of this book may be reproduced, stored in a retrieval system or transmitted in any form or by any means, without the prior permission in writing of the publisher, nor be otherwise circulated in any form of binding or cover other than that in which it is published and without a similar condition, including this condition, being imposed on the subsequent purchaser. All characters in this publication other than those clearly in the public domain are fictitious, and any resemblance to real persons, living or dead, is purely coincidental.
Cover design: Tamara Kokic
Photographer: Lanefotograf
Models: David and Isabelle
Editing: Heather Long (content) and Dolly Jackson (line).

For Heather Hardass Long and No Pants Katie... without whom this book never would have been written. I could be working at Bunnings right now but nope... finished another book instead. Yay.

PREVIOUSLY IN
THE VALENSHEK LEGACY...

ILLUSTRATIONS BY JOANNA HADZHIEVA

THIS PAINTING SUCKS ASS
HE'S THE PROFESSOR?!
HEY TRIS, WANNA FUCK?
DEX
OH, SHIT!

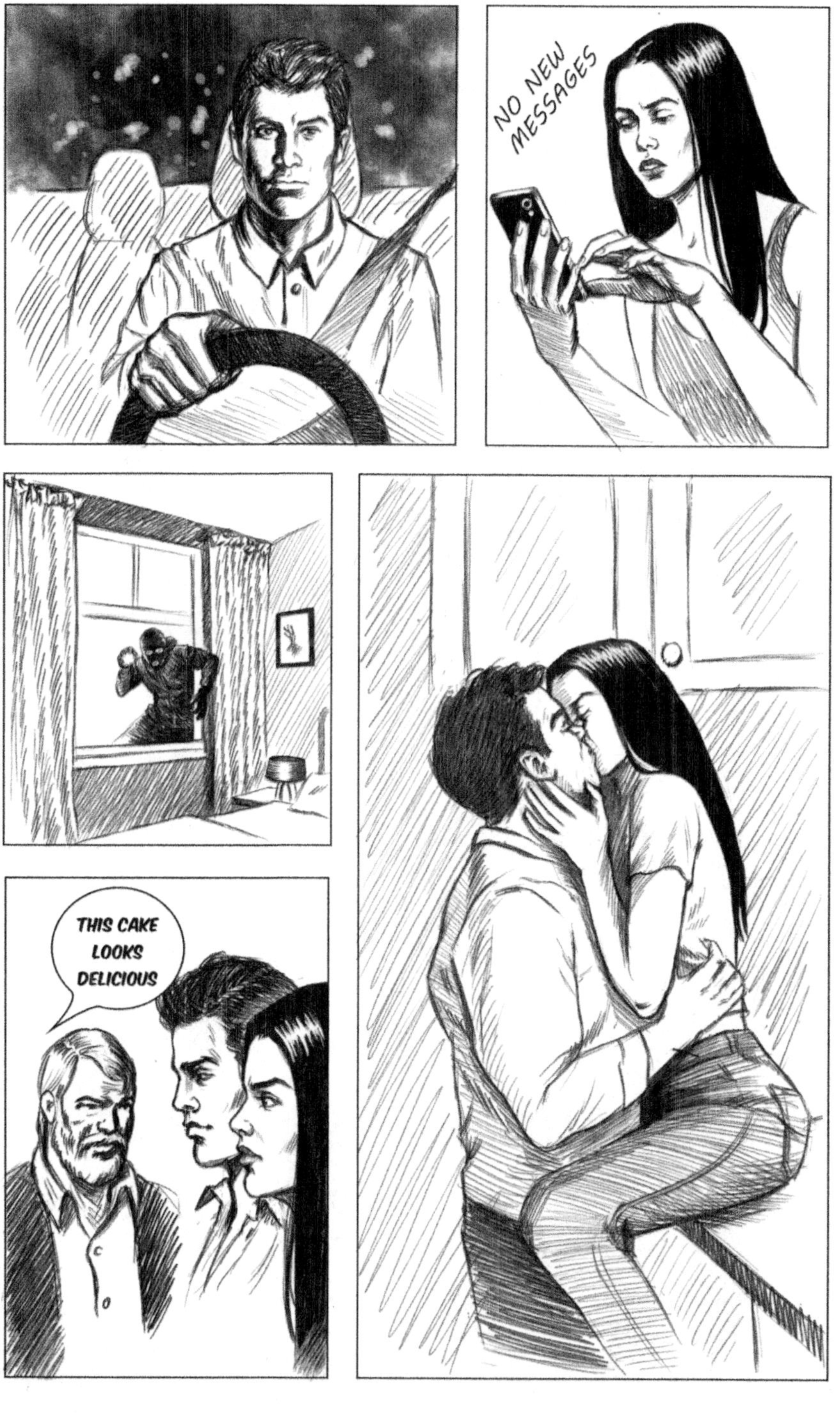
NO NEW MESSAGES
THIS CAKE LOOKS DELICIOUS

The Slippery Lips

BUT I'M HORNY, DAD

DON'T TOUCH TRISTIAN AGAIN!

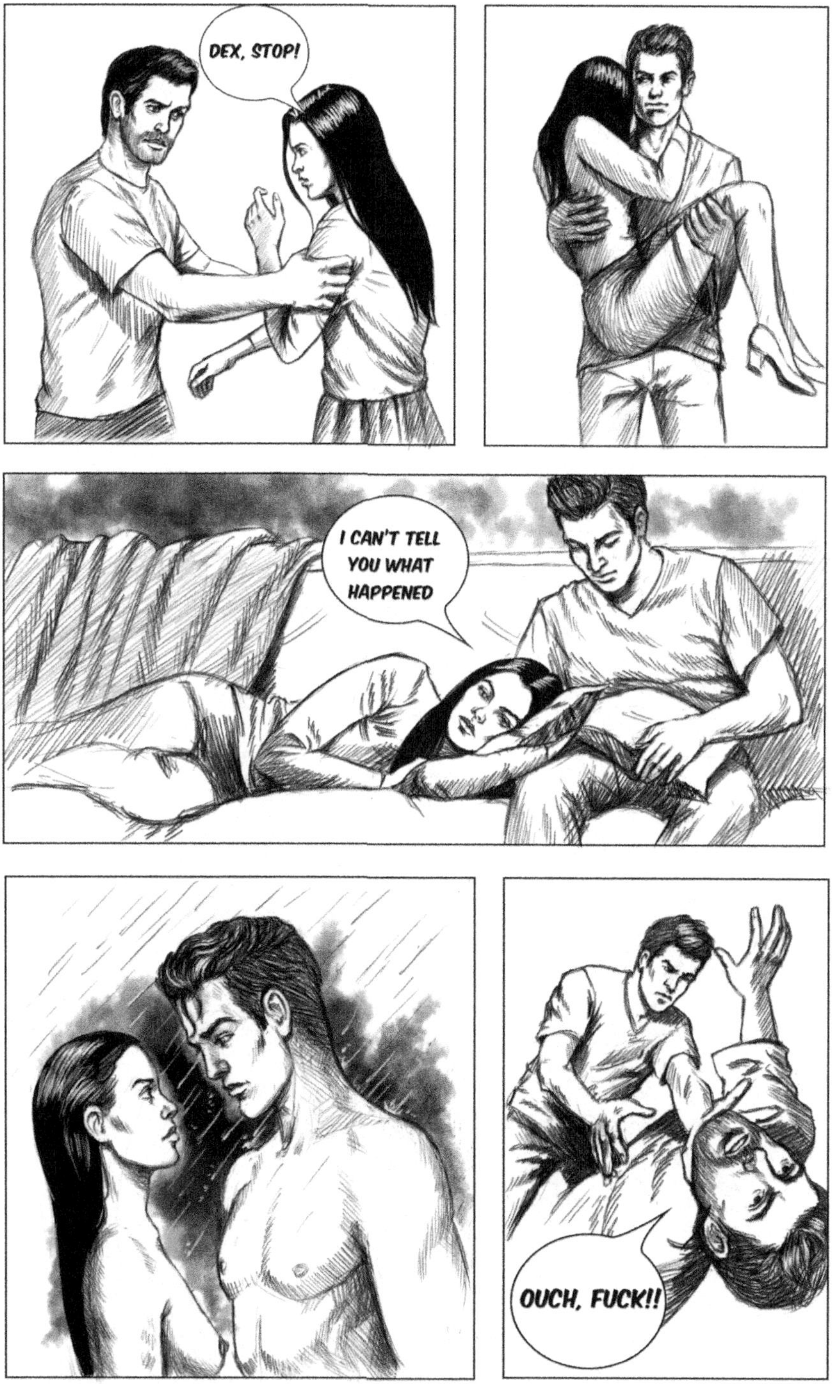
DEX, STOP!
I CAN'T TELL YOU WHAT HAPPENED
OUCH, FUCK!!

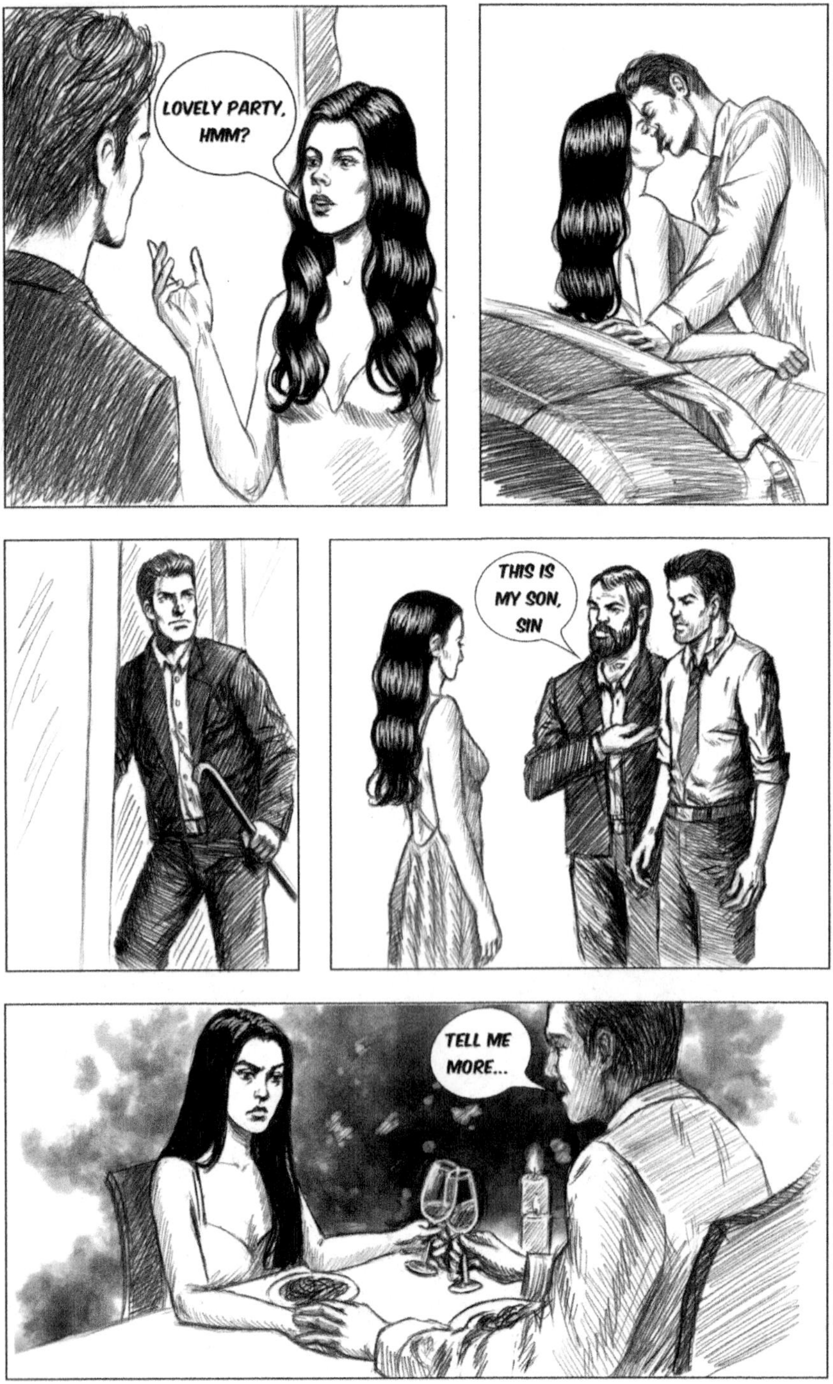
LOVELY PARTY, HMM?
THIS IS MY SON, SIN
TELL ME MORE...

WHERE THE FUCK ARE ALL MY VIBRATORS?!
FORGET HIM, HE'S A CUNT
ART THIEF RELEASED!
Ding Dong
OH, SHIT! I'M DEAD.

FORGERY

VALENSHEK LEGACY #2

TATE JAMES

Tris

one

Breakups sucked. Like, they really sucked. But they were just a shitty byproduct of love and relationships, right? And anyone willing to put themselves and their heart on the line enough to really *feel* something, risked being hurt. Right? I wouldn't know, because I'd never let myself be that vulnerable with a romantic partner before. I'd never let my walls down enough to really be hurt by a breakup.

Until now.

John's betrayal cut me open and left me bleeding. His betrayal was so much more than just a relationship breakdown, because he'd left me standing in front of a firing squad to take the bullets for him. All the while, he skipped off into the sunset with that fucking painting.

The cold realization that he'd been playing me from day one—that I was nothing more than a mark for him, a means to an end and a convenient scapegoat at that—hurt more than just a breakup.

So yeah, I was feeling pretty fucking sorry for myself. I didn't want or need company, but Katinka didn't really give me the option to say *no* when she showed up on my doorstep with a big bag of Royal Orchid Chinese take-out, and an even bigger shoulder to cry on.

Then I'd seen that fucking news report and panic spiraled.

"Alleged art thief released by authorities after priceless Van Gogh was found to be a forgery," Katinka read aloud from the TV screen while my breathing turned shallow. "Wait, is that the one stolen from the Grimaldis?"

Panic didn't even begin to describe where my head was at. My whole body broke out in cold sweat, and a thousand worst-case scenarios flashed through my mind in a fucking *instant*. Trembles shook my hands as I reached for my phone and dialed Nelson. He was more than just my neighbor and father figure; he was also my best friend and partner in crime.

My pulse rushed in my ears as I tried to catch him

up to speed. "Nelson...he got arrested by the FBI Art Crimes Division. They *arrested* him...and he was just released."

We hadn't banked on this. My forgeries were impeccable, some of the very best and utterly impossible to be recognized as fakes to the naked eye. Hell, not even under the magnifying glass of a routine inspection. But Art Crimes was a different beast, one I couldn't fool. They'd put paintings up to tests that could—and would—confirm or reject authenticity.

Nelson said something, but I couldn't hear anything outside of the ringing in my ears. My phone dropped into my lap. I was so fucked. *We* were so fucked. Because if Art Crimes had confirmed the painting John stole was a forgery, then he also knew he'd been duped. And it'd only be a matter of time before Mr. Grimaldi was told... which would then beg the question why *I*—as his restoration expert—didn't know it was a fake.

Obviously I did. My employer wasn't an idiot; he'd know I'd been the one to switch his authentic Van Gogh with a forgery. The only question would be what he'd do to me now. Would he shoot me? Clean and simple, get it over with?

Katinka was staring at me with confusion, but I couldn't find the words to explain it all to her. How the hell did I tell my new friend that I'd dedicated my life to being a fake? To perfecting forgeries of countless masters, and swapping them for the originals with no one any the wiser. No harm done, until someone was *stupid* enough to be picked up by Art Crimes of all fucking departments.

What an *idiot*. Was John some kind of fucking amateur? That'd be just my luck, having one of my latest forgeries, one that Nelson had only *just* switched for the original, stolen by a dumbass wannabe cat burglar who couldn't even cover his tracks after the theft.

"Tris, what's going on?" Katinka asked, clearly puzzled at my panic attack. I didn't blame her, but I also had no words to answer.

Then my intercom doorbell buzzed.

Oh fuck. Was it Mr. Grimaldi coming to gut me for stealing from him? Or John, freshly released from custody and on a warpath for letting him steal a forgery? Or someone else entirely? None of the options were good.

I didn't move. I couldn't.

The intercom buzzed again, and nausea rolled through me.

"Do you want me to get that?" Katinka asked, rising out of her seat.

"No!" I exclaimed, shooting my feet. My phone hit the floor—probably breaking—and I knocked over a box of shrimp fried rice on the coffee table. *Fuck*. I wet my lips, my breathing harsh as I looked to the door in horror. Nelson wasn't even home, but that was a good thing, right? It meant that he wouldn't get swept up in my mess.

Yeah. That had to be my focus. Keeping Nelson and Hank's hands clean. It was too late for me, my fingerprints were all over this theft, but they didn't need to suffer with me. But that meant I needed to take the full blame, and take it quick before the old goats decided to do it for me.

"Tris, babe, what is *going on*?" Katinka reached out to touch my arm, her expression creased in deep concern. "You're freaking me out. Just talk to me."

I shook my head, my mind made up. "It's fine, I'm fine. I just... I think my luck has finally run out."

The doorbell buzzed again, and I forced my feet to move. Hey, maybe I was totally wrong and it was just a delivery or... something. Maybe I ordered more wine and forgot about it?

"What does that mean, Tris?" Katinka pushed, following me as I reluctantly crossed the floor to answer my doorbell. "Are you in some kind of trouble? Whatever it is, I can help. Just tell me what happened."

It was such a sweet offer, but this wasn't just a simple boy-trouble issue. It wasn't even a money issue. I'd been walking a dangerous line for a long time, and really this day had been coming since the moment Nelson started teaching me the art of forgery for my twelfth birthday.

"I wish you could," I groaned, sweat rolling down my spine. "You have no freaking idea how much I wish this was something you—or anyone—could fix."

Before I could chicken out, I pressed the *answer* button on my doorbell intercom. The video screen lit up and I held my breath, desperately clinging to the hope that I'd see a delivery driver. My heart sank right out of my chest, though, when I recognized one of Mr. Grimaldi's men glaring back at me.

"Hi," I squeaked.

"Miss Ives," the man snapped. I couldn't remember his name, or maybe I never knew it, but he was one I often saw involved in violence at the manor. "Come downstairs, please."

My chest was so tight it felt like I couldn't breathe. "Um, I can't right now. I'm naked."

"What the fuck?" Katinka whispered, bewildered, and I just gave her a *I don't fucking know* shrug.

"Miss Ives," the Grimaldi goon barked again. "I'll make this simple. You come downstairs and accompany me back to the manor, or I will come inside and shoot one of your neighbors. You have five minutes to decide."

I watched on the video screen as the goon stepped away from the doorbell camera, then paused to speak with my elderly neighbor from downstairs, Mrs. Bordeaux. Shit. She was such a nice old lady and brought me gingerbread cookies at Christmas.

"Oh fuck," I groaned, wringing my hands. Nelson was already on his way home, too. Either I womaned up and faced my own mistakes, or there would be collateral damage and I'd *still* have to face up. Fucking hell, this part of being an adult sucked so hard.

"Tris, you're scaring me," Katinka stated, picking up her phone. "I'm going to call Sin."

I nodded my head like one of those bobbly dogs. "Yeah. Call Sin. But I'll probably see him at RBD's anyway so probably don't bother. Or do, whatever. Won't make a difference. Fuck. I'm fucked. Ummmmm, okay. Come on Tris, be a big girl."

"Babe, talk to me!" Katinka snapped, coming over to shake my shoulder. "You look like you're short circuiting. Whatever happened, whatever you did... it can't be that bad. We can work it out."

Oh geez, if only I'd met her at another stage of life, we could have been really good friends. I knew it. But... wrong time, wrong place.

"I just..." I raked my shaking hand through my hair and winced at a snag. Time was ticking, though, and I couldn't keep stalling. "I've gotta deal with something at work. Thank you for coming over to check on me. I appreciate it. Just, um, lock up when you leave." I mumbled that last bit, my hand already on the door.

"Tris, wait!" Katinka exclaimed, but I was out of time. I left my apartment in a daze, striding past Nelson and Hank's apartment without looking at it, my focus on the elevator. If Mrs. Bordeaux got shot because I was dithering, I'd never forgive myself.

I swallowed hard as I pressed the call button. "I'm fine, Katinka. I'm just... probably getting fired. Sorry for, um, freaking you out. I'm fine. It'll be fine. So fine." I was rambling, but like... whatever. The elevator doors opened and I jumped in before I could chicken out.

The doors closed behind me, and by the time I reached the lobby I was on the edge of hyperventilating.

I almost talked myself into slipping out the back door and running a dozen times, but if I didn't take the heat, Nelson would. And I'd do anything to save that old badger. So I forced my feet to move, putting one foot before the other until I reached the blacked out town car sitting outside my building. Goon dude stood beside it with a deep scowl on his face and no attempt to hide his gun.

"Wise choice, Miss Ives," he grunted, opening the back door. "Get in."

I nodded, then did as I was told, sliding into the back seat with my jaw clenched.

And I thought the breakup had been the worst ever before.

John

two

My strides ate up the small room as I paced back and forth, trying to make sense of what I'd just been told. Not only had the FBI *released* Igor the previous day, it was done on *lack of evidence*. Because *Poppy Flowers*—the Van Gogh I'd spent fucking months tracking down and stealing—was a forgery.

"How?" I demanded, my fists balled at my sides. "How is this even possible?"

The Special Agent in charge of the Art Crimes division, Davis Waterstone, just arched a bored eyebrow in my direction. "It's more common than you think. These criminal types buy a painting at black market auction, their people verify the original, then the auction house makes a switch. Smart collectors would wait until they had possession to verify authenticity but... most criminals are dumb."

I shook my head. "Not this one." Luther Grimaldi was far from an idiot, nor was he complacent enough to take the word of an auction house. Not to mention *Tris*. Fuck, that sneaky little... "Are you *sure*?"

Davis sighed, annoyed at me now. "Yes, I'm sure. The paint analysis doesn't lie. You should know that." There was an edge to his statement that made me narrow my eyes.

"What's that supposed to mean?" I glowered, folding my arms.

He shrugged. "Just that the rumors about you must be grossly exaggerated if you couldn't tell a fake from an original. You're this mythical boogeyman in the Art Crimes world and you've probably stolen dozens of forgeries and never even known."

Anger blistered through my flesh and my jaw clenched so hard it hurt. Or maybe that was because of the heavy layer of bruises left by Igor's ambush the night I left Whispering Willows. Fucker nearly killed me, which was in strict violation of the Game rules. Not that I'd go tattling to the committee, since I'd hit him back by calling Constance D'Ath and leaning on her Art Crimes contact to have my father arrested. My plan had been to steal the painting back out of evidence, but lo and behold, it was a motherfucking forgery.

"This one was flawless," I growled, trying to fight the urge to feel impressed. I'd *never* been so thoroughly fooled by a replica. Ever. If I wasn't the one being ripped off, I'd be doing everything possible to put that woman on permanent retainer. The possibilities of what we could do together nearly made my dick hard.

Davis grunted, nodding. "You're right about that. Can't fool science, though. I'd love to get my hands on whoever made this forgery... I'd bet my house this isn't the first master they've duplicated."

So would I. Tristian... the little mystery.

"Sorry, can't help you there," I lied. I wasn't *positive* it'd been Tris who made the swap, but my gut told me she was responsible. Even if I was one hundred percent sure, though, I wouldn't be giving her up to Art Crimes. No way in hell. She was all mine.

Except, she wasn't. I'd made my choice when I left her and took that painting, leaving her to deal with the fallout. She *knew* that was me, and that I'd dropped her like a hot rock. I couldn't just swan back into her life like nothing had happened, so I'd have to satisfy myself with—hopefully—building a professional, mutually beneficial relationship.

"Anything else I can help you with while you're

here, Hermes?" David asked with a curious look. "I have to admit, when Con told me she needed a favor, I never thought I'd have one of our most wanted in the office."

I huffed a short laugh. "Well, let's keep that between us. I appreciate the assistance."

Davis nodded, turning his attention back to his computer screen. "Righto. Leave the way you came in, and I never saw you here."

My skin was itching just from being inside the FBI office, so I wasted no time slipping back out through the air conditioning vents—preventing my image being captured on CCTV—and winced at how tight the squeeze was. What I would give to be Tink's size for shit like this.

Once I was free of the building, I made my way back to my accommodation at a nearby hotel. I'd been staying there for a few days, since Igor's guys had jumped me, but now that he'd been released and the painting was in the wind, I'd need to reassess my plans.

The Game was still in play.

I wondered if Tink knew, or if she'd skipped town the minute she saw me escaping into the night with the painting in tow. Obviously Igor knew, and he wasn't playing by the rules. Damn it. Why'd he have to be in the final round? He wasn't remotely good enough to have beaten the other competitors. If I were to put money on it, I'd say he'd dabbled in a heavy amount of sabotage.

My room was on the seventeenth floor of a high-rise hotel—I always requested a high floor and it wasn't for the view—so the elevators took a minute to get there. My head swirled with possible scenarios of how the paintings got switched. Maybe Tris wasn't involved? It'd fooled me, maybe it fooled her too?

But how did that make sense when she was working on *cleaning* the painting? The one I'd taken was clean, and I'd put that down to her having finished the job she'd been assigned to do. But if it was never dirty to start with—because it was just painted—then she'd have had nothing *to* clean.

No matter which way I looked at it, Tris *had* to have known.

Unless, maybe, on some slim chance, someone had stolen it and made the switch *right* before I broke in. Maybe. Anything was possible, right?

I swiped my door key and waited the second it took for the light to blink and lock to deactivate, then I pushed open the door.

Almost immediately, I needed to duck out of the way to avoid a ham-fist smacking into the side of my head. I twisted and retaliated as the door closed softly behind me, leaving the room dark as I grabbed my intruder's arm and spun him into a wrist lock against the wall.

"Give me a good reason why I shouldn't do the world a favor and kill you, Igor?" I asked in a quiet voice. The fact he'd tried to surprise me *again* wasn't a shock in the least. Typical Igor.

My father gave a mocking laugh despite his position. "Oh please. You're no killer, son. It's why you're going to lose this Game, and lose my pathetic father's legacy because you don't have what it takes to win *no matter what*."

He was wrong about me losing. I never lost. But to my irritation, he was right about me not being a killer. I preferred to outsource those tasks to my extensive list of contacts within the mercenary guild and keep my own hands clean to some degree.

Though the temptation to break his wrist was almost too hard to resist.

"Go on, Ivan, show me how tough you are," Igor taunted as I tightened my grip on his wrist. "Maybe you're more like your old man than you think."

Fuck. That idea made me physically nauseated, and I released him with a shove. "I'm nothing like you, Igor. Get the fuck out of my room before I call someone who would be more than willing to toss you out the window."

"Oh yeah? Who'd that be then? One of your dirty little FBI contacts? Or one of those pretty mercenary girls you keep doing favors for?" He rubbed his arm as he eyed me like a caged animal.

I bit my tongue, not willing to give him any reaction. It disturbed me that he knew more about my habits than he should. All my work was confidential, whether it was paid or pro bono. I didn't have a *team* to leak information, either, so his knowledge made me think he was following me in some capacity.

"Get the fuck out, Igor. You're out of your league on this Game, and you fucking well know it. Otherwise you wouldn't be breaking rules left right and center to steal from *me*." I opened the door and held it. "Out."

Igor squinted at me for a long moment, then smirked. "Those bruises look painful, son. You should be more careful."

I stifled my eye roll, keeping my expression blank as I waited for him to exit the room, then I closed the door and locked it. Not that locks would keep Igor out, but it was just a habit.

I peered through the peephole, watching as my father stood out in the corridor a moment, checking his phone. Then he casually strolled away toward the elevators. Fucking hell… he had some kind of tracking device planted on me. I was sure of it now.

For the next hour I searched through my belongings with a fine-toothed comb, looking for a bug of any description. This wasn't my area of expertise, though. Bugs, surveillance, listening devices, trackers... none of those were thief-level shit. The only time I ever used that kind of technology was when I was assessing a mark and gaining intel to manipulate them into letting security slip. I'd never needed to *find* one before.

Frustrated and annoyed, I ended up abandoning half my possessions. When I left the hotel, I only took my essentials and placed a call to someone infinitely more qualified in searching for bugs than I was. Because until I could be *totally* sure Igor wasn't listening, watching, following... I couldn't return to Whispering Willows.

Fuck the timeframe of the Game, if Igor found out Tris was—most likely—the one who'd taken the original Van Gogh? Shit, I hated to think what he'd do to make her hand it over.

Sliding behind the wheel of my Mustang I sighed heavily. Even if I showed up on her doorstep tonight, she'd likely throw a potted plant at my head, then shove one of her huge vibrators up my ass for the insult of daring to care.

My call went unanswered but that was standard

procedure. I left a voicemail and headed that direction anyway. Then I placed another call.

I drummed my fingers impatiently on the steering wheel while waiting for the call to connect, then had to swallow the urge to berate my contact when he finally picked up.

"How is she?" I growled, desperate for any shred of information.

"How do you think?" the little twerp asked. I should have pushed for a more experienced bodyguard to watch Tris after I left, but on short notice Bram was all they could offer. He was only twenty-two(??) which was hopefully too young to hit on Tris but too old for being so green as a merc. I should have waited longer, until they could send a better seasoned merc.

I swallowed back the urge to swear at him. "I think I'm asking you because it's your fucking job, Bram. How *is she*?"

"Wrong," he snapped back. "My job is to keep her alive, and she is. Reporting back on how heartbroken she is after a breakup is not part of the contract. If you were really worried, you'd call her yourself, not me."

Technically, he was right. Giving me updates on how she was handling my disappearance was *not* part of his job description. But I was going out of my mind with worry.

"Just tell me *something*."

A heavy gust of a sigh sounded down the phone. "Fine. She's fine. Some sexy blonde chick showed up a few hours ago with takeout, then Tris went to work. See? Totally fine. Now fuck off and stop calling me with your *Dear Bram* bullshit, I'm not your girlfriend or therapist."

He ended the call, leaving me seething. The sooner I got cleared of trackers, the sooner I could return to Whispering Willows and protect Tris myself.

If she'd let me.

Tris

three

No one spoke to me for the drive to RBD's, but I also wasn't trying to make small talk. Why bother, right? Better to keep my cards close to my chest and maybe... *maybe* I could somehow wiggle myself out of this mess with my head still attached to my shoulders.

It was a slim chance, but it was a chance. Mr. Grimaldi was a smart man; he might see some value in my skills. Enough to overlook the theft of a priceless painting? Well, I could hope.

When we arrived, my guard escorted me through the front door of the manor and down the corridor to the ballroom. I shivered. How many times had I seen men being beaten bloody in the middle of the ballroom, hanging by their wrists from the chandelier? Not to mention the man who'd been shot in front of me as he'd tried to escape.

Suddenly that slim chance seemed to evaporate.

"Sit," my guard ordered, giving me a shove toward the heavy wooden dining chair in the middle of the ballroom. So dramatic, but I expected nothing less from the Grimaldis.

I did as he said, parking my butt down on the upholstered seat. "What now?" I squeaked, unable to help myself. Nerves were getting the better of me, and I clasped my hands together in my lap.

"Wait," the guy snarled, retreating to the doorway where he positioned himself across the opening, his back to me.

I rolled my eyes and huffed. "Sit," I muttered to myself. "Wait. I'm not a dog, dickhead."

Aside from me on my chair, the whole room was empty of people and furniture. I glanced at the windows, briefly debating and immediately dismissing the idea of making a break for it. For one thing, I knew how tight the security was outside the manor, and for another... well. I'd seen what happened to people who ran.

Boom. Splat. No thanks. Not when I still had that microscopic chance to make myself too valuable to kill.

I wrapped my arms around myself, trying really

freaking hard not to let my imagination run away with itself as I waited. I spent a while silently cursing out John, though. Fucking amateur. Was it too much to expect that he was good enough to evade capture? He was clearly good enough to steal from Mr. Grimaldi *and* stage the scene to somewhat clear me of suspicion.

As if using me for my security access wasn't bad enough. The part that stung the most was that last visit... He crept into my bedroom and fucked me *right* before skipping town. Why? He probably already had the painting by then, so why the hell did he feel the need to rub salt in the wound with that one last visit?

Typical fucking man, thinking with his dick. Fuck. I'd laugh if that was why he got caught...

Or, I guess I couldn't laugh if I was dead. But my ghost would find it amusing as hell. Except for the part where his utter incompetence got me caught as a forger.

My guard shifted from the doorway, and I sucked a breath as Mr. Grimaldi strode into the room with a troubled scowl set across his features. He was accompanied by two of his usual bodyguards, and they took their positions slightly behind him when he stopped in front of me.

"Tennison, get me a chair," Mr. Grimaldi said after a long pause. He didn't look away from me as his bodyguard disappeared to do as he was told, and I was too scared to look away.

We held that stare off for an extended moment until the sharply suited goon returned with a matching dining chair for Mr. Grimaldi to sit in.

My employer finally broke eye contact as he cleared his throat and unbuttoned his blazer to sit down. It always fascinated me how men couldn't seem to sit with their suit jackets buttoned. Was it uncomfortable or just habit?

"That will be all," Mr. Grimaldi told his men. "You can wait outside."

The second guy frowned his objection. "Sir..."

Mr. Grimaldi swung his glare in the man's direction. "I gave you an order Anders. Tristian is not a threat to me, and she is smart enough not to try anything foolish. Aren't you?"

I nodded quickly. "Yes, sir. Nothing foolish."

"You see?" Mr. Grimaldi gestured then waited expectantly as his guards retreated out of the ballroom. He didn't seem in any hurry to speak, adjusting his position until he was comfortable in the chair opposite me then glancing over to check his men had actually followed his order and left the room.

I swallowed hard, my arms folded tightly to hide how badly my hands were shaking. I'd wait for him to speak before opening my mouth, though. Defense was my best offense right now.

"So, Tristian," he finally said with a sigh. "You stole from me."

Ah crap. This wasn't a great start. Could I play dumb and pretend I had no clue what he was talking about? Maybe?

"Please, Tristian, don't insult my intelligence by denying this. We both know you are the one who swapped my Van Gogh for a fake. I'm guessing if the painting wasn't stolen, I'd have been none the wiser, too." He arched a brow, his hands clasped casually in his lap. "This puts me in a very uncomfortable position, Tristian."

I gave a nod. "Yes, sir. I understand."

His brow dipped with a frown and he studied me for a long moment. Then shook his head. "You look awful, Tristian. Like you got dragged through a ditch on the way here. Did my men mistreat you?"

Why... would he care?

"Uh, no sir. I was..." I trailed off, figuring he really didn't care to hear about how my heart got broken by a smooth-talking British art professor who moonlighted as a thief. Mr. Grimaldi just waited, though, so I swallowed and wet my lips. "Um, I was going through a relationship breakup. So I, uh, wasn't feeling myself."

The old mob boss just nodded in an understanding way. "The art professor?" I nodded. "Anything to do with this nasty business of forgeries?"

My breath stilled in my chest. As mad as I was at John, I couldn't bring myself to drag him down with me. So I shook my head. "No, sir. Just... personal differences."

"Hmm," Mr. Grimaldi murmured, looking thoughtful as he shifted his position. "That's good, then. I liked him. He's too old for you, though, Tristian. Too serious and conservative."

What I'd give to see John's face when he got called *conservative*. Funny.

"So... what happens now?" I asked in a moment of bravery.

Mr. Grimaldi drew a deep breath. "Well... I should shoot you, shouldn't I? You stole from me, Tristian. Worse than that, you abused my trust to do the deed, and that is something I can't let slide. You understand, of course?"

Sheer terror filled my chest to the point of choking me. But still, I nodded. "Yes, sir," I whispered in a strangled voice. "I understand."

His gun was at his hip, easily visible. But he didn't reach for it. Not yet, anyway.

"See, that's something I really like about you,

Tristian," he commented thoughtfully. "You take responsibility and don't try to make pathetic excuses. I like that. Shows strength of character. You're the kind of woman who could really go places in my line of work."

I swallowed the lump of fear in my throat. "Thank you, sir."

He blew out another frustrated sigh, drumming his stubby fingers on his knee. "I'd really hate to have to kill you, Tristian." He tipped his head to the side, considering me with his calculating gaze. "Tell me, where is my Van Gogh now? Do you still have it?"

I wet my lips. "I can get it..." I evaded, not wanting to implicate Nelson and Hank. "I can return it to you."

"That would be a good idea," Mr. Grimaldi murmured. "And the others?"

My spine stiffened. "Hmm?"

His lips curled in a smile. "Tristian... don't start playing stupid now. I really will shoot you if you start to disrespect me like that."

Ah shit. "It might just take some time," I whispered. "But I can get them all back." Because of course *Poppy Flowers* was not the first painting I'd switched from his gallery and he damn well knew it now.

"Your work is very impressive, Tristian. Much better than my last artist. Flawless." He was still looking at me with that same calculating gaze and a small spark of hope ignited within me.

"Thank you, sir."

He stared at me a long moment, thinking, and I sat quietly to let him consider my worth. Eventually he nodded to himself, then reached for his gun.

My heart slammed to a halt as I watched him pull the weapon from his holster, and cold sweat drenched my skin. I guess my worth wasn't enough to let my infractions slide, after all.

"Tennison!" Mr. Grimaldi called out, glancing over to the ballroom doorway. "Fetch Simmons and bring him to me!"

He held his gun casually, resting it in his lap, but I couldn't tear my eyes away from the barrel pointed right at me. I'd thought maybe I would have more moments of epiphany at the end. Wasn't I supposed to see my life flash before my eyes or something? Instead, all I could focus on was how *pissed* I was that this was all John's fault.

Was that seriously going to be my last thought? John's smug, sexy face?

"Tristian... I'd like to not kill you," Mr. Grimaldi told me, like he was confessing a secret.

My brows shot up in surprise. "Um, sir, I'd also like that."

His lips tugged in a smile. "Good, so we are in agreement? I'm glad."

Suspicion rippled through me. I wasn't big on looking the gift horse in the mouth but... "Um, yes? I think so? Er, not to sound ungrateful, sir, but what exactly am I agreeing to here?"

His sly smile spread wide. "Smart girl. See? I knew I liked you. Not letting this cloud your decision making." He waved the gun and I flinched. "I think you will agree that you're in no position to negotiate terms, hmm? So, here's what we will do. For one thing, you will do whatever is necessary to recover my *original* artworks, yes?"

I nodded quickly. "Yes, absolutely, goes without saying, sir."

He gave a grunt of acknowledgement. "Good. Then I think I might have some use for your *unique* skills, Tristian. A way for you to win my forgiveness, if you'd like to do that?"

My eyes widened and my heart fluttered. "Yes. Anything. I can be very valuable to you, sir."

In the back of my mind, I recognized that this was a turning point in my life. That if I went down this rabbit hole, there would be no backing out. Once I started working for Mr. Grimaldi in an illegal way, there would be no escaping his world.

Fuck it. I'd rather be in the Grimaldi crime family than dead.

"Anything," I reiterated. My skin was worth saving, even if it meant shifting my allegiance to a new master. It wasn't like my previous forgeries had been anything less than illegal anyway.

Mr. Grimaldi smiled again. "Excellent. A certain business associate has been trying to track down a particular painting for a long time, and to no avail. I am led to believe that if someone were to *gift* this painting, my very influential associate would be forever indebted. I would like that debt."

Understanding rang clear, and a huge weight of tension eased from my shoulders. He wanted me to forge another painting. Easy. "Of course. I can do that for you, sir."

He nodded. "Yes. You can, and you will. But first there is the small issue of this theft... I think you've worked for me long enough to know that I can't let any infractions go unpunished. Unfortunately, Tristian, when a fifty million dollar painting goes missing from my gallery, it's the sort of thing that goes noticed. And as such..." He trailed off, shrugging helplessly.

I winced. "It needs to be punished." My voice was hoarse and raw. Maybe he wasn't going to *kill* me, but that didn't mean I was walking out of his house unscathed.

"Indeed," he murmured.

His guard from earlier, Tennison, entered the room then with his hand on another man's arm. The other guy was dressed similarly but more rumpled and stained, and a dark bruise had formed on the side of his face.

"Thank you, Tennison," Mr. Grimaldi said, glancing up at the two men. "That will be all."

His guard jerked a nod, then left the bruised man swaying on his feet there as he retreated out of the ballroom once more.

My employer cleared his throat. "Tristian, my dear. As you know, someone recently stole a very valuable painting from me."

I frowned my confusion, but nodded slowly. "Yes."

"Good. *Someone* needs to be held accountable." He gave me a pointed look, then shifted his gaze to Jones, who simply looked resigned. "How far are you willing to go to stay alive, Tristian? Who is paying the price of breaking my trust? You? Or him?"

Oh shit. I had a really bad feeling about where this was heading. But...

"Him."

Mr. Grimaldi smiled again, and this was no longer the kindly old man who loved paintings. This was Luther Grimaldi, mob boss. "I hoped you might say that, my dear." Then he handed me the gun. "Shoot him, then."

My jaw dropped, and my gaze dropped to the gun in my hand. Holy shit. He wanted *me* to do it? Fuck, of course he did. I knew that was too easy. I was free-falling down that rabbit hole now, and pretty sure I didn't pack a parachute.

"Tristian, it's you or him. My time is valuable, so make your choice quickly." There was no cold threat in my employer's voice, he could just be discussing the need to trim his lawns for how affected he sounded.

I bit my tongue hard enough to draw blood, my mind in a turmoil. John was no longer front and center, though. No, it was Nelson, and Hank. I swore to Nelson years ago that I'd do anything to protect them if we ever got caught and now was the time to follow through. If I died today, who was to stop Mr. Grimaldi from taking them next, questioning them on what I might have done with the paintings? It would only take a casual question to my neighbors to know they were a surrogate family to me.

I had to live, to protect those old men. Because I loved them a hell of a lot more than I loved myself.

So before I could second guess myself and panic into paralysis I raised the gun and pulled the trigger.

The shot rang out through the ballroom, deafening me. Shock ripped through me instantly, and the gun fell from my hand. Mr. Grimaldi caught it before it hit the floor, though, then patted my hand reassuringly.

"...proud of you, Tristian." I only made out the end of his sentence as my ears rang painfully. Simmons was dead, blood pooling from around his body as he lay on the marble floor. Fuck, no, he wasn't dead yet. His chest heaved as he gasped for air, and blood stained his mouth, bubbling.

Mr. Grimaldi followed my line of sight then stood up and fired another bullet through the man's head to end his suffering. Thank fuck for that. He yelled for Tennison again, indicating to me and totally ignoring the body. "Get Tristian set up in the jade bedroom, please. Let Naomi know that I need to speak with her about the wedding plans."

Tennison gestured for me to exit the ballroom, and I stumbled to my feet, totally numb. I made it halfway to the door before those words sunk into my panicked brain.

Holy shit I killed someone.

"What plans?" I squeaked, spinning back to Mr. Grimaldi in horror.

His mob-boss smile was back. "Your wedding, my dear. You're family now, so it seems only right that we make it official. You and Sin will make a beautiful couple." He strode over to where I stood rooted to the ground, then *hugged me*. "I couldn't be happier to welcome you as a daughter, Tristian."

John

four

My contact in the Mercenary Guild took longer than I'd have liked to get back to me with a rendezvous point, and even longer to arrange her tech specialist to meet up with me. What I'd hoped to be a *quick* detour was turning out to be an exercise in frustration and irritation.

I checked into the dodgy motel on the side of the road near the California–Oregon border and searched my shit all over again. When I came up blank *again*, I nearly hurled my phone at the wall. But I couldn't break it before getting it scanned for tracking devices. God damn it.

The need to put more research into my target, to thoroughly trace the *Poppy Flowers* history as it changed hands, was making me crazy. It was still possible that the forgery had been switched out years ago, wasn't it? That would mean the *forgery* could have needed cleaning and Tris was just understandably fooled by what was an impeccable copy. Like I was.

The idea that Igor was watching me had me too paranoid to use my computer, though. Anything that could give him a hint about what I was planning was too risky. So I just had to turn on the crackly cable TV and watch *CSI: Miami* for *hours* while waiting for the tech specialist to arrive.

At some stage I fell asleep and jerked awake when my phone vibrated on the bedside table. I grabbed it, answering the call before I was even fully awake. I assumed it was the tech dick calling to say he was finally here, so the woman's voice on the line had me all kinds of confused for a moment.

"...did you hear me?" she asked after a pause and I scrubbed the heel of my hand on my eyes.

"Tink?" I asked, my voice a sleepy groan. I hadn't slept much since Igor's guys jumped me, and it was all starting to catch up.

"Yes, idiot, it's me," she snapped back. "Did you hear what I said? Tris is in trouble, and it's your fault."

I sat up, swinging my legs over the side of the bed. "Huh?"

Tink gave an annoyed growl. "Fucking forget it. I'll save her myself."

"Wait, wait, wait," I hurried to say, stopping her from hanging up. "You just caught me half asleep. Start again. What happened?"

"Tris. Is. In. Trouble. *Dickhead*. There was a whole news report about an art thief being released—which I have to assume was Igor, not you, because only a moron gets picked up by Art Crimes that easily. Then she started having a fucking panic attack and some guy showed up to take her to the Grimaldi mansion. John, I swear to fuck if you've left her to take the fall for you—"

I scoffed a laugh before I could stop myself. "Me? She made her own bed with the Grimaldis. Besides, why do you care? Why are you still hanging around Whispering Willows? You saw me take the painting, the Game is over."

There was a long pause on her end, and I held my breath while I waited for her to buy my bullshit. To assume I did, in fact, have the original. She breathed a short sigh. "I stayed because I knew you were going to break her heart, John. She doesn't seem like the kind of girl with a lot of friends, so I stayed to make sure she was okay."

Fuck, that struck me way too deep. Tink was a much better person than I was.

"But *now*," she continued, "I'm hanging around because I don't think the Game is over after all. If it was, we'd have been notified and if you had the original you'd have already turned it in. Which leads me to think *you* got duped and stole a forgery." Tink snickered a mocking laugh. "How *embarrassing*, Hermes."

"Shut up," I muttered, swiping a hand over my head. It was pointless to try and persuade her to leave town; she was too smart. And one hundred percent correct. Besides... I liked the thought of Tris having a friend in her. Way more than I should.

She huffed. "Okay well, if you care about her at all, you need to do something. Grimaldi's goon picked her up hours ago, and she hasn't returned to her apartment yet."

I glanced at my watch, my brow dipping when I saw it was past midnight. That wasn't good. She never stayed late at work... not ever. Had Grimaldi held her accountable for the theft? If he had... she was probably already dead.

A pained gasp sucked at my lungs, and I doubled over in pain at that thought. Had Tris been killed because of my theft? Something told me that would be a mistake I wouldn't easily heal from.

"Is she—" I could barely get the words out.

"I don't fucking know, John!" Tink yelled down the

phone. "If I knew, I wouldn't be fucking calling *you*! I've tried everything within reason to find out, but fucking Dexter is out of town right now and no one else takes me back to the manor for *extra services*."

Extra services, aka sex. Tink leveraged *all* of her assets to get the job done. She was determined like that.

"Call Bram," I told her. "He's moved into Tris's building in apartment number—"

"I know the guy," she cut me off. "I met him in the elevator this morning. Handsome guy. Is he... Guild?"

I wrinkled my nose, hating that I was admitting this. I still didn't know if the line was bugged, either. But... shit. Igor already knew I cared too much about Tris, so this was surely no great shock if it was overheard. "Yeah. I just wanted someone watching her in case this shit blew up on her once I was gone."

"Consider it already blown," Tink snapped. "Fat load of use he was in stopping her being taken, by the way. Maybe ask for a fucking refund."

Christ. I knew he was too green for this job, but it *should* have been an easy one. I'd staged the scene enough that it was a clear robbery, *not* an inside job. There should have been no reason to suspect Tris. Unless...

"Shit, Grimaldi must know it was a forgery." I said it out loud before I could catch myself, then winced. I really didn't need to be giving Tink any extra help on beating me.

She let out a low whistle. "How would he know? He couldn't exactly have reported the break in and admitted to all the stolen art he's in possession of. So surely your buddies in Art Crimes wouldn't have given him a courtesy call to let him know it was a dupe."

She had a point. But... "Someone must have told him," I muttered, "which probably means she's already dead." *Oh fuck, that hurt to say.*

"Bullshit," Tink snapped back. "I refuse to believe that, and neither should you."

The thick determination in her voice made me sit straighter. "What are you going to do, Tink?"

"Fuck if I know, but I'm not just going to write her off. The least I can do is check on her, somehow. I might have thought you'd want to do the same, but I guess the whole thing between you two really is over. You're a hell of an actor, Hermes." Someone spoke in the background and a car revved. "I've got to go."

Tink ended the call before I could think of anything else to ask her. For a moment, I stared at my blank screen with a heavy feeling of dread and guilt sitting on my chest. Was Tris already dead? I hoped more than anything Tink was right and she'd talked her way out of it. She could make herself useful to Grimaldi, I was sure of it.

Blowing out a long sigh, I considered the merit of rushing back to rescue her. To what end, though? Gritting my teeth in anger, I sent an urgent message to Bram. It was his fucking *job* to keep Tris alive. That was the whole point of hiring a mercenary and placing him inside Tris's building.

He read my message but didn't reply. Dick.

Irritated, I went back to pacing my room again. What the fuck was taking this tech dude so long? Maybe I hadn't been clear that I was in a hurry to get this bug sweep completed. Trying to pass time, I flicked the TV back on and groaned when I saw it was an all night marathon of *Gilmore Girls*. Worse yet, it was the Rory and Dean era. Needless to say, I turned that off again straight away and pulled a notebook out of my bag.

I needed to get my head straight, so I started recapping everything that had happened since I arrived in Whispering Willows. Everything that had happened since meeting Tris. I was no wordsmith, so I sketched out some little cartoon people in scenes, smiling to myself when I made Sin Grimaldi look like a gawky teenager.

That whole process made me suspect something. Tris wasn't working alone. If I were to put money on it,

I'd think at least one of her elderly neighbors was involved in her extracurricular activity. After all, one of her passwords had been Royal Pelican which was the name of the casino where she'd first met Nelson.

I sat there a long time, staring at my wobbly cartoon sketches. Staring at the one of Tris painting naked, and remembering one of the many nights I'd broken in to watch her sleep. Her wrists had been splattered with dried paint in yellows and greens, but the painting on her easel didn't have *any* of those shades. *Poppy Flowers* did, though.

Sneaky, sneaky. She must have had the forgery hiding right there in plain sight within her studio and I'd just never seen it.

At some point, I gave up waiting for the tech guy and went back to sleep. If nothing else, that was a decent use of my time, right?

When I woke the next morning, I nearly jumped right out of my skin to find a tattoo-covered dude lying on the bed beside me as he scrolled through his phone casually.

"What the fu—" I mumbled, clambering out of bed with my pulse racing. Adrenaline coursed through my body, but the stranger just quirked a brow like I was acting crazy. "Who are you? How did you get in here?" *Without me knowing...* "Oh. You're the guy Danny sent."

"That would be me," he replied, finishing whatever he was doing on his phone then smoothly getting up from the bed. It was a fluid movement, like he was a hell of a lot more than a tech merc. It made me instantly suspicious.

"What's your name?" I asked, my spine stiff. Not that I had any hope of fighting off a Guild killer, but surely if he was here to hurt me he'd have done it in my sleep.

The guy gave me a lop-sided smile, like I was joking. "None of your business. You're *Hermes*, though, aren't you? Can I ask you about how you did one of your jobs?"

I narrowed my eyes. "Which one?"

He grinned wider. "Stanley."

Ah yes, one of the favors I'd done a while back. One of the Guild leaders wanted me to return her stolen potted plant to her. Of all the ways to get a woman's attention, I'd never have thought stealing her *plant* was the way to go. Mercs were fucking strange individuals, though.

"None of your business," I shot back. "Did she tell you what I need done?"

The guy gave a nod. "Yup. Bug sweep. Easy, when you have the right tech." He started strolling toward the motel door, like he was ready to leave without actually doing the job.

"Wait, aren't you going to do it?" I was already pissed as hell for how long I'd needed to wait for the guy, and now he was playing games? Fuck that.

The odd dude spun back around to face me, a confused frown on his brow. "It's already done. You snore, by the way."

Shock held my tongue. He'd checked *all* my stuff for bugs while I'd slept and never alerted me to his presence? That... was scary.

"You were right, if that helps. You're bugged. A good one, too. GPS, audio, the whole package. The only thing it didn't give the receiver was video, but if I were you I'd probably get a new car and accommodation just in case of static cameras."

My jaw dropped. "Where?" I looked at my small pile of belongings that didn't look disturbed at all.

The tech guy tapped his neck, just under his right ear. "Here. I fried it with a magnet—you're welcome—but if I were you, I'd cut that sucker out." He opened the door then gave me a wave over his shoulder. "Have a nice day, Hermes!" Then he was gone.

Tris

five

Once I was "escorted" to my room—a polite way of saying I got shoved inside so hard I hit the carpet—the adrenaline drained out of me so swiftly I was left a trembling mess on the floor at the end of the bed. For a long time, I just lay there all curled up in a ball. I wasn't even processing what'd just happened. I was compartmentalizing. Big time. I was taking all the scary things and shoving them into lockboxes where I didn't have to face my feelings over them.

Like how I'd just killed a man.

Or how Mr. Grimaldi casually announced I'd be marrying his son.

What the fuck did he think I was, a camel ripe for breeding? He couldn't just announce I was going to *marry* someone like he was a medieval lord. Could he? Oh wait, I just killed a guy and now that my head was clearer it was pretty fucking obvious he would have some kind of camera surveillance in that room. Therefore, yes. I suppose he could play Lord and make me do pretty much whatever he wanted. I thought I was in hot water with art forgery and theft? Murder was a step up.

Life in prison was *not* on my list of goals, thank you. Any idiot would agree arranged marriage and a little bit of indentured forgery was preferable to that, so Mr. Grimaldi wasn't being totally unreasonable. And yet... logic and reason seemed to be impossible to hold onto as confused pigeons flapped around my brain cooing about how *I just murdered someone in cold blood.*

Sitting the fuck back down and thinking through my next steps would have been an amazing idea, but instead I crossed to the huge windows and tested the latch. Most of me expected to find them nailed shut, maybe even some prison bars. But nope... the damn things glided open without any effort at all. Like fate was taunting me with the illusion of freedom.

It was a trap. It had to be.

"Don't do it, you idiot," I whispered to myself, my eyes glued to the open window. I was on the second floor for fuck's sake, I couldn't just jump from here.

Leaning out, I peered down the side of the house. If there was a fire escape or a convenient ladder it'd confirm my suspicion that it was a test, but there wasn't... and my hopes plummeted faster than a lead balloon.

"Probably for the best," I grumbled out loud. I wouldn't have been able to resist a seemingly clear path to freedom, even if it was obviously too good to be true. Also, with my level of athleticism I'd probably break a leg just trying to climb out the window.

So why *the fuck* was I staring at the rainwater down pipe like it was my ticket out of here?

I glanced over my shoulder at the bedroom door, sure that Mr. Grimaldi would come bursting through at any second and correct his mistake. When he said *jade bedroom*, he must have meant *jail below* and his guard and I simply heard wrong.

"Fuck it," I groaned, already halfway out the window. "Now or never."

Instantly I regretted my choice. I hadn't thought it through. The ledge in the stonework of the house was barely wide enough for half my shoe, and as soon as I shuffled away from the window, I had nothing to hold onto properly.

My stomach swooped, and I plastered myself

against the rough façade, whispering pathetic prayers to gods I didn't believe in… but I didn't go back.

"Stubborn bitch," I whimpered, insulting myself as another choking wave of fear rippled through me. "What were you thinking?"

Oh yeah. Forced manslaughter, arranged marriage, threats of death… or worse? A girl did crazy things under duress, and I felt like those factors applied. My mind wandered, just for a second, and my shoe slipped.

A squeak of terror escaped my throat and my fingertips tried to fuse with the rough stone wall as I shifted all my weight to my other foot.

"Fuck," I whimpered. "Holy fuck. This is insane."

It was all insane. Getting caught out on a forgery for the first time since I was fifteen was insane. *Shooting a man* was insane. Barely blinking at the implication of an arranged marriage? Insane. So in the scheme of things, attempting to scale the side of a house? It was on par.

I shuffled across further, one inch at a time, racing the clock as my fingers started to sweat. The downpipe was still fucking *miles* away, though, and I whined pathetically as if that would get me there any faster. My stupid boobs were preventing me pasting myself close enough to the wall, every passing second made me feel more and more off balance. If I didn't get to that drain pipe soon, I was done for. Could I survive the drop from here? Probably. It'd hurt, but I wouldn't die.

Eyes on the prize, I kept shuffling along the tiny ledge, inch after inch until finally my fingertips reached the downpipe. Hope soared in my chest, and I inhaled deeply with relief, shuffling faster to get a better grip. I hardly dared to breathe until both hands wrapped around the old drainpipe. Only then did I exhale heavily as I rested my forehead on the stupid fucking pipe.

Except... *now what, you genius?*

What the hell was my plan? Shimmy down the drainpipe? This wasn't fiction, for fuck's sake, and it wasn't a damn stripper pole. It was a pipe that had been bracketed *to* the wall. Meaning I couldn't wrap my hands or legs around it to go all fireman down to the ground. But what the fuck else was I going to do?

In a moment of weakness, I glanced back to the window. Should I give up?

No way. Quitting was for quitters. I'd come this far; I had to see it through.

A quick glance at the ground below told me I'd be landing in bushes. Hopefully soft bushes. Bushes of marshmallows and clouds.

"Now or never, Tristian," I muttered. "Shit or get off the pot." One of Nelson's favorite sayings never seemed more appropriate.

Closing my eyes, I gripped the pipe as hard as I could with both hands, then took my feet off the ledge. For a split second I thought I'd lose my grip and just go crashing down, but I didn't. I dug my toes into the side of the house and slowly started doing a backwards tree climb to get down.

It was working! Holy hell, of all the crazy plans, I could hardly believe this was actually working.

Until it wasn't. A small pop was the only warning I got, and then the whole drainpipe detached from the side of the house. My eyes widened in horror, but I managed to swallow my scream, clinging to the pipe like a monkey as it swung out into thin air. Then it dropped, taking me with it.

A small squeak escaped me as I hit the bushes, which were absolutely *not* made of marshmallows and clouds… but the landing wasn't as hard as I expected. Nothing broke, except my dignity for such an embarrassing escape. Why couldn't I be all graceful and athletic like girls in espionage movies? Those girls probably would have cartwheeled out of the window in a miniskirt and stilettos then walked away with sass.

Meanwhile, I just lay there in a tangle of limbs, drainpipe, and the scratchiest bushes known to man. Groaning. Regretting my life choices. Crying a *tiny* bit with frustration and embarrassment despite the fact no one could see me.

Wait. No one *could* see me, right?

Footsteps scuffed over grass, and my whole body heated with an intense rush of fear. There was no way I could quietly scramble out of the spikey bush and hide, I simply had to stay *still* and hope the darkness hid me. Maybe they'd just walk straight past?

I mean... sure... the broken downpipe might draw a little attention. But if I stayed *really still*...

"Tris?"

What the fuck?

I knew that voice. But that wasn't possible... he was gone. Long fucking gone. No way was he returning to the scene of the crime after being released by the FBI, right?

"Tris, are you okay? That looked like it had to hurt." The insufferable asshole had the absolute *audacity* to sound amused. "Here, I'll just..." The pipe shifted from above me, then there he was, smug fuck, looking down at me with a lopsided grin. "Hi."

My lips opened and closed but no sounds came out. This *motherfucker*...

"Did you hit your head?" John frowned, his expression lit up from house lights and moonlight. "You made a whole lot of noise on that escape. You're going to want to get out of here."

I blinked, trying to make my brain connect. "What the fuck are you wearing?" He was in all black, a damn turtleneck top that was sinfully tight and a knit cap like some kind of... well, like a *thief*.

"Tris, we need to get you out of here," he tried again, speaking carefully and low. "I had to knock out six of Grimaldi's guards to stop them from finding you on what had to be the slowest escape in history, but they won't stay knocked out forever. Come on, yell at me when you're safe." He offered a hand, and I stared at it like he was offering a fucking viper.

Distant voices shocked me into motion, though, and I struggled to free myself from the most uncomfortable bush ever grown. Dozens of twigs scratched my skin, but eventually I found my feet *without* the help of John's traitor hand. Asshole.

He indicated for me to stay silent, laying a finger to his lips and gently wrapping his hand around my arm. I started to jerk away then realized he was ushering me around the corner and into the darkness of an inset doorway.

"John, there's—" I started to protest, but he clapped a hand over my mouth, hissing at me to *shh*.

I rolled my eyes, batting his hand away and pointing

at the security camera *right* above the door. The camera that was all of a foot away from his fat head. He glanced over his shoulder but didn't seem even remotely worried. Maybe he was blind as well as a prick? I pointed again, glaring hard to get my meaning across.

He rolled his eyes this time. Actually, I was guessing. It was way too dark and his face was entirely in shadow, but I could *feel* the eye roll. He crowded me into the corner of the small alcove, his head dipping low until his lips brushed my ear.

"I already disabled all the cameras on this side of the house, Tris. What do you take me for, an amateur?" He whispered those words so softly there was no risk of being overheard... but they sent shockwaves through me so hard my toes curled.

"Yes," I hissed back. "That's exactly what I take you for. What kind of bumbling idiot gets picked up by Art Crimes?"

His chuckle rumbled low, doing sinful things to my insides. "Not me, that's for sure. Don't underestimate me, Tris, it'd be a huge mistake."

"I could say the same about me," I shot back, ready for a fight despite our current situation. I started to say something else, but he laid a gentle finger across my lips. A split second later I heard voices and footsteps approaching, and stiffened.

John's huge hands shifted to my waist, holding me like he was scared I'd disappear in a puff of smoke. Like he had. The backs of my eyes burned with unshed tears over how badly he'd hurt me, but I refused to let them fall. Fuck him, he didn't deserve to see how deeply he'd cut me. So I swallowed back the lump of emotions in my throat and tried to ignore the stroke of his thumb across my skin between my stained sweatpants and sloppy sweatshirt. Oh yeah, I looked *hot*.

The guards passed us by a moment later, neither one of them even so much as pausing.

"They won't come back this way for another fifteen minutes or so. If we're running, we'd better run now." John gave my waist a little tug, shifting back but not releasing me.

I didn't move, though. "What do you mean *we*? I'm not going fucking anywhere with you, John Smith. That's not even your real name, is it?"

He paused a moment, then gave a vexed sound. "No."

A bitter laugh escaped me. "Of course it's not. Literally every single thing about you is bullshit. I can't *believe* I fell for it all."

"Look. We can argue about who double crossed *whom* somewhere else, but right now we need to run. Grimaldi has massively increased his security since my last visit, and you're damn lucky I was out there to deal with guards while you—"

"Shut up!" I snapped, way too loud, then cringed and clapped a hand over my mouth. "Shit. I mean, *shut up*." I hissed it this time, keeping my voice low. "I don't need your fucking lecture, John. I was doing just fucking fine on my own. Not that you even care, or did you *not* steal from *my work* by using *my access codes* then leave me to deal with the repercussions? Hmm?"

He stepped back ever so slightly, enough that I could see the scowl set across his brow. "That's not quite what—"

"I said *shut up*," I snarled, cutting him off again. "You think you can swoop in to save the day with a charming fucking smile and that infuriating accent? I wouldn't be in this shit show if it weren't for you! You're lucky I don't scream for those security guards right now and see a bullet through that thick skull of yours."

"So why don't you, then?" he retorted, calling my bluff with a frustrated gesture. "Go on, Tris. Scream."

My lips parted, but no sound escaped. I couldn't do it. Just like I couldn't tell Mr. Grimaldi about John's involvement when I thought my life was on the line. I just... couldn't do it.

"That's what I thought," he said in a harsh, emotionally charged whisper. Then he gripped my throat, pushing me against the door as his lips crashed into mine. I whimpered in shock, melting into his touch as his demanding kiss erased all sanity from my fucking brain.

Weak as it was of me, I kissed him back. Our tongues met, each giving as good as we got, and intense waves of heat pulsed through me. The adrenaline crash from this would be intense, but I couldn't seem to stop myself as I kissed him like I was starving.

Then reality came crashing down like the broken drainpipe. John had *used* me. Not only that, but he took off without a single word of warning for what he'd done and was probably only here tonight chasing the real *Poppy Flowers*.

Worse yet, I couldn't run from Mr. Grimaldi. It wasn't only my life on the line with that deal I'd made. I couldn't ask Nelson and Hank to go on the run with me in the middle of the night, not at their advanced age. Maybe ten years ago things would have been different, but they were settled now. Comfortable. Hank had an incredible career, and if I ran they'd either be killed or forced to run with me.

John's kisses were fast making me forget it all, and I needed not to forget.

I needed to *stay angry*.

It was the only thing helping me survive.

John

six

One minute I was kissing Tris like she was the very air I breathed, then the next her knee slammed into my balls like a fucking freight train. I stumbled backward, a pained yelp escaping my throat before I could silence my reaction.

"Fuck you, John," she spat with absolute venom. "I am not here for your amusement, nor will I be your pawn in whatever game you're playing. You've got three seconds to disappear before I alert the guards to a thief on the grounds."

"Tris, I wasn't—" Fuck, I couldn't get the lie past my lips. I was using her. Then *and* now. Someone still had the original painting, and I'd bet my bruised balls it was her. But that didn't mean I didn't care as well...

"Three..." she hissed, stepping past me warily and out of the alcove.

Ignoring the pain radiating through my groin, I grabbed her arm. "Tris, we can talk about this. I'll explain it all. But we need to go." Now. Or we'd both be caught.

She shook her head, the stubborn, infuriating little...

"Two..." She jerked her arm out of my grip, taking another step out of hiding.

I shook my head, so frustrated I could put my fist through a wall. "Dammit, Tris, you don't get it. You're in danger here."

"I'm well fucking aware, John. Who the hell do you think is responsible for that? Scurry away into the night like the thief you are, but *do not* come back here again. I catch sight of you, I'm telling Mr. Grimaldi who you really are." Her words were loaded with hurt and betrayal, and my response just about gutted me when I let the words pass my lips.

"How can you, when you have no idea?"

Tris reeled back like she'd been slapped, and I instantly wanted to take it back... even if it was the truth. She didn't know me, she only knew the version of me that suited her best. And damn if that didn't cut like a knife in my chest.

Her response was soft, but devastating. "I never

want to see you again, John Smith. The painting is long gone from Whispering Willows, so you've got no reason to hang around. Do us both a favor and disappear for good this time."

Then she strode away, casual as anything, stepping out into the lit area of the grass where I couldn't follow. I almost did anyway. My body twitched with the need to chase after her and *force* her to listen and hear me out, consequences be damned. But I wasn't so stupid as to think that'd work. Even if I could force her to listen, I couldn't force her to forgive me.

Without her forgiveness, what was the point?

The painting was long gone... then that's what I needed to be as well. Long. Gone.

Swallowing the urge to scream her name, I swiftly strode away, slipping into the shadows as seamlessly as a ghost. It was the only smart thing I could do.

My lips buzzed with the phantom touch of her kiss, and I nearly choked on regret as I retreated off the Grimaldi property without leaving a shred of evidence that I'd ever been there. I *should* have lied to her... should have played dumb and acted like I had no clue what she was talking about.

For the first time in a *long* time, I'd found I couldn't make the words form. I couldn't lie to her. Not anymore... and how the fuck I would have explained my presence at Grimaldi's house in the middle of the night, I had no clue.

I scrubbed a frustrated hand over my face and grimaced. She hadn't noticed my bruises and cuts, but that was thanks to the darkness and heavy duty concealer I'd used to disguise the purples and blues blooming down the side of my face. My neck was a fucking mess, too.

That smug asshole of a tech specialist had either been absentminded when he indicated where the tracker was located, or he'd been fucking with me. Because after cutting up the right side of my own neck and finding *nothing*, I'd taken a chance on the left side and found the metal chip almost immediately.

The *when* of the tracker being placed had my skin crawling. How long had he been keeping tabs on me? No way had Igor planted it himself. He wasn't that stealthy. He must have outsourced the task to a professional... but *when*? The obvious moment was when his guys jumped me a couple of days ago, but that didn't account for how he'd ambushed me in the first place. Nor how I failed to notice the injection and the tracker itself. It would have hurt after it was in, right? Fuck, had he heard my conversation with the Art Crimes guy?

Nah, those FBI buildings had enough tech in place that I'd bet the signal was blocked while I was inside.

Igor would have known where I was, and nothing more. Hopefully.

Cheating motherfucker.

Popping out of the forest at a rest stop a mile or so away from Grimaldi's manor, I spotted my brand new Cobra. Tech dude had warned me to ditch my car and accommodation—because cameras—so I'd traded the Mustang in at a Ford dealership on my way back to Whispering Willows. I'd way overpaid for the Cobra, but I was too anxious to get back to Tris.

Fuck.

No.

I was anxious to get back to *Whispering Willows* and find that goddamn painting so I could win the Game. Yes, that was why I felt the burn of urgency to return to that interesting college town. I hadn't even quit my position at the university, but it'd only been a week. I planned to bribe the dean with more feet pics and convince him I was just sick. Now that Tris said the painting was long gone, though... I didn't know where that left me.

Barely five minutes later as I drove toward town, my phone rang. I hesitated a moment before answering, then decided the tech guy wouldn't have missed something as obvious as a phone bug.

"Hello?" I said, taking the call through the car's speakers.

A crackle, then a beep, then cold dread trickled down my spine as a computer voice spoke. "Contestants of The Game. This is a message from the judging panel. Please cease all movements immediately."

"Shit," I groaned out loud, flipping on my indicator and pulling my brand new car over into the shoulder. When the judging panel said *cease movement* they meant right fucking now. These calls were rare but needed to be taken seriously. More often than not, they were to inform the players of a disqualification due to rule breaks.

Not one of the three of us were clean in this round of the Game, though. If someone was being struck from the Game... shit it could be anyone's guess at this point.

The phone line tinkled with elevator music, and I waited impatiently for the judging panel to connect to the call. We didn't know how many were on the panel, nor *who* they all were, but rumors had circulated. Of course I knew my grandfather used to be the head judge until this year. I was curious to know who'd taken his position.

They made us wait a full ten minutes on hold, and then the music finally ended and someone cleared their throat.

"Finalists, thank you for all following directions and ceasing movement for this conversation." It was a distorted electronic voice, totally hiding the speaker's identity. I couldn't even be confident in saying whether it was a man or woman.

I smiled at the clear implication that they had some kind of eyes on us at all times. Maybe that was a bluff, but it was enough to make someone like Igor pay attention.

"What is this about?" my father snapped, his voice filling my car like a bad smell. "You're interfering and that—"

"Igor, do not speak unless specifically called upon." A different distorted voice cut him off, with zero lenience for his bullshit. This one felt more feminine. Interesting.

"We won't keep the three of you in suspense," a third voice said with an accent. French, maybe? "Rules have been broken, but as each of you have been guilty of your own infraction, we cannot disqualify all three or there would be no winner. Instead, we are suspending the challenge."

My brows shot up with surprise. Questions burned on my tongue, but I wasn't going to risk the judges' wrath given what *my* infraction had been. Involving law enforcement to trip another player was one of the worst rule breaks in the book. I was lucky I hadn't already lost my collateral and been kicked to the curb.

Trust Igor not to keep his mouth shut, though. "Suspend the challenge?" he shouted in outrage. "What the hell does that mean?"

"It means, we are *suspending the challenge*," the woman—I think—snapped.

"We as a judging panel need to assess the damage the three of you have already had on the town of Whispering Willows," a new voice said. "Then we will decide if the objective of the Game needs to be revised."

That didn't sound good. If they changed the objective then *Poppy Flowers* would no longer be the painting to steal. Did that mean I had no reason to stay in Whispering Willows? Shit, Tris already said the painting wasn't here, but if I chose to ignore her tip then no one could blame me for staying.

"Do you have any questions?" A different voice again. How many were on the judging panel?

"When will we know your decision?" Tink asked.

"Soon," someone replied, keeping it succinct.

I blew out a breath, running a hand over my face and wincing again at the bruise ache. "What should we do in the meantime? Do we proceed as we are?"

There was a short pause, like the judges were conferring behind the scenes.

"You may continue in your existing cover identities to minimize suspicion and social impact, but all attempts and schemes to locate the current objective must be suspended. I'm sure we don't need to remind you three, if you break the rules again you'll be disqualified *and* your collateral forfeited."

I winced. All Game players—and accomplices—had to put something of *substantial value* on the line to ensure compliance with Game rules. Sometimes it was monetary value, sometimes it was emotional value, but it was always something you didn't want to lose.

"Understood," Tink replied.

I nodded to myself, then echoed her. "Understood."

There was a pause, then someone sighed. "Igor...?"

"Understood," my father gritted out, sounding *furious*. Whatever he'd been in the middle of, he was not happy to be put on ice.

"Good. We will inform you of our decision in due course." I'd lost track of which voice was which, but the call ended a moment later anyway.

Well... at least they'd given permission to continue with our established cover identities. For Igor, that meant poker dealer and general shit kicker for the Grimaldis as he tried to weasel into the organization. For me, I could go back to my day job teaching at the university... and seeing Tris?

For Tink, it meant she was still stripping at the Slippery Lips and blowing Dexter on the regular. Shit, I actually felt sorry for her. As easy as girls had it for cat burglary... I couldn't imagine relying on sex appeal and seduction to build a cover ID.

On impulse, I brought up the number she'd called me from and hit redial. It rang out, which was frustrating, so I left her a quick message asking if she had any new information. Then I sent the same to Bram, though my tone was considerably more terse to the amateur mercenary. Yes, I had my own confirmation that Tris was alive and well, but I wanted more. What had gone down between her and Grimaldi? What deal did she cut to keep her head? Why the fuck had she changed her mind about escaping when I was right there, offering her my hand and a chance of freedom?

I wasn't allowed to actively go after *Poppy Flowers* for the time being, but I could remain in Whispering Willows and attempt to rebuild some burned down bridges. Right? Or at least attempt to smooth things out with Grimaldi to have Tris cleared of blame. Somehow.

The relief that I'd experienced when I saw her climbing out of that window—alive—was hard enough I'd almost passed out. Half the reason I'd gone straight to Grimaldi's house was to find out if he'd killed her, and a horrible dark part of me believed he already had.

But to my intense relief, Tink was right when she said Tris was too smart to go down so easily. She was still alive... for now.

The same probably couldn't be said about me when she got her hands around my throat, though. I could bullshit all I wanted to retain my job at the university, but my luck had well and truly expired with her. She knew full fucking well that I'd double-crossed her and left, so I'd gotten off lightly with just a knee to the nuts.

Besides, before that she'd kissed me back. Mad as she might be, she couldn't fight the attraction any more than I could. We were fated and all that dumb shit, so I had to believe that she'd eventually forgive me. She just needed space and time, but then we'd be good.

The thought of us together, *actually* together as master-thief and impeccably talented forger? Oh yeah, that was the kind of partnership that got my dick hard.

Tris

seven

Walking away from John actually felt good. Fuck him and his inflated sense of self-worth, swooping in here to try and *save me* after it was his stupidity that got me caught in the first fucking place. The audacity of the man made my blood boil. So much so that I didn't notice one of Mr. Grimaldi's loyal guards leaning against the side of the house, smoking, until I was almost on top of him.

"You owe me fifty bucks," the gray-haired man said, not even the slightest bit surprised to see me standing there.

I stopped dead in my tracks, startled, confused, and more than a bit scared. "Um, I what?"

The guy dropped his cigarette butt and ground it out with his toe. "Not you, Miss Ives. Him."

I glanced over my shoulder in the direction he nodded, finding a second security guard approaching out of the shadows of the trees.

"Yeah, yeah, smart ass," the second guy drawled, pulling his wallet out as he approached. He sighed as he withdrew a fifty and handed it to the smoker, then glared at me. "Now *you* owe *me* fifty bucks. Who was the guy?"

My mouth went dry and a cold sweat broke out over my skin. "What guy?"

The second guard, sporting a salt and pepper beard and weathered lines around his eyes, just arched a brow. "The guy that you just kneed in the balls while he was trying to give you mouth to mouth. I couldn't catch a good look." He tipped his head at me thoughtfully. "Guild merc, right?"

Confusion fuzzed my brain. "What?"

"Ahh, doesn't matter. Seems like you made your choice pretty clear. Will he be sniffing around here again?" Bearded guard didn't even seem slightly worried. Had he watched the *whole* time? Including when I fell into the bushes? *Fuck.*

I swallowed hard, trying to get some kind of moisture back in my mouth. "N-nope. No, he has no reason to return."

"Good. Let's hope you're telling the truth, kid."

Bearded dude clapped me on the shoulder, then headed inside the house. "You still owe me fifty bucks, though!"

Speechless. I had nothing to say.

"We took bets whether you'd actually make it off the property," smoking dude informed me.

"I worked that out," I whispered. "Thanks."

"Miss Ives, I understand you have been doing your utmost to keep your head down and your blinkers on during the last year of working here, but it's our job to monitor everyone in close contact with Mr. Grimaldi. You know... get a good sense of who they are. What motivates them. Where their decisions will lean. This," he said, holding up the fifty dollar note, "proves I'm better at reading people than Stevens is."

Holy fuck. I knew it was too easy.

"Are you going to tell Mr. Grimaldi?" I asked, focusing on the important shit.

He gave me a long look. "About your aborted escape attempt or about your boyfriend?"

I cringed. "Both."

He shrugged, pulling out another cigarette. "That is my job. Head on inside, get some sleep, Miss Ives. It's late and you look like shit." He lit up, effectively dismissing me, and I bit my tongue as I stepped inside the house.

I passed by several more guards on my way back to

the jade bedroom, but they all just gave me a nod, like they'd known where I was the whole damn time. Apparently I'd underestimated how on the ball the security team here were.

So how in the hell did John keep getting past them? Obviously tonight wasn't the first time, probably not even the second. And had they even tried to catch *him*?

The bedroom door was unlocked when I tried the handle, and a shiver ran down my spine as I stepped inside. Willingly putting myself back into my jail cell. I'd been so close to escape before John showed up...

But I hadn't, had I? The security guys had eyes on me the whole time, just waiting to see what I'd do. Giving me enough rope to hang myself with, if I chose wrong.

"Fuck," I whispered, anxiety curling through my gut like a venomous snake. Now I'd made myself all the more dangerous and untrustworthy by meeting with a mystery man in the dark. A man who clearly wasn't my nice, well-mannered Art History professor with how he'd disabled the other guards and avoided any alarms or cameras.

It definitely made me curious why the two older guards didn't raise an alarm. Was their fifty-dollar bet more important than house security? If so... I couldn't let my guard down. I wasn't safe here, and it'd do me good to remember that.

The guest room I'd been assigned was decorated in really tasteful jade green, which was weirdly soothing and I guess explained the name. It housed a huge bed with more than a dozen pillows, a love seat, and a pair of closed doors that I hadn't explored before jumping out the window.

Opening them, I found a huge—empty—wardrobe, dressing room complete with makeup mirror, and enormous en-suite bathroom.

"At least it's comfier than the typical prison cell," I muttered aloud, then winced when I caught sight of myself in one of the mirrors. That guard, and Mr. Grimaldi, had been downright flattering when they said I looked awful. My roll in the bushes didn't help, either. I looked like I'd been dragged behind a rabid moose through bracken and forest for six miles then tossed down a steep hill.

"Wow," I whispered, peering at the nasty tangle my hair had somehow ended up in, and plucked a twig from the mess. The dark circles under my eyes were so heavy I looked like a cartoon character. And yet, I was still alive. My lips curled up in a satisfied smile. I was still alive... and I'd do whatever it took to stay that way, including marrying into the Grimaldi family.

Thank fuck Dex was already married with a baby on the way, otherwise I'd rather take jail time or a bullet.

Sin, I could handle. I *liked* him. So yeah, Mr. Grimaldi was being more than reasonable with his requests. I could do this.

With that renewed sense of determination, I stripped out of my stinky, coffee-stained sweats and stepped into the shower. It was time to stop sulking over John. That man didn't deserve my fucking tears any more. I hoped his balls were bruised purple from my knee by now.

Halfway through my shower, I got a visit from Naomi—Mr. Grimaldi's personal assistant—who knocked politely on the open bathroom door. It was already past midnight, but apparently she was on call twenty-four seven for her employer.

"Just me, Tristian," she called. "Sorry for the time, I heard the shower running so figured you were still awake. I'm just dropping off some clothes for you. They're from Rose Bella in town, so it's easy to swap if they don't fit."

"Thanks, Naomi!" I shouted back, not bothering to cut my shower short. Clean clothes actually sounded great now that I was showering—and had somewhat made my peace with staying for now—so I was appreciative. Also, Rose Bella was the highest end boutique in Whispering Willows, stocked full of designer labels and charging triple figures for fucking socks, let alone full garments. So if that was going on Mr. Grimaldi's tab, I wouldn't argue.

With quite literally nowhere to be—because Mr. Grimaldi and his scary calm guards made it pretty fucking clear I wasn't permitted to leave—I took my time in the bathroom. Then I tried on the clothing Naomi had delivered. It was only a handful of things, but she'd included underwear that thankfully fitted and some satin pajamas, which I put on. I usually slept nude, but that just seemed like a seriously bad idea while captive in a mob boss's house.

Then again, it also seemed like a bad idea to let my guard down at all, but I couldn't stay awake forever. So I crossed the bedroom and tested the door handle, expecting to find it locked now. I was a prisoner, after all.

When it turned easily and the door opened, my jaw dropped. I pulled it open further and peered out into the hallway, expecting to find armed guards. But nope. Nothing. No one. *What the fuck?*

I stood there in the hallway like a statue, confused as fuck, until someone came around the corner. Startled, I started to retreat into my room until I realized it was Naomi again.

"Hey, Tristian," she said with a smile. "Clothes fit?"

I nodded, "Yeah, they did. Thanks. Uh, don't you sleep?"

She gave a tight nod. "Rarely. Good about the clothes, though. I'll pick up some more in the morning when they're open. In the meantime, Mr. Grimaldi asked me to give you this." She held out a key, and I took it with a perplexed frown. "For your door. He thought you might feel more secure if you were in charge of your own safety, with a house so full of armed men."

"Oh." I didn't expect that. "Um, thanks."

Naomi flashed me a quick smile. "Are you hungry? The chef has already left for the night, but you're welcome to help yourself to anything in the kitchen. You know how to get there?"

I glanced along the corridor, trying to work out where in the manor I was. "I think so, yeah."

"Great. Well, if you need anything else...?" She left that open, waiting for my response.

I nearly told her I didn't need anything, then I decided to test the limitations of my new situation. "Actually, do you think I could make a phone call?"

"Of course, there's a house phone beside the TV. Just hit nine for an outside line." She indicated past me, and I felt stupid for not having even *looked* for a phone. Then again, how long had it been since I even *had* a landline?

"And Mr. Grimaldi asked me to get you set up on the family mobile plan tomorrow. I'll drop your new phone with the clothes, if that's okay?"

Stunned, I just nodded. "Yeah, that's totally fine."

"Okay, well if you think of anything else you can reach me using the house phone with extension seven. Any time of day, no request is too big or small. Have a good sleep, Tristian." She started to walk away, and I blinked rapidly to clear the confusion.

"Wait!" I called after her, making her pause and spin back to look at me. "Why... uh... Naomi, I'm really confused. Why is Mr. Grimaldi being so... um... hospitable?"

She gave a light chuckle. "You're engaged to his son; why would he not be? You're not a prisoner, Tristian. You're family now."

I swallowed the thick lump of dread in my throat. "Thanks. Good night."

She gave a small wave and continued along the hallway, leaving me to close my door and lock it with shaking hands. Somehow, I'd have almost preferred the presence of guards and locks. There was no doubt in my mind that I was *not* permitted to leave... so this illusion that I was a guest just freaked me out. Mr. Grimaldi was confident enough in his power that he didn't *need* to lock me up, because I'd stay put all of my own accord.

The phone was exactly where Naomi said it would be, and I stared at it in my hand for a long time, chewing my lip. I needed to call Nelson, to let him know I was *okay* before he launched a rescue mission. But I wasn't dumb enough to think the line was in any way secure.

He needed to hear from me, though, so I dialed his number and held my breath as I waited for him to answer. Any other night he'd be fast asleep, but the call connected in just a couple of moments.

"Yes?" he answered cautiously, since I was calling from an unknown number.

"Hi Nelson, it's Tris from next door," I replied, keeping my voice light and impersonal.

He paused only a moment before catching on. "Tris, yes hi. It's very late... is everything okay? Do you need an emergency repair?"

"No!" I quickly replied, reading between the lines. "No, no repairs necessary. I just wanted to let you know that I have had a work thing come up and won't be home for a while. Could you take care of my house plants until I can work out how long I'll be gone?"

I held my breath, anxiety filling my chest as silence stretched down the phone line as Nelson processed my message.

"Of course," he finally muttered. "Are you sure there is nothing else we can do for you?"

"Nothing at all," I replied firmly. "I have things totally under control. Just... look after my, uh, house plants."

"Do you need me to let the university know that you're out of town?" he asked, and I winced. This was getting too personal for a courtesy call to my landlord.

I swallowed hard, desperate to tell him everything. "Nope, no need. I have it handled." I reiterated. "Everything is under control. I should let you get back to sleep, it's late. Thanks for... everything. I appreciate you."

Nelson's voice was rough when he replied. "You too, kid."

I ended the call before I could start sobbing, and placed the phone back on its cradle. Then I crawled into the big plush bed. Would I ever see those two old men again?

If I wanted to keep them safe, I needed to play by Mr. Grimaldi's rules. No more climbing out the window, no more confusing visits from John under the cover of darkness. Play by Mr. Grimaldi's rules, stay alive, keep Nelson and Hank safe. Simple.

I just had to convince the ache in my chest that I was doing the right thing.

The sound of my own sobs soothed me to sleep.

John

eight

Force of habit saw me drive back to my accommodation on campus, but I hesitated before getting out of the car. There was every chance Igor—or whoever he paid—had bugged that too. So I sat there in my new Cobra, searching for available rentals within Whispering Willows. There were a few, but they looked like crappy university student housing, so I switched my browser to the dark web and searched for a Hestia safe house instead.

They were pricey, but I wasn't short on cash and their security was unparalleled considering their whole business model was like Airbnb for criminals and people with targets on their backs. They were safer than even witness protection, and better stocked, too.

To my surprise, there was one available only a few

blocks from Tris's building, so I submitted my booking request and sat back to wait for confirmation.

Movement outside my car pulled my attention, and I squinted into the darkness. It was nearly one in the morning and the whole campus was closed up tight until the librarian returned at six. So it made me think whoever was creeping across the lawn right now was up to no good.

Not that I really gave a fuck about university vandals. Just because I was temporarily teaching at Boles, didn't mean I was dosed up on school spirit. So I shrugged it off and turned my attention back to my phone, sending a message of thanks to my Guild contact who'd sent the tech guy out.

He'd been a bit of a dick, but he found the tracker. Appreciation was due.

Ten minutes later, when I was thoroughly bored, my phone pinged with the Hestia booking confirmation and entry codes... along with a sizable deduction from my linked credit card. Someone must make absolute millions from their network of safe houses, but I was glad for the option.

Another movement in the dark saw me hesitate with my finger on the engine start button, and I frowned. It was the person from earlier, now creeping back out of the administration building. They were definitely up to no good... Igor?

"Shit," I whispered aloud. "Motherfucker never follows directions."

Determined to catch my father in the act of defying the judges orders, I slipped quietly out of my car and crouched low as I made for the tree line myself. He wasn't leaving, he was creeping around the perimeter of the building looking for something. Any entry point? Or something else?

The judges had been crystal clear when they said to stop pursuing the painting, but I'd put money on it, that was what Igor was doing here. Why here, though? Unless he'd overheard enough to suspect Tristian as the one who'd swapped the forgery in. Then maybe it'd make sense if he thought she was hiding it in the Boles art studio? There was a secure safe in the back of that room, but it wasn't *that* secure.

I rounded the corner where I'd just seen him skulk around, and paused. He was nowhere to be seen... Where the fuck did he go?

Confused but cautious, I took a few steps forward, peering along the side of the building. There were no doors... nowhere to hide. I hadn't heard any glass breaking. What the shit? Where'd that rat go?

A faint scuff of a shoe on grass gave me a split

second warning, and I dodged right as a brutal punch flew at my head. I was too slow to avoid it entirely, but at least it only glanced off the side of my cheek rather than knocking me out cold.

But *shit* it hurt. This wasn't Igor.

I swung back reflexively, aiming for the anonymous guy's gut, but he spun faster than I'd thought possible. My fist met air and I stumbled, off balance. He darted back in and delivered a brutal jab to my ribs that made me grunt. He'd somehow managed to hit me right on a nasty bruise from Igor's guys only a week ago.

"Fuck," I coughed, staggering to the side in an attempt to avoid getting hit again. It was a lost cause, though, with the shorter guy coming at me like a pit bull. I was no MMA star but I generally held my own, when push came to shove. Unfortunately, whoever I'd picked a fight with tonight was proving that my skills had slipped... a lot.

In my defense, the dude attacking me was *deadly*. He wore a mask, revealing nothing but his dark eyes, absolutely no other features to identify him later. Not that I was inclined to go running to the cops about getting my ass kicked for the second time in a week.

My head snapped back with a jarring uppercut, and I tasted blood. This fucker wasn't messing around. Before I even regained my balance, a follow-up right hook saw me hit the grass, and stars danced across my vision before I passed right the fuck out.

The soft brush of feathers on my face woke me. I groaned, my face throbbing, and opened my eyes. I don't know what I thought I'd find—maybe a naked Tris in my bed, tickling me with a feather? But instead I found myself staring right up the asshole of a pigeon perched on the end of my nose.

"Shoo!" I growled, batting the dumb bird and getting shat on for my efforts as the startled avian took to the sky. "Fucking pigeons." I wiped the spat of bird poo from my cheek with disgust, grimacing as I cleaned my fingers on the wet grass. The sun was only just peeking over the horizon, but that still meant I'd been unconscious on the grass for several hours. How hard had that dickhead hit me?

The ache in my head as I staggered to my feet said it was *too hard*. I needed painkillers and sleep.

My head throbbed so hard I could barely see as I made my way back to the Cobra, sliding into the driver's seat with a long, pained moan. My rib might be broken. Wasn't that fun?

So I'd definitely been wrong about catching Igor

creeping around Boles at night... but who the fuck *was* that? Tink was too small and delicate, and the power behind those punches said it was a man. Who the fuck *else* would be in town and up to no good?

It was a puzzle for another day. I blinked carefully to try and clear my vision, driving slowly across town to my new apartment. Trying to read the email from Hestia with my access codes nearly sent me cross-eyed for how bad my headache increased, but eventually I got inside, deactivated the alarm system, locked the door, reactivated the alarm, then staggered into the kitchen. Hestia houses were always fully stocked, so it only took me a minute to find the paramedic-level medical kit beneath the sink and raid it for painkillers.

I washed the pills down with a glass of water, then kicked my shoes off and headed for the bedroom.

Despite my aches and pains, and my nearly overwhelming exhaustion... sleep evaded me for far too long. All I could think about was Tris, and whether this new player was a danger to her.

Tris

nine

A flash of unexpected light across my eyes woke me, and I jerked up out of bed with a gasp. Someone had just entered my room; that light had been from the hallway.

"Shh, Tris!" a woman hissed in the sudden darkness. "It's me. Tink."

A huge sigh rattled through me as I sank back onto the bed. "Holy shit, Katinka, you scared the crap out of me," I complained. My half-asleep brain had been one thousand percent sure it was Dexter Grimaldi, come to attack me in my sleep.

"Sorry," she apologized, coming to sit on the edge of the bed. "I had to come check on you. With the way you were when you left your place, and then you never came back... I got worried. But you seem totally fine. Is everything... okay?"

I scrubbed the heel of my hand into my eye sockets. "Yeah. I mean... no. But yes. I'm alive, right?" I gave a hollow laugh before realizing I was talking to someone who had *no idea* what kind of trouble I was in. "Sorry, um, bad joke. What time is it?"

"Like six-ish," she whispered. "I can't stay long or someone will see me here; the sun is just coming up now, so people will be starting work."

Ugh, no wonder I was all groggy. I hadn't had nearly enough sleep for coherent brain power. "Were you here with Dex?" It explained why she was in the house, even if that thought did make my skin crawl. But also, I wouldn't begrudge Katinka whatever he was paying. Each to their own.

"Uh, yeah. Yep. Easiest way into the manor." I got the general vibe that she was winking. Don't ask me how; it was too dark with my curtains closed to be sure. "Fuck I'm glad to see you're okay, though. The Grimaldi family can be very, um, trigger happy. You know? I was really worried something bad had happened."

Okay, so maybe she knew more about that side than I gave her credit for. "Yeah, I know. But I think Mr. Grimaldi and I have reached an agreement that we can both live with. Live being the key word there."

She gave a little chuckle, and I found myself grinning. This really wasn't a laughing matter, and yet...

"Well, I'm glad," she told me with a sigh. "I better sneak back out before I get caught."

Katinka stood and took a few steps toward the door before I gave a confused sound. "How'd you get in here, Katinka?" I asked, frowning as I squinted at her, my eyes having adjusted to the low light.

She tilted her head to the side. "With Dex, remember?"

"No..." I shook my head. "I mean in *here*. This room. I locked the door. Didn't I?" I squinted at the door but couldn't see the key sticking out. What the—

"Are you sure?" she replied, pointing to the door key lying on the bedside table beside the cordless house phone that I hadn't put back in the cradle "But you really *should* keep it locked, so do it after me. I'm glad you're okay, Tris."

She slipped back out into the hall, the door closing softly behind her. This time I made sure I was awake as I locked the damn thing. Securely. And then tested the handle to check. I couldn't afford to fuck this up. I crawled back into bed with the house phone in one hand, but the reality I'd been sleeping with the door unlocked meant falling back to sleep was impossible.

I LAY IN BED FOR HOURS, STARING AT THE CEILING AND WAITING for my stupid brain to shut off enough to let me sleep a little more, but I was shit out of luck. No one came to drag me out of my bedroom, either, and eventually hunger—and curiosity—saw me making my way down to the kitchen. The white-uniformed chef eyed me as I hovered in the doorway, then grabbed a tea towel to dry his hands.

"You must be Tristian," he said by way of greeting. "I'm Chef Tony. Naomi said to expect you some time this morning. What can I get you for breakfast?"

There was no menace or threat in his tone; he was just treating me like a *guest*. It was overwhelming, confusing, off putting. And it saw me dithering on making a decision to the point where I probably looked like I'd just had a brain malfunction.

Chef Tony just squinted at me. "How about we start with coffee, eh?"

He guided me over to a breakfast bar area with comfy upholstered chairs lined up along the front. Another staff member popped out of nowhere to lay out a place setting complete with silverware and a linen napkin. Chef Tony told the woman—she was older than me—to get me coffee, then headed back to whatever he was cooking.

"Thanks," I murmured when hot coffee filled the bone-china mug beside my silverware.

She gave me a polite smile. "No trouble. I'm Dana, you'll find me here most mornings till mid-afternoon."

"Thanks, Dana," I corrected myself. "I'm Tris."

She smiled wider. "I know. You *have* worked here almost a year, but I guess you never hang around for mealtimes."

That confused me. "Do a lot of staff stay for meals?" I'd never even known that was an option. Not that I ever would have, even if I'd known.

Dana nodded, circling around the breakfast bar to put the coffee pot away. "Yeah, absolutely. Chef Tony used to work in a Michelin-star restaurant, so his food is better than anything you can get in town. Breakfasts are quiet, but dinner time is often a busy affair."

"Huh," I mumbled, picking up my coffee and reflecting on how little I had paid attention in the year of working in Mr. Grimaldi's gallery. I always parked around the side of the house with an access door closest to the gallery. I came in and went straight to the gallery, spent my entire shift locked in there, then left again the same way. I rarely spoke to any staff besides Naomi, and never went wandering around the manor. Mainly because I was terrified of stumbling over more bodies. Or getting cornered by Dexter.

That thought reminded me of my late night—or early morning—visit from Katinka. Which meant Dex was somewhere in the house. Or maybe he'd already gone to work? I could hope.

"Here," Chef Tony crossed over to us and set a plate in front of me. Then he gave me a hesitant frown. "You aren't allergic to anything?"

I shook my head, my stomach growling loudly at the incredible aroma of baked cheese. "No allergies. Thank you, Chef, this looks amazing."

He gave a short nod. "Nothing fancy, just a croque monsieur. You tell me what you usually like to eat for breakfast and I'll sort you out tomorrow, clear?"

I licked my lips, already cutting into my breakfast. "Yes, Chef."

He huffed a satisfied sound, leaving to go back to his work. Dana was gone, too, leaving me alone to eat my food and sip my coffee. No one came looking for me, or yelled at me for being out of my room... It was almost like I'd imagined that whole messy scene with Mr. Grimaldi in the ballroom.

But I couldn't forget. I'd killed a man to save my own skin. I was trying hard not to think about that... but it was a permanent stain on my mind. Because as awful as I felt for taking that man's life, I also knew that I'd still make the same choice again and again. Anyone would do the same... they'd just lie to themselves until push came to shove.

No one else talked to me while I finished breakfast, but Dana circled back once to refill my coffee. It wasn't a tense silence, either. It was comfortable and polite, and it was freaking me the fuck out. Everyone was acting like this was some kind of five-star hotel and I was a VIP guest. Or like I owned the house. Had I somehow pulled a *Freaky Friday* with Mr. Grimaldi?

I needed answers, because this psychological game was making me twitchy. Sliding off my stool, I tried to carry my dirty dishes to the sink, but a young kitchenhand whipped them away for me and assured me it was taken care of.

My plan was to hunt Mr. Grimaldi down and ask what he was playing at. But I had no idea where to even start looking for him. The ballroom? Only if someone was being tortured... or shot. Damn it, he'd made me a murderer and seemed to now be rewarding me for it.

"There you are, Tristian," Naomi called from along the corridor as I stood there at a loss for where to start. "I just delivered some more clothes to your room, along with a phone. Was there anything else you needed?"

I shook my head, still bewildered. "No, that's great, thank you."

"Good. Did you get something to eat?" She nodded past me to the kitchen.

"Yes, I met Chef Tony, too. I was actually hoping to speak with Mr. Grimaldi. Do you know where I might find him? If he's here, I mean?" It just occurred to me, he had plenty of businesses to run outside of his home, so it was unlikely he just hung around the house all day.

Naomi checked her delicate gold watch. "Yes, he should be in his office. He usually leaves around nine o'clock, so you'll have to be quick to catch him." I had no idea what time it was but took her word for it. "Head down that way, turn right at the Grecian statue, then take the small staircase up to the double doors."

"Got it, thank you." I hurried in the direction she'd sent me, eager to work out what in the fuck was going on.

The statue she'd mentioned was hard to miss; it looked like something lifted straight out of Rome. Knowing Mr. Grimaldi, it probably was. I hurried up the steps and paused outside the double office doors. Then I pulled up my big girl panties of courage and knocked. Lightly.

"Yes?" Mr. Grimaldi shouted back, and I took that as an invitation.

Hesitant, I opened the door just enough to peer inside. "Good morning, sir. I wondered if you had a minute to speak?"

He looked up from the papers on his desk and smiled. "Tristian! My dear, yes for you I always have time. Come in."

Okay, I was definitely creeped out now. The guards had told him about my rather inglorious descent into the bushes and the encounter with John, right? Frowning my confusion, I entered the office and closed the door behind me before crossing to his desk. "Thank you," I murmured.

"Sit, please," he indicated one of the chairs where I stood. "How did you sleep? Has Naomi delivered your wardrobe?"

I flicked my tongue against my teeth, reminding myself to remain polite and professional. This was the same man who casually handed me a gun and a scapegoat less than twelve hours ago. Maybe my aborted escape was something he'd already anticipated too?

"Yes, actually I wanted to ask you about that..." I started slow, hoping he would just explain without me needing to be rude.

His brows lifted. "Ah, you don't like her selections? If there is another color palette you prefer, of course she can exchange anything, but I think you look lovely in red."

I glanced down at the crimson, almost *blood-red* knit sweater I wore, and shivered.

"Um, no. That wasn't what I meant," I murmured, shifting forward on the chair nervously. "Sir... I know you have places to be so I'll cut to the chase." Then I lost my nerve and bit my lip nervously.

Mr. Grimaldi just waited patiently, hands clasped loosely on the desk in front of him.

Well... if he didn't kill me when I stole from him, he wouldn't kill me now. "Sir, what the hell is going on? I'm very confused. After our chat last night, I was under the impression that we had a business agreement?"

"We do," he agreed. "Have the staff not been treating you well? If someone has been rude—"

"That's not the problem. Quite the opposite. I was under the impression that I'm your pri— uh, that I'm here under duress. But everyone in your household staff is treating me like a guest." I pursed my lips, trying not to freak out. Because he was messing with my head and I didn't fucking like it.

Mr. Grimaldi arched one bushy brow. "Tristian, my dear... you are not a prisoner here. Your room was not locked from the outside, was it? Nor were you prevented from exploring freely? You are free to leave any time you like." He let the silence stretch between us, his stare unblinking. When I said nothing, his lips twitched. "Of course, then I couldn't protect you any further, and it's such a dangerous town."

And there it was. Leave this house, get killed. Maybe that was all he had to say on the subject of my midnight "run." Maybe. Whatever. I got the message. Loud and clear, boss.

"Shall we discuss the little art project I mentioned?" He watched me like a hawk, searching for any sign of weakness.

I wet my lips. I'd rather discuss that casual comment he'd made last night about a *wedding,* but I also didn't have the lady-balls to bring it up. Part of me wondered if he was just testing me, and if I didn't mention it then neither would he.

"Sure, what's the painting you'd like replicated?" I folded my legs, interested in the project despite my situation.

Mr. Grimaldi smiled. "It's a Picasso."

Cubism. Fuuuuck. My weakest style. "I see. Which piece?"

My boss opened a drawer in his desk, rifling through some papers then pulling out one sheet, which he slid across the desk for me to take. I leaned forward, picking it up.

My lips parted in surprise when I recognized the piece in question. "*Le Pigeon aux Petits Pois.*" It was a relatively well-known Picasso for the fact it had been taken in a museum heist and never seen again since. Not even on the black market. Rumor was that it'd been destroyed but... "You have this? Where?" Because it certainly wasn't in the gallery that I'd worked nearly a year in.

"I do not," he replied with a sigh. "No one does. Which is why this painting in particular would be such a valuable gift."

My jaw dropped. "You want me to replicate a Picasso from *photos?*" That was not how I worked. An authentic forgery required hours on days on weeks of close study of the *original* to perfectly emulate the direction of brush strokes and amount of pressure and... this was *Picasso* for fuck's sake.

"Yes, Tristian, I do." His eyes narrowed, like he was daring me to back out of the deal. Which, of course, wouldn't end well for my plan to remain breathing at all costs. "Is that going to be a problem?"

Yes. A huge one. Massive. This was an impossible task, and he fucking well knew it.

"Nope," I lied, giving a tight smile. "It might just take a little more time than first anticipated." Like... a *lot* more, because it couldn't be fucking done!

Mr. Grimaldi shrugged. "That's okay, I am in no rush. Perfection takes time, Tristian, and I'm a very patient man. Right now, though, I do need to head out for some meetings. I've asked Naomi to order supplies for your studio, but it might take a couple of days to be set up."

He pushed back from his desk, standing and reaching for his blazer. I took his cue, standing up myself and starting for the door.

"Uh, sir, what would you like me to do in the meantime?" Because surely I wasn't okay to just hang out and eat Chef Tony's food all day.

Mr. Grimaldi gave me a warm smile, tugging his shirt sleeves into place. "Nothing at all, Tristian." Except, of course, that I couldn't leave the manor. Got it. I gave a nervous nod, exiting the office ahead of him and walking down the small stairs with him following. As much as I might want to check to see if the guards told him and what he knew, I also didn't want to highlight it if they hadn't told on me. No, better to assume he knew and to be a good girl. We paused beside the Grecian statue where we would go separate ways.

"I understand this new arrangement is an adjustment for you, Tristian," he said thoughtfully, "but I believe it will be very mutually beneficial. And you're a smart woman, I think you agree. Oh, and I'm very pleased to hear the staff have been welcoming of you; however, they aren't treating you like a guest, my dear."

My brow furrowed. "They aren't?"

"No, of course not. You aren't a guest here, Tristian. You're family." He gave me a pointed look, daring me to deny it. To argue that point. But the words froze on my tongue and my eyes involuntarily flicked to the gun holstered under his jacket.

When it became clear I wasn't going to say anything, he gave a nod of approval and headed for the front door. "Take some time to relax, Tristian. Check out the pool. It's lovely."

I stood there, staring after him, for what felt like forever. His words echoed through my head like a life sentence. *You're family.*

So... the whole marrying Sin thing was still a thing. Good to know.

Come to think of it... where *was* Sin? Surely he'd also have something to say on this matter. Lord knew Dex would, but that was an interaction I'd very much prefer to have Sin backing me up on. Maybe it wasn't such a bad idea after all. Especially seeing as I was single now...

John

ten

With permission to proceed with our cover identities, I felt totally justified when I broke into Tris's apartment as soon as I recovered from my killer headache. I'd slept most of the day, only waking to dose myself on painkillers around midday. It was only just after sun down when I got to Tris's apartment, so I went through the motions of knocking first, just in case Tris had been released and returned home during the day.

No one answered, though, so I made quick work on her lock and let myself inside quietly. The lights were all off—which I'd already noted from the street level—and I flicked them on. If I was going to search for a hidden Van Gogh, I couldn't do it in the dark. Besides, it was a hell of a lot easier to make an excuse for my breaking and entering if I wasn't sneaking around in the dark with a flashlight.

It did occur to me that I was doing exactly what I'd tried to catch Igor out on—disobeying the rules of the Game—but I figured no one would know. Tris and I had been dating, sort of, so I had plenty of excuses about what I was doing in her home, should anyone question me.

The logical place to search was her studio, so I started there. The painting she'd been working on before I skipped town was no longer on the easel, and I wondered if she'd finished it. Curiosity burned hot in my gut as I gravitated over to her racks of stored—finished—canvases. I flipped through them, admiring her undeniable talent in a massive range of different styles. Now that I knew she was forging the masters—or at very least I was ninety percent sure—it made sense that she was proficient in so many styles. Except cubism. She was not amazing at that, but it was clearly something she was forcing herself to work on, despite the lack of passion in those projects.

That said, she was still *good* at it. I seriously doubted there was anything she couldn't do.

When I eventually found the canvas I was searching for, my mood soured. It *had* been a beautiful pop-expressionist painting of me, even if she hadn't admitted it was me. The focus had been my back, the curve of my shoulders and slope of my spine as I lay in her bed, splashed with bold reds, striking grays, warm golds and interwoven with iris blooms. Now, though, it was ruined with an enormous neon purple dick and balls splashed across the entire image.

If I was holding onto any illusions that Tris had been pining after me, that cleared it up. Yeah... we were over. Seeing the destruction of her art drove the point home much harder than her knee in my nuts had.

Damn it.

With a sigh, I gave up on the studio and headed through to Tris's bedroom. Why? She wasn't likely to have *Poppy Flowers* stashed under her bed. So why did I find myself looking through her drawers and straightening the sheets on her bed? Christ, sometimes I creeped myself out.

"What the *fuck* do you think you're doing in here?" someone snapped, and I stiffened in shock. No freaking way had Nelson just managed to sneak up on me without my noticing. Why was my nose buried in Tris's pillow? When did I pick that up?

"Uh, I knocked..." I offered lamely, quickly dropping the pillow back to the bed, then turning to face the old man. He folded his arms and glared absolute death my way. "The door was unlocked. I just came to see if I'd left something here last week."

He wasn't buying it. His bushy brows rose, and he gestured to Tris's bed. "In here? What did you lose? Your favorite boxers? Or maybe your sense of fucking decency when you stole a priceless painting and skipped off into the night while leaving Ivy to take the heat? Huh? Which was it? I should call the authorities right now."

Oh good, he knew *everything* then. Great. Still... no harm in trying a little denial. I'd already started constructing a cover story for the university, and now was a great time to try it out.

"What?" I gasped dramatically. "Steal a... Nelson, what on earth are you talking about? I was in a car accident, but I sent a message to Tris to let her know. Didn't she get it?" I gestured to my bruised up face, and the bandages on my neck. It sure as fuck felt like I'd been in a car accident. I hadn't bothered to cover up my fresh bruises, and now I was glad for that laziness.

A flicker of uncertainty passed across his face as he scanned my injuries, and satisfaction warmed my chest. I had him; he just needed a little more of a push.

"Bullshit," he huffed. "Don't try telling me you conveniently ended up in an accident the same night that painting got snatched from Grimaldi. Coincidences like that don't exist, John, and *that* is when you disappeared so... bullshit."

I widened my eyes, a picture of innocence and confusion. "Nelson, I swear to you, I have no clue what's going on. I've been trying to call Tris all week from the hospital, but she hasn't been answering her phone. What is going *on*? What painting got stolen?"

Nelson's brow furrowed, and more uncertainty flicked through his eyes. The difference between bullshitting a stranger and bullshitting someone like him? Nelson *liked* me. He *wanted* to believe me. All I had to do was craft a vaguely plausible excuse and his own imagination would fill the gaps. Thanks to Igor's thugs and the lethal stranger last night, I had evidence to back up my story.

"*Poppy Flowers,* the Van Gogh... you really didn't know?" He was squinting at me now, ready to swallow my excuse whole with just a touch more encouragement.

I spread my hands wide, shaking my head in disbelief. "I had no idea! That's awful. And Mr. Grimaldi thinks Tris was responsible? She would *never* do something like that!"

Nelson scrubbed a hand over his face, looking exhausted. The dark circles under his eyes said he wasn't sleeping and probably hadn't since Tris left. Did he know what she'd been up to with the forgeries? I bet he did. I'd bet he was the one who'd taught her everything she knew... It stacked up with them meeting in a casino when she was a child.

Once a con man...

"I can't discuss this with you, John. Ivy's in enough trouble as it is without you trying to ride in there and save her."

Got him. Hook, line, sinker.

"In there?" I repeated. "Where? Grimaldi's house? She's there now? Is she okay? I get the impression Mr. Grimaldi is involved in some dangerous business..."

Nelson huffed a laugh. "What gave you that impression?" Because of course, Professor Smith should be oblivious to the dodgy shit going on in this town. Right?

I frowned. "Just a feeling. I've noticed some of his security guards carry a lot more weapons than usual rich old guy security... and the amount of priceless *missing* artwork he owns is enough to raise some eyebrows. You can't be an upstanding citizen and also bid on stolen paintings at black market auctions, you know?"

He nodded his acceptance of my reasoning. "Yeah, I guess you could say his business is not all aboveboard.

I'm fucking worried about Ivy, but she insists she's fine."

Surprise rippled through me. "You've spoken to her?" Was that before or after she attempted to escape the manor, then changed her mind? She couldn't have gone back the way she left, so Grimaldi must know she tried to run. He can't have been happy about that.

"Yeah, last night." He sighed, seeming older than ever. "She called to let me know she was okay and not to go launching a rescue attempt."

"She *called*? Well... that's good, right?" Then I glanced around her apartment, confusion creasing my brow. If she had that much freedom, why was still staying? "Why is she still there, though? When did she leave?"

Nelson headed through to Tris's kitchen, grabbing a glass of water. "Yesterday. She called me in a bit of a panic after..." He glanced at me with narrowed eyes. "After she saw some news report about an art thief being released from custody. Apparently whoever pinched the painting from Grimaldi took a forgery. Now Grimaldi must think she had something to do with it. Which she didn't, obviously."

I carefully conveyed appropriate levels of shock and disbelief, whilst filing away my curiosity. Did he really not know, or was he acting just as hard as I was? "Holy shit, imagine that. It must have been an impeccable forgery. I saw it in Tris's workshop just last week, and I'd have never guessed it wasn't the real deal. She had no idea?"

Crap. A news report? That explained how Grimaldi knew about the forgery. I had no idea it'd been on the news. Art Crimes must have an info leak.

Nelson's demeanor shifted to offended. "Of course not. What are you trying to insinuate, John?"

I shook my head. "Nothing! No, nothing at all. I just thought she spent so much time working on that painting, it must have been an incredible forgery for her not to know it was a fake. I bet whoever made it is one bloody talented artist himself."

It was a deliberate attempt to provoke a response, assuming the forger was a man. I hoped Nelson would try and correct me to *her*self.

"Well, if she has her phone maybe I'll try calling her again," I mused aloud. "If she didn't get my messages about my car accident then she probably thinks I just cut town without a word. I probably have some groveling to do."

"You're right about that," Nelson muttered with a huff of laughter. "She was pretty broken up for a few days there, thinking you *used* her. You wouldn't do that, would you, John?"

Yes. I would. And I'd probably do it again, if she ever let me close enough.

"What? No, never!" I bullshitted. "Shit, I hate that she was thinking that of me... I need to talk to her. I'd better call... or maybe I can drive over there and—"

"No, you can't," Nelson cut me off. "She was very firm about leaving her be. Besides, it wasn't her number she'd called from, have to assume it was the landline at RBD's, so I don't think she has her phone."

So... she had enough freedom to call Nelson but not enough to have her own phone. Interesting. Something wasn't adding up. I wanted to check if she'd packed any clothes or possessions to take with her—which she would have if she was staying at the manor by choice, or at least before she ordered me away, that had definitely been her choice—but I couldn't just go searching her closet while Nelson was here grilling me. He believed my story... to a degree. I could tell he was still a bit uncertain and wary, so I needed to avoid raising more suspicion.

"Hmmm, I don't like it," I admitted, honestly. "But she should be at class on Monday, right? So I can talk to her then." If she was free to continue classes, though, why'd I catch her climbing out a window? This puzzle was missing too many pieces.

Nelson grimaced. "I'm not so sure. Even without

this nasty business with the Grimaldis, she said something the other day about submitting a transfer request. Apparently she tried a few weeks back and the administrator lost her form. I tried to talk her out of it, but she was pretty firm that she wants to leave Whispering Willows."

Damn it. Yes, the administrator lost her form because I fucking well ripped it up. If she filed again while I was gone, it'd probably already been submitted for assessment. What the hell would I do if she moved to another city? I'd have no reason to continue pursuing her. Unless the Game changed in a way that kept her in play. I could only hope.

I needed to get my ass over to Grimaldi's and check on her. Even if it was at a distance, I wanted to ensure she was still alive and well. Grimaldi wasn't known for his patience or understanding. If he genuinely thought Tris stole from him... well fuck, she'd already be dead, wouldn't she? So the fact she went back into the house, undoubtedly alerting security to her attempted escape, and *then* called Nelson meant... what?

They must have reached an agreement. Somehow.

"Uh, I was just looking for a pair of cufflinks I left here last week," I explained to Nelson, jerking a thumb over my shoulder toward the bedroom area again. "You mind if I take another look? They were my grandfather's so I don't want to lose them..."

He gave a brief frown but nodded. "Yeah, sure. I just came over to water her plants. I'll get on with it." He fetched a little watering can from under the sink and started to fill it as I retreated to the bedroom.

As subtle as possible, I searched for any signs that Tris had *known* she would be gone from home for an extended period of time. It was hard to know, but all her favorite outfits were accounted for, so she either packed clothes I'd never seen her in, or she'd been taken by surprise. According to Tink, it had been unplanned. But that didn't mean she hadn't returned...

I flipped up her comforter as if I were looking under the bed for my "cufflinks" and sucked a sharp breath when I spotted Tris's favorite little purple bunny ears vibe dropped on the floor. It had a dumb name, from memory. Bang, Bang, Bunny. That was it. She kept replacing it with the same style after I'd stolen its predecessors, so it must be a good one.

She wouldn't have left it behind if she was going anywhere on a planned overnight. Not with her high sex drive. Gritting my teeth, I shoved the little critter in my pocket because I was quite honestly addicted to stealing Tris's toys at this stage. Why change that, just because we were no longer together?

"Find them?" Nelson asked, and I straightened up with a jerk.

"No. I guess I must have lost them somewhere else. Thanks for letting me look, though." I started toward the door, then turned back to him with a frown. "You can make sure the door is locked, right? It's worrying that she left it open..."

Nelson's answering smile was cautious and suspicious. "Sure can. If you hear from her..."

"I'll let you know," I agreed with a reassuring smile. Then I escaped before he could pick apart my flimsy excuses. I wanted to get over to Grimaldi's and see Tris. Just *see* her. To reassure myself she was still alive.

That reminded me... that fucker Bram hadn't given any updates. Useless rookie merc.

Tris

eleven

When Mr. Grimaldi told me to relax and check out the pool, that was actually what he meant. After I returned to my room I found Naomi hadn't just delivered *some* clothes for me: she'd cleaned out the entire clothing store and then some. The huge wardrobe of the jade bedroom was fully stocked with garments, all still with tags attached, and several swimsuits had been included.

As odd as it felt, exploring the manor and going for a swim seemed more appealing than just sitting in my room and waiting for the other shoe to drop. So that was what I did.

Chef Tony made me the most delicious lunch and told me to come back for dinner at seven, because he was making spinach and ricotta cannelloni. Sounded amazing, and by seven I was hungry enough that I forgot Dana's comment about how many staff show up for dinner. So when one of the other kitchen crew directed me into the dining room, I nearly swallowed my tongue.

By "staff" Dana meant Grimaldi goons. Not household staff. The dining room was packed with maybe twenty or thirty suited men all sharing a meal like one big suit-loving family with Mr. Grimaldi in the middle of them all.

"Tristian! You made it for dinner. Good. Alfonzo, move over and make space for my new daughter-in-law." Mr. Grimaldi whacked the heavyset goon to his left and gestured me over to take the vacated seat. "Gentlemen, you already probably know Tristian, but she is now *family*, alright. You all treat her as such."

The men all mumbled their understanding, and I tried to make myself as small as possible in my seat. Fucking Chef Tony and his lure of great food, he clouded my brain and made me let my guard down. If I'd been thinking straight, I'd have avoided this scene like the plague.

But... now that I was here... it wasn't really so bad.

No one forced me into awkward conversation, Mr.

Grimaldi returning to whatever he'd been discussing with the scarred man across the table and leaving me to my meal. Alfonzo to my left silently handed me dishes to serve myself from, and one of the other guys across the table poured red wine into my glass. Gentlemen, indeed. Most of the guys around the dinner table were older than some of the goons I'd had interactions with, and none of them gave me uneasy, threatening vibes.

Hell, it was the opposite. By the time I finished my dinner, I was relaxed and comfortable. Maybe that was down to the two glasses of wine I'd had.

When I excused myself, I got a casual chorus of well wishes for my evening, and that was it. Like I belonged, rather than being forced to be there.

Mr. Grimaldi had a very strange approach to extortion, that was for sure.

Red wine always helped me sleep well, so after locking my door—and triple checking that it was, in fact, locked—I collapsed into a deep, dreamless sleep.

When I woke, I found a folded note on the pillow beside my face.

A cold trickle of fear zapped through me, and I looked to the door. It was closed, just as I'd left it last night, but I scrambled out of the sheets to check it was locked. It was.

Wetting my lips, I reached for the note still lying innocently on my pillow and unfolded it cautiously. What I thought was going to jump out at me from a simple piece of paper, I had no idea, but I still handled it like a ticking time bomb.

I'll be watching you.

That was it. Four words scrawled across the page with no further information. A deep chill ran through me as I crossed to the window. Was that how my visitor got in?

Maybe not. If this was a message from Mr. Grimaldi or his security, they could have just unlocked my door. Surely I didn't have the only key to that lock. That'd be stupid. But he hadn't said a word about my failed escape attempt, so maybe this was the game he'd chosen instead? Or had his security not actually told him... and this was them, warning me not to try again?

Either way, someone had been in my room while I slept. Someone had stood right there beside the bed, close enough to smother me in my sleep, and had chosen to leave a threatening note instead. Was this psychological torment?

It was working.

Swallowing the lump of fear in my throat, I ripped up the note and went for a shower. Some part of me seemed to think I could wash off the anxiety. Like I could exfoliate away my fear.

I was utterly unsurprised to find it didn't work, and I was just as paranoid and on edge after my shower as I was before.

With a resigned, stressed-out sigh, I dressed in comfy clothes—silent thank you to Naomi's good choices—and headed down to the kitchen for breakfast.

Chef Tony had prepared me vanilla polenta porridge with rhubarb compote, which did a hell of a lot more for my mood than the shower had achieved. Yum.

"Good morning, Chef!" Mr. Grimaldi boomed as I scraped the bottom of my bowl some time later. Would it be rude to lick the plate?

"Morning, sir," the chef replied with a warm smile. "Can I get you another coffee?" He snapped his fingers at one of the other kitchen staff who dropped what they were doing to fire up the barista machine once more. Yesterday over lunch, Chef Tony had pumped me for information on all my favorite foods and drinks, promising to incorporate my preferences into his menus. One of those comments was about *real* coffee, so this morning I'd been handed a latte rather than yesterday's filter coffee.

Apparently Mr. Grimaldi also preferred espresso over drip.

My boss chatted with Chef about kitchen admin crap for a while, something about stock levels and wastage, and I got the distinct impression that Mr. Grimaldi treated his kitchen just like a restaurant to ensure there was no money slipping through the cracks within the house. Smart, really.

Once the kitchen hand passed him a coffee cup on a delicate saucer, Mr. Grimaldi turned to me with a smile. "Tristian, I only have a few minutes but wanted to get you set up in your studio. Shall we?"

Surprise and suspicion had me nodding and sliding off my breakfast bar stool in a hurry. "Yes, of course. Thank you for breakfast, Chef!" Was this where I faced the music for my escape attempt?

"My pleasure, Tris," Tony replied over his shoulder, already turned away to do something else.

I followed silently through the house as Mr. Grimaldi casually sipped his coffee on the way, until we reached a staircase I hadn't explored yet. We ascended, and it took us up to an attic area with a locked door.

"This is for you, dear," Mr. Grimaldi said, handing me a key from his pocket. "You can keep that one; I have another. No one else will be permitted entry, same as the gallery."

"Understood," I murmured, unlocking the door at his gesture. I pushed it open and stepped inside to find a fairly sparse art studio setup with a gorgeous view over the manor gardens from a big circular window. All thoughts of being scolded for climbing out my window evaporated. This wasn't a punishment. Not even close.

"It will take a few days for the rest of the supplies to arrive, but I thought you'd like to organize the space yourself. As deliveries arrive, they'll be left in the mail room for you to collect so no one else is entering this room." He glanced around, his lips pursed. "Will this do?"

I made my way further into the room, assessing the few things already set up. Work tables, a large easel, a short backless stool, and a stack of plastic wrapped canvases. "Yes, the room is lovely," I confirmed. "For the task you've asked, I'll need some specialized equipment, but a lot of that is already in the gallery studio."

He nodded. "Well, I'm sure you can understand why you aren't permitted access there, but if you give Naomi a list I will arrange for the relocation of those items."

Ah. Yes. That answered my question of why he was setting me up a studio here... and not just sending me back to the existing workshop. He wisely didn't want to give me any further access to his art, in case I decided to switch to something else. Understandable, given my history.

"I can do that," I agreed. "Then in that case, this should be fine. I need to be totally transparent with you, though, this will be a *very* time intensive project. Without the original to study, it will take a lot of attempts to get it convincing and even then..." I shrugged.

Mr. Grimaldi gave a small hum. "Well. You may not have the original to study for a replica, but neither does anyone else have it to compare for inconsistencies. I trust you will do your best, Tristian, even if it takes years." He checked his watch, then sighed. "My apologies, I need to be going."

Years. Of course, because if he was serious about marrying me off to his son then why would there be any urgency?

"Sir, sorry, just a question..." I *needed* to ask. "Where is Sin? Does he know about our arrangement? I had the distinct impression he was otherwise spoken for."

Mr. Grimaldi's face clouded with anger, but it faded to irritation quickly. "Well it's about damn time he let that torch die. He's out of town on a business trip right now. I'll inform him when he returns." He gave me a curious look, his brow furrowed. "You don't need to worry, dear. Sinister is an obedient boy and does what his father tells him. Dexter could learn a thing or two."

My chest tightened and I swallowed hard. I really, badly didn't want to see Dex again. But it was an inevitability now that I was *family*. The fact I hadn't seen him around the house already was some kind of miracle, but I had no doubt the clock was ticking on that confrontation.

"Um, does *he* know? Dex, I mean."

"I don't see why he needs to," Mr. Grimaldi replied, shaking his head. "He's more than busy right now preparing for his child to arrive."

That was right: Dex's wife was pregnant, and he was screwing around with Katinka. What a gem.

Mr. Grimaldi bid me farewell and left me there in my studio, taking his empty coffee cup with him when he exited. For such a rich and powerful man, he was very considerate of his staff, and I liked that about him. It was hard to remember he was the same man who'd handed me a gun and told me to shoot someone.

And yet, there it was, right back in the front of my mind. *I killed a man.*

The fact I wasn't a bigger mess about that surely meant there was something wrong with me. Maybe Mr. Grimaldi had a therapist or psychologist on staff that could analyze me. Maybe I was broken. Normal people would not be coping... would they?

Reluctant to return to my room, I set to work

organizing the studio in a way I wanted things arranged. In one of the boxes I found a gorgeous watercolor palette, some charcoal pencils, and a sketchbook. If I were to guess, I'd say Mr. Grimaldi was setting this studio up for more than just one forgery.

I wasn't complaining, though. I ripped the plastic off the sketch book and flipped it open to a blank page. My sense of duty to the task saw me trying to sketch out as much as I remembered of *Le pigeon aux petit pois* from memory, but it wasn't detailed. After a few attempts, I tore the pages out and crumpled them up. Fuck it, I'd try again once I had reference images to work off.

My pencil continued gliding over the page anyway, my hand working with a life of its own as I sketched absentmindedly. Until I paused and sighed when I refocused on what I'd drawn.

"Fuck you, dickhead," I muttered, tearing the portrait of John out and balling it up. Stupid fucking muse kept wanting to draw him, though, and I found the slope of his shoulder and tilt of his mouth appearing on my page as I tried to draw Chef Tony instead. "Dammit."

More and more pages got ripped out and crumpled up, but all I was achieving was frustrating myself. John was on my mind, like it or not, and I needed to purge him. What I wouldn't give for my vibrator right now, though. A quick self-pleasure session was *exactly* what I needed to clear my head.

Annoyed at John's overbearing presence in my mind, and at Naomi's oversight in stocking my room with everything under the sun *except* a vibrator, I slouched to sit on the floor beneath the big circular window. An armchair right there would be amazing, so I could look out on the garden below.

Blowing out a breath, I decided to settle for second best and slid a hand inside my pants. It wasn't as quick as the Bang Bang Bunny, but my fingers could get the job done. Biting my lip, I tipped my head back and tried to picture anyone *but* John as I rubbed my clit with my thumb. My middle and ring fingers slipped into my pussy, giving that added sensation of being penetrated while my clit stimulation got the goal. As mad as it made me, I only managed to climax when I let my mind embrace John. Replaying that hot, sexy, sleepy fuck we'd had right before he skipped town, then morphing into the kiss we'd shared in the dark just two nights ago. Right before I tried to pulverize his balls with my knee.

I hated that my imagination had conjured up that last time we slept together, because that visit was so unnecessary. He had probably already taken the painting, he could have just *left*... but no, he needed to leave his touch on my skin, his kisses on my lips. Like he wanted to ruin me.

"Fuck," I moaned out loud, my body quivering with endorphins even as disgust rippled over my skin. I needed to forget that prick, like he'd forgotten me.

If only his touch were as easy to wash off my memories as it was my skin.

John

twelve

It'd taken me longer than I liked to break into Tris's bedroom during the night. Then by the time I finally got inside, I froze. She was sound asleep, snoring softly like some kind of sharp-tongued angel. I couldn't bring myself to wake her up, but I also couldn't risk getting caught. So I panicked and left her a note instead. Just a quick one to reassure her that I wasn't leaving town just yet.

Hopefully if she knew I was keeping an eye on her, she would stop doing dumb shit like climbing out of a second floor window.

After sneaking back out, feeling calmer for having left that cute note for Tris, I headed out of town to stage a car crash. Nelson was ninety percent of the way to believing me, but he was also shrewd enough to fact check my story. So apparently, I was buying back my old Mustang just to crash her. That hurt a little, I wouldn't lie.

Once the sun went down that evening, I put some time into patching up the cuts on my neck with steri-strips then gave up on trying to hide the rest of my bruises. Even before encountering that mysterious stranger outside Boles, the concealer wasn't doing much to mask the damage.

As reassuring as it'd been to see Tris alive, unharmed, sleeping peacefully... it'd left me with even more questions. Like why the fuck she seemed to have moved in there, and why she hadn't given Nelson any explanations. Bram wasn't answering my calls, which was making me stabby, but even as green as he was I wasn't dumb enough to go picking a fight with a Guild mercenary. I'd lose.

So my next option was Tink... and Dex. Which was why I strolled through the front door of The Slippery Lips a little after nine that night.

"Here for a dance, big boy?" a mature woman with enormous breast implants asked with a wink. She ran a hand over my upper arm, giving it a squeeze. "Wanna let Jolene take care of you tonight?"

Ah hah, yeah I saw the theme now. With her big blonde hair and massive tits, she was vibing the Dolly

Parton look. Good for her, switching things up from the tired old naughty school girl costume that strippers seemed to love.

"Sorry, no. I came to see someone in particular." But of course, I had no clue what name Tink was dancing under. I did know she was using her full name when befriending Tris, though. "Is Katinka working tonight?"

Jolene rolled her eyes. "Tinkerbell? She's one popular girl. Not until ten. You want a dance from someone else in the meantime?"

I wanted to tell her to go away, to leave me alone in my foul mood so I could sulk. But that wasn't the right way to win friends in a place like The Slippery Lips. So I glanced around the room until I spotted a girl who caught my eye. "Yeah, maybe her?" I pointed at the brunette across the room.

Jolene patted my arm again, then indicated to a vacant table near the main stage. "Take a seat, big boy. I'll send her over."

I did as I was told, then ordered a drink from one of the passing waitresses. A minute later, the petite brunette dancer I'd selected sashayed her way over to me with a coy smile on her painted lips. Her face was nothing on the perfect beauty of Tris, but it was dark in the club and if I squinted... yeah, good enough.

She dropped into my lap, grinding and rolling with

the music pumping through the club. I sat back, sipping my Negroni and *pretending*. She flipped her long dark hair, and I caught a whiff of floral shampoo, not totally dissimilar to the one Tris used. My dick hardened, and I tucked a twenty into the side of her micro-skirt.

The dancer—whose name I didn't get—increased her enthusiasm after that, touching me all over as she danced and grinding her ass on my boner. I wasn't even mad about it, either, because in my head she was Tris and *goddamn* I wanted Tris on my dick.

What I didn't want was to get castrated with a butter knife, and since Tris had been pretty fucking clear we were *done-done*, I'd have to settle for the Wish version of her instead. A stripper at The Slippery Lips wearing a tiny blue skirt. This sure felt a whole lot like rock bottom, if I were being honest.

I lost track of how much time passed, as I sipped drinks that magically refilled, and routinely added more and more cash into not-Tris's outfit. When she leaned in close and whispered a proposition to join her in a private room in my ear, I realized I'd taken things too far.

"Thank you," I gritted out, my stomach curling with self-disgust and my erection deflating, "but no."

I lifted her out of my lap, depositing her carefully on the seat then standing up before she could protest. A glance at my watch said it was just after ten, so Tink should be here somewhere... but I needed to visit the restroom first. One, to take a piss. Two, to splash some cold water on my face then stare into the mirror and question what the actual fuck was wrong with me.

That process only took a few minutes, but when I returned to the bar Tink was up on the main stage dancing around with silly little fairy wings on. Fucking Tinkerbell. She met my eyes with a glare, and I shook my head in disbelief. Talk about leaning into a physical stereotype, Tink.

Her set went for fifteen minutes, and I grew increasingly annoyed while waiting for her to get off the stage, but eventually the MC announced a new girl and they swapped out.

"You've got a whole lot of nerve showing up here, John Smith," Tink growled under her breath as she sidled up to the bar beside me. Her chunky Perspex eight-inch heels brought her up to my shoulder, which was adorable in a scrappy fighting terrier kind of way.

"Good to see you, too," I muttered. "Can I buy you a drink?"

She glared up at me. "Obviously. Why ask stupid questions, John?"

With a grin, I nodded to the bartender to order us both a drink. "So... why'd you stay in Whispering

Willows after I took off with the painting? Surely you had no idea it was a fake." I kept my voice low, cautious whether anyone else could hear us.

Tink seemed to be thinking whether to lie or not, then blew out a breath as she drummed her fingers on the bar top. "You're right, I didn't. But I figured if the Game was over then... why not stay? I like this town, and I knew you'd break Tris's heart, so I thought maybe she might like a friend. We're not all as disconnected from human emotions as you are."

I grunted at the insult. "Ouch. Low blow, Tink. You really don't know me well enough to make that observation."

Her laugh was cold and judgmental. "Oh, I think I do. You're not as mysterious as you like to think."

"Bullshit," I protested. "I'm very mysterious. But... I'm glad you stayed. Have you got any news? I saw Nelson last night, and he mentioned she called..." I wasn't in the mood to tell her about my own visit to Grimaldi's manor, or Tris's less than enthusiastic response.

She laughed, taking her drink and swallowing it with one gulp. "Like I'd fucking tell you. In case you aren't comprehending, Mommy got custody of Tink in the divorce. Thanks for the drink, you look like shit, by the way. Did you get in a fight with a lawnmower?"

I scowled and she just tossed her head back with a laugh, then left me at the bar to return to work. As frustrating as it was to get no answers out of her, I was glad she'd taken Tris under her wing. Tris needed a friend, and despite Tink's shady morals, she had a good heart.

I debated hanging around to try and pressure Tink for more answers, but the middle finger she extended my way from across the room sort of told me all I needed to know. She wouldn't be giving me anything useful tonight.

Leaving my drink untouched, I headed out of the club. I had huge plans to try and spy on Tris *again*, but I changed direction halfway to my car when I recognized a familiar frame down the street.

He was on the phone, not paying attention, so he never even saw me coming. Well, not until my fist connected with his face and he got knocked on his ass.

"What the *fuck*?" Igor roared, holding his hand to his busted nose. Blood dripped off my knuckles, and I shook my hand in disgust.

"Don't worry, old man, there's plenty more where that came from. Just settling the score." I turned to walk away, then changed my mind. Spinning around, I leaned down and punched him again. Then again, because he fucking well deserved it.

Screw it. One more wouldn't go astray.

Igor groaned, nearly unconscious, and I forced myself to step away before I killed him. Fucker wasn't worth that level of trouble for myself. "You're a disgrace to the Valenshek name, Igor," I spat with hatred. "Do my grandfather's memory a favor and disappear for good this time."

"Found the tracker, huh?" Igor groaned from behind me as I started to walk away. "No need to throw a tantrum, son. It's just business."

My fists tightened, and I ground my teeth together to fight the urge to stomp on his face. Still, I turned back to sneer at him. "Just business? You mean cheating. But that's one and the same to you, isn't it? You couldn't abide by the rules if your life depended on it. Hell, maybe this time it does."

"I'm not giving up," he groaned, blood pouring from his face as he lay there on the sidewalk. "Not this time. That inheritance should have been mine, and you fucking know it."

A cold, hate-filled laugh bubbled out of me as I shook my head. "You're fucking delusional, old man."

He was trying to get under my skin, so I shut out his voice while I stalked away, leaving him lying there in his own blood. If I was lucky, maybe a stray wolf would wander down the road, smell blood, and eat him alive. It was nice to dream.

Sliding into the driver's seat of my new Cobra, I sighed. Then I wiped my bloody knuckles on my t-shirt because I didn't want Igor's stink tainting my new car. He'd actually done me a favor, planting that tracker and forcing me to trade in the Mustang... I loved this car.

First good thing that'd ever come from Igor Valenshek.

Useless prick.

Tris

thirteen

After rubbing one out, I spent the rest of the day sorting out my studio and experimenting with watercolors just for fun. A delivery of equipment arrived while I was having lunch, and Chef Tony assigned one of his kitchen hands to carry it up the stairs for me. After that I happily wallowed in denial about my coerced living arrangements and pretended I was there by choice, humming as I organized my new studio.

I stayed up there so long that I was running late for dinner, racing into my room to rinse off the paint and charcoal from my hands and changing my shirt. A glance at the time on my phone—which I wasn't brave enough to actually use as anything but a clock—said I was already ten minutes late, and Chef Tony was making lasagna.

Tony gave me a nod as I came sprinting into the kitchen a whole fifteen minutes after dinner started, out of breath and only halfway into my sweater. "Tris, chicken, you're fine. I saved you a plate. Here." He pointed to my breakfast bar spot. "Sit here, or someone will swipe your garlic bread."

My mouth watered as he put the plate down in front of me. "You're the best, Chef. Have they already demolished the garlic bread? I'm not *that* late am I?"

He quirked a brow. "On lasagna night? On time is late. They're almost finished in there." He tipped his head to the dining room, where raucous laughter erupted. "Anyway, eat. Timmy, get Tris some of the wine." He snapped his fingers and one of his staff headed for the wine cellar. Chef Tony paired wines with all the main meals, and it was amazing.

Dessert was tiramisu—as if there were any other options—and by the time I slid off my stool with a belly full to bursting, I was having a hard time remembering that I was a prisoner. A really hard time. Sure, I'd killed a man, and I might be killed if I tried to leave, but where were the other negatives? So far, Mr. Grimaldi and his staff were going out of their way to make me feel welcomed and included. What was so bad about that?

My *only* regret was leaving Nelson and Hank behind. They were my family. But I refused to put them in danger just to satisfy my own wants. That would be selfish as fuck.

A few staff bid me good night on my way back to my room, and I smiled back. I fished in my pocket for my door key as I approached, then remembered I'd left in such a hurry I hadn't locked the door... which was fine, since I had nothing of value in there to keep safe. The most important part was making sure I locked it when I was *inside*.

Yawning, I let myself in, then closed the door and locked it carefully, testing that it was definitely locked. Between John and Katinka, I was developing a complex about whether I was locking doors properly. So now I had taken to locking, then checking the handle.

Lock. Check. Secure. Tuck the key into my pocket and then—

A hand wrapped around my mouth from behind, an arm pinning me to a bigger, stronger body, and I screamed into the man's palm. He grunted, tightening his grip and lifting me off my feet with his superior height. Panic flooded my limbs, and I thrashed, kicking backward and clawing at the hand on my face.

"Stop it," a familiar voice snarled, and a glacial chill

chased down my spine. I should have fucking known I wasn't safe. Not here.

Terrified and desperate, I sank my teeth into his hand and tasted blood. He grunted and spat a curse but didn't let me go. Not that I gave up, though. I continued fighting and thrashing until finally my heel caught him between the legs and he roared, tossing me onto the bed.

"You little bitch," Dex spat, inspecting his bleeding hand while his other one cupped his junk. "You think you can get away with this?"

"Get away with what?" I exclaimed, scrambling backwards and fumbling my pocket to try and find that goddamn door key. "You attacked me!"

He grabbed my ankle, jerking me back to him and making my teeth snap on my tongue when my chin hit the bed. "You think marrying Sin puts you out of my reach, Tris? You're wrong. So fucking wrong." He gave a low, cold laugh, pinning my ankle with his knee, making me cry out when he leaned his weight into it. "He is *always* traveling for work, Tris. That means you'll be left all alone, here, in *my* house. Defenseless. At my fucking mercy, every damn night, and there won't be a thing you can do about it."

That idea nearly made me vomit. I knew Dex had

developed a bit of a fixation, but this was a serious escalation.

I did the only thing I could, considering my disadvantaged situation. I screamed. Loud. I *screamed* so hard it hurt my throat, and Dex panicked. He slammed my head forward into a pillow to muffle my scream, but effectively suffocated me at the same time. Either he didn't notice, or didn't care, but he held me like that, face down in the pillow with my lungs rapidly tightening at the lack of oxygen while he unbuckled his pants.

"...letting that asshole take what's mine..." he muttered, only bits of his words reaching me through the rush of panic and oxygen starvation in my head. "...gonna take this from me. I *earned* this!"

I wanted to scream and fight, I really did, but right now my primary objective was not suffocating. Which was becoming increasingly more urgent as Dex shoved my head harder into the pillows. All of a sudden, a *boom* shuddered through the room, and I gasped a greedy lungful of air as my hair got released.

My ears rang and I blinked rapidly against the tears in my eyes, while trying to get my bearings. Someone had kicked down my bedroom door, the frame splintered and broken where the lock had been forced through the wood. Holy shit.

Arguing voices pulled my dazed attention, and I refocused on my attacker. Dex. Fucking hell, there was the other boot I'd been waiting to drop. He swung a punch at the second man—one outfitted in a Grimaldi goon suit—but the man deftly sidestepped the punch and twisted Dex up in an arm lock.

"Let go of me, you sorry piece of shit!" Dex howled as the security guard marched him out of my bedroom. "You can't touch me! I own you! I own all of you!"

"Sorry, sir, just doing my job," the guard responded in a bored tone of voice. There was something vaguely familiar about his voice but I didn't care enough to think about it as I curled up in a ball on my bed. Their voices faded away along the hallway and Dex's outraged protests echoed along the hall... but the guard who'd saved me was totally unfazed.

I hugged my knees, burying my face as tears leaked from my eyes, the rush of adrenaline making me tremble and shiver.

"Tris?" someone said, and I gasped so sharply that I choked on my own saliva. My eyes were blurry from crying, and I blinked frantically while coughing up half a lung.

Then I wrinkled my nose as I recognized why the guard sounded familiar. "Bram?" I asked, confused as fuck. "What are you doing here? Did Nelson send you?"

His brows rose, his expression curious as he looked up at me from his position kneeling beside the bed. "No... should he have?"

My lips parted, but I caught my tongue before I could say anything dumb. "N-no, I'm just... what are you doing here?"

"Uh, saving you, apparently." He gave a lopsided smile, then winced. "Sorry, no joking matter. I just got a job here. Tonight was my first shift and *probably* going to be my last if that douche has anything to say about it."

A hard shudder ran through me and my mouth went dry. "Dex... he was... he'll try again. Every time he gets denied, he comes back harder. More determined. Fuck... I need to get out of this house." My voice trailed into a pathetic whine that made me cringe. Because I couldn't leave.

"You want me to drive you home?" Bram offered. "I'm getting fired anyway, so I may as well get you to safety first."

I gave a hollow laugh, warm at his sweet, totally well-meaning offer. It really must be his first day on the job. "I wish," I whispered, shaking my head. If I left with him, God only knew what would happen. Not to me... but to him, Nelson, Hank... It wasn't worth the risk.

Then again, living here where Dex could try to finish

what he just started? Made my stomach knot and twist. My eyes shifted past Bram to the splintered door frame. Fucking hell, now I couldn't even lock the door.

Bram gave me a worried look but didn't try to talk over me and pretend he knew better. He just nodded slowly and reached out to pat my arm gently. "Are you okay for two seconds while I check in with my supervisor? I won't leave you, I promise. I'll be right outside in the hall."

"Y-yeah, of course, I'm fine." I mustered up a watery smile, still hugging my knees. "I'm fine." Maybe if I kept saying it, I'd believe it.

He scrubbed a hand over his cheek, looking uncertain, but when I murmured another *I'm fine*, he slowly nodded. "Okay. I'll be *right* outside. No one will come in here, alright? We'll sort it out, Tris. I've got your back."

I believed him. I'd only met the guy twice, but for some reason I *believed* him. There was a grounding quality to him, a level of confidence that said he kept his promises. So I bit my cheek to hold in the needy *don't leave me alone* bullshit that wanted to pour out, and watched him step out into the hall.

Uncontrollable trembles wracked through me, tears pouring steadily from my eyes, but no sounds escaped me. I just silently shook in a little ball on the edge of the bed and lost track of time as I listened to the low hum of *calm* voices in the hallway. Calm, but not content. I got the sense Bram was keeping his voice low and steady deliberately to save frightening me, and *damn* I appreciated it.

Eventually, he returned to my pretty green bedroom and crouched back down beside the bed.

"Hey, neighbor," he said softly. "So, good news."

I raised my head slightly, trying to pull myself together. "You're not fired?"

He shook his head. "Not today. But my boss agrees we need to move you for tonight... since I broke your door and it won't lock. Is that okay?"

I nodded quickly. "Y-yeah, of course. Lemme just... I just need some stuff." I scrambled off the bed and crossed to the wardrobe to grab some pajamas. Why the fuck that seemed important right now, I had no idea. It just was. Bram waited patiently, then offered a reassuring smile as he indicated for me to leave the room with him.

In the hallway, several other suited guards lurked around, and I hesitated until Bram touched a gentle, non-threatening hand on my elbow to silently tell me I was safe. Now.

He got me situated in a new room, then flicked on the enormous flatscreen TV and told me to relax. Then he and another security suit went about installing an interior deadbolt on the door and made a visible show of checking *every* crack and corner of the room.

I sat there in silence as Bram introduced another older security guy who checked me for bruises. He smeared some peppermint scented cream around my neck where Dex had grabbed me, but I was otherwise unscathed. My tongue throbbed where I'd bit it, but that would heal itself.

Despite my shock, and residual fear, I slept easy when they were done.

John

fourteen

For what seemed like the first time in my whole damn life, I was *excited* to go to work. Not my night job—I was always excited for that—but my day job. I loved the academics and material—my interest in art history was genuine—but I didn't *enjoy* answering to a superior or holding scheduled hours. I liked sharing knowledge with students but hated having to actually interact with them.

But as I strode into the Boles University campus on Monday morning, a flutter of anticipation filled my chest.

Was Tris going to be here?

The infuriatingly brief report I'd gotten from Bram the night before said she was still being accommodated as a valued guest rather than a prisoner. So did that mean Grimaldi would allow her to return to school as well? If he wasn't going to kill her for stealing from him... but then why make her stay at the manor in the first place?

Maybe I was being foolish, thinking that he was just... what, exactly? Forcing her to stay in his home and drink tea all day? The *not knowing* was driving me insane, so I held onto hope that she would be there today. Even if her school transfer got accepted, it would take some time and she'd be expected to continue her classes here in the meantime.

That was the hope I clung to as I made my way to Dean Lawrence's office to bullshit my way out of being fired. It'd only been a week, but I suspected I wouldn't get the warmest of welcomes.

"John!" the dean's assistant gasped when I strode into the administration office. "Oh my gosh, what happened to you?" She brought her hands to her mouth in horror, and I put on my most pathetic expression.

I'd really leaned into the bruises today, not covering any of them up since they were right in that lovely dark purple and vibrant green stage of healing. It added to my car accident story that Nelson had been so eager to believe. If I could fool him, then dean should be a breeze.

"Unfortunate car accident," I replied with a wince,

"is Lawrence available? I fear I need to make apologies for my absence this past week."

Marla shook her head and flapped her hands. "Oh my goodness. No, John, I think this is a very understandable reason. You poor thing, how horrible. Hang on, I'll just—" She knocked sharply on the dean's door, then opened it without waiting on a response. "Larry, hon, John is here, and my goodness the poor duck has been in an accident. Come in, John, come in."

She gestured me into the office, and I bit back a smile at her grandmotherly fussing. I should have known she was the one to win over, not Lawrence.

The dean himself was halfway out of his chair with a deep scowl set on his face, but even he gasped when he saw my face.

"Oh, I see," he grimaced. "Yes, come in, John. Thank you, Marla, you can close the door."

His assistant hovered a moment longer, then huffed a sigh as she exited, closing the door softly behind herself. I put a visible stiffness into my movements as I shuffled to the seat in front of Dean Lawrence's desk and groaned a little as I sat down.

"John," he said with a puzzled look on his weathered face. "What on earth happened to you?"

I let out a heavy, exhausted sigh. "Car crash," I replied mournfully. "Last weekend, I was heading out of town to visit a relative in Cloudcroft and hit a deer. My car went off the road and I took a pretty hard knock to the head. I should have called and let you know, I can't apologize enough..."

Dean Lawrence frowned but shook his head. "No, don't be silly. This is... goodness, you look terrible. Are you in pain? Do you need more time off? We have Professor Gregson covering your workload, and I'm sure he can handle a few more days."

I grimaced, and this time it wasn't faked. "Professor Gregson? Why not my TA, Tristian?"

Dean Lawrence shrugged. "She resigned from the position last week. I assumed that something had happened..." He gave me a pointed look, and I chose to ignore it. "And that she'd decided to resign rather than file a complaint. I believe she has requested to transfer her credits to Shadow Grove University, but they haven't accepted yet. That school thinks it's more prestigious than all the Ivy's combined, like they weren't founded by a scumbag just five years ago."

The scowl set on Lawrence's face said he held some grudges against someone at Boles' closest tertiary neighbor. He'd probably applied there and been rejected.

Still, this was good information that they hadn't

rushed Tris's transfer papers. It meant she was still here… for now.

"Huh," I murmured when the silence stretched between us. "I didn't know. Maybe I can change her mind."

Lawrence's expression turned sly and accusing. "I have no doubts. You seem like a very persuasive man, John. One who gets what he wants."

I smiled, meeting his gaze without flinching. "I am. I should get going if I want time to prepare for this morning's classes. Let Gregson know that I have it handled but appreciate his assistance."

Not waiting for the dean to dismiss me, I gave a pained groan and stiffly exited. Marla gave me a worried smile as I passed, but I just nodded back and continued on my way. Better not to hang around and give Lawrence any reason to second guess my story, though the bruises were convincing. Igor really helped me out by setting his goons on me. The car accident excuse was flawless. Especially now that I was driving a new vehicle.

Internally, I smiled with satisfaction at a story well sold. Now I just had to somehow win over Tris… which would be a whole lot more challenging. She knew me too well already, and there was no way I could pretend I didn't fuck her and leave with that painting, no matter who else believed my innocence. Hell, I'd basically admitted it to her face the other night. Something about her made it impossible to lie, though.

Step one would just be getting to *see* her.

I had some time to kill before my first lecture of the day, so I took up residence at the desk inside the lecture theater. Somehow I managed to review the vague, scribbled notes Gregson had made in the last week, and came up with a weak but passable plan for the lesson today.

As students started filing into the room and taking their seats, my senses were all on high alert. I stared at the door so hard I could have set it alight with the force of my gaze. Would she come to class?

Come on, Tris... please show up.

Tris

fifteen

"Again? Seriously?" A man's irritated voice jerked me from my deep sleep, and panic flooded my veins like acid. "How many times do I have to tell that prick, I'm not interested in —" The frustrated rant cut short as I sat up in a frightened jerk. "Tris?"

I scrubbed sleep from my eyes and pushed my tangled hair out of my face. "Sin? What are you doing in here?" I glanced at the clock on the side table, shocked at how late I'd slept. I would normally be in class right now... with John. Prick. Had he resumed his fake teacher role? Doubt it. He'd be halfway across the country by now, still chasing the stolen Van Gogh.

Sin arched a brow, tucking his hands into his trouser pockets. The irritation had seamlessly melted into amusement. "What am I doing here in my bedroom? I could ask the same of you. Also, why'd my father's security need to give me a deadbolt key for my own room?"

Understanding dawned and I wrinkled my nose. "*Your* bedroom. Of course it is. Fuck, I'm sorry, Sin... they didn't tell me..."

He gave a chuckle, sweeping a hand over his hair. "I'm not even a little bit shocked, Tris, don't worry about it. I'm just glad it's you and not one of the countless women my father has tried to *distract* me with in the past few years. At least I know you're not going to try and molest me in the shower."

There was so much relief in his voice that I wondered how hard Mr. Grimaldi was pushing his son into moving on from his broken heart. And *why*. But also...

"You don't think I'm confident enough to molest a pretty man in the shower? I'm insulted." But also, he wasn't wrong. I would *never*, even if that had been Mr. Grimaldi's intention in forcing us together.

Sin scoffed a laugh, unbuttoning his shirt as he disappeared into his walk-in closet. "Confident enough? Absolutely. Lacking in self-respect and dignity enough to make a move on a man you're not even remotely attracted to? No way in hell. Give me five minutes, I just got off a long haul flight."

He popped out of the walk-in closet with his shirt unbuttoned and a stack of clean clothes in hand, then disappeared into the bathroom. He was wrong about me being *not even remotely attracted* to him, because I wasn't fucking blind. He was a gorgeous man, all dark and brooding with tattoos and abs for *days*. But I was also relieved to know he'd acknowledged I wasn't *interested*. Similar, but different. While yes I could appreciate he was visually appealing, there was no chemistry between us. No spark. He was just a really good looking friend. Or had the potential to be, at any rate, since we really didn't know each other that well.

Hell, who knew what the future might bring if we really went through with getting married. The spark could grow... one day. Maybe? I could do a lot worse, that was for fucking sure.

A deep shudder rolled through me, remembering the forceful way Dex had grabbed me last night. Rubbing my bruised neck, I thanked my lucky stars for Sin.

The sound of the shower running gave me the confidence to slide out of bed and change from my pajamas into the clothes I'd been wearing the night before. But then I grimaced as my fingers snagged on a tear in the seam of my ribbed sweater. I needed to talk to Mr. Grimaldi today... If he wanted me to stay here, I needed some kind of reassurance that I'd be safe. Otherwise I'd take my chances on the run.

The shower shut off, but it was another couple of minutes before Sin returned to the room in a casual pair of jeans and a faded *Seventeen Daggers* concert t-shirt. I waited cross-legged on the edge of the bed, which I'd neatly made.

"Alright. What have I missed?" he asked, flopping down into the armchair under the window. His dark eyes studied me carefully, but it was with concern rather than anything sinister. "The last I heard, you were home with the flu. Catch me up."

I blew out a heavy breath, my shoulders sagging at the casual, non-threatening way he spoke to me. I didn't feel so vulnerable in this house with Sin on my side.

"Okay so... did you hear about how the stolen painting was a forgery?" I bit the edge of my lip, watching for his reaction under my lashes.

His expression was genuine shock, which surprised me. "I did not," he replied. "Wow. It was a... *oh I see*. Tris..." He started laughing, shaking his head. "Really? You?"

I scowled, my cheeks heating with shame. "What's

that supposed to mean? You don't think I have the skill to replicate Van Gogh?"

He laughed harder, snorting a little. "That I don't doubt. But holy shit, the *balls* that must have taken..."

I rolled my eyes. "Balls are weak, Sin, use a better analogy. But *anyway*... your father was, um, not super happy about it all."

"You're kidding," he deadpanned, a grin still sitting on his lips. "I'm so shocked. But you're still breathing, which genuinely is a surprise if he even suspected you'd stolen from his gallery. Which must mean you're still useful to him. I take it you haven't given the original back?"

I shook my head. "No, not yet."

"Good," he murmured, thoughtful. "Don't. It's probably the only thing keeping you alive right now."

I grimaced, rubbing the bridge of my nose. I couldn't exactly leave to get any of the paintings anyway. At least not yet. "That, and he wants my assistance forging another painting for some business contact or some shit."

"Ah, yes. That checks out. My father is smart enough not to let his emotions ruin a potential asset to the Grimaldi house. You do know he'll never let you leave, right? You either make yourself invaluable enough to remain alive or, you know…" He mimed getting his throat slit, and I cringed.

This wasn't *news* to me, though. I was well aware how close I'd come to dying just a few nights ago, and I never wanted to be back in that seat. Even if it did mean signing a contract in blood. Or, shit, maybe I already had when I shot that man.

"Yeah…" I murmured, wetting my lips. "About that. Turns out Mr. Grimaldi saw my *worth* in more than just my artistic talent." I gave him a pointed look, silently begging him to work it out and save me saying it out loud.

Sin stared back at me, blank. Then eventually glanced from me to *his* bed. Then at the door with the deadbolt, and a heavy sigh gusted out of him. He dropped his head into his hands and gave a low groaned curse.

"*Yeah*," I confirmed. "So… surprise! We're engaged. Bet ya didn't see that one coming, because neither did I."

I expected an explosion of anger. For outrage and denial. I did *not* expect laughter, but that was what I got. "Of fucking course we are. Wow. This is…" He trailed off with a chuckle, scrubbing a hand over his dark stubble.

"Insane, I know," I agreed, shifting uncomfortably

where I sat. "So we're totally clear, there was a gun to my head when I agreed to this, so I'm not trying to marriage-trap you or anything."

Okay, not *literally* to my head. But close enough.

Sin's brows shot up. "I never would have thought that of you, Tris. This is not the first time my father has tried to interfere in my life. We have issues, and you're just getting caught in the cross-fire, but honestly... this could work out. Of all the insane meddling the old man's done, I don't *hate* this."

My jaw dropped. "You don't?"

He shrugged. "Why would I? I might not know you *that* well, but I do know you aren't a social climber out for my family money, nor are you a bloodthirsty psychopath wanting to become a mob queen, or a prostitute."

"Wow, the bar is that low, huh?" I bit my lip to hold back the laugh trying to escape. This was no laughing matter.

Sin nodded mournfully. "It really is. So this actually feels like a reward. You're... you know. Normal. Are you still seeing that professor guy? John?"

I shook my head. "Definitely not. If I accidentally ran him over, I'd probably reverse and do it again just for good measure. What about the girl who has your heart? Won't she have something to say about this arrangement?"

He slouched back in his seat, looking at the ceiling. "Honestly? I don't even know if she's still alive. No one has seen or heard from her in two years, and I'm starting to think I'm chasing a ghost. We weren't even dating."

"Oh." I frowned my confusion. "Yeah, okay. Well... so we're doing this? Seriously?"

He shrugged like this genuinely wasn't a concern for him. "Why not? It's just paperwork and neither of us are dating anyone so what's the harm? I'm not going to suddenly get ideas about fucking you if that's what has you worried." My jaw dropped *again* and he squinted at me. "Sorry, I didn't mean that in a bad way. You're gorgeous, just not... my type." That awkward pause told me what he really meant.

Just not *her*.

Fine by me, though. If we were both on the same page then there really were very few reasons *not* to play along with Mr. Grimaldi's game. At least for the time being. It gave Sin a break from being set up with undesirable women, and it kept my head attached to my shoulders.

"Um, *if* we are coming to a mutually beneficial agreement," I said slowly, picking anxiously at a thread in the ripped seam of my sweater, "I need to know how I can be safe when you're not here. I know you travel a lot, and—"

"Safe *how*?" he demanded, cutting me off as he sat forward with concern. "Did something happen?" He glanced at the door, seeming just to compute that the deadbolt was on the *inside* and he was likely given the only key. "Who hurt you, Tris?"

I swallowed hard, not meeting his furious gaze. "Dex."

Sin surged out of his chair in a rush of fury. "I'll fucking kill him."

A strangled squeak escaped my throat. "What? No, you can't!" Because like it or not, Mr. Grimaldi was always going to choose his son over the girl who stole from him, no matter how admirably sneaky. "It's fine. Bram, one of the security guys, came to my rescue and got rid of him. I don't totally know how. But that's how I ended up in here, because the door to my bedroom was busted up."

My attempt at diffusing the situation only seemed to make it worse as Sin's eye twitched and his fists curled at his side. "Tris, let's get something perfectly fucking crystal clear. If we're getting married, I'm responsible for your safety. Regardless of whether we're fucking or not, *no one* lays their hands on you. My brother is no exception to that. Now, if you'll excuse me, I need to commit fratricide. We can chat more about our arrangement when his body is in the ground."

I barely even managed to croak out a weak protest before he was slamming the door behind himself, leaving me alone in his room once more.

For as strange and unconventional and bewildering as our situation was... I suddenly felt a million times better. The other shoe had dropped, and now I had an ally. Maybe Mr. Grimaldi knew what he was doing all along.

John

sixteen

She didn't come to class. I fucking phoned in that whole lecture, barely even paying attention to the course material as my eyes remained glued to the door. For some reason my foolish brain kept reasoning her absence. She had car trouble and was running late. She stopped to help an injured kitten. She slept through her alarm. Something like that, and she would come running into the lecture all flustered and embarrassed about being late.

But nope. She never turned up. Even after the lesson ended and students filed out, I kept waiting for her to show. Janie slithered over, batting her lashes and hinting that she wanted to apply for my now vacant TA position, but the idea of spending time with anyone other than Tris made my chest hurt.

I'd really fucked up. Didn't she get my note? If it fell off the bed or something, then she'd never know I'd been there... so she must think I'd left town to chase the painting. Which was a fair assumption, since she didn't know the Game was paused.

The worst part was that I'd probably do it again. Fuck her over to get the prize, I mean. Winning the Game meant more to me than any potential love interest. It wasn't just the status and satisfaction of winning, this was my grandfather's *legacy*... and he was the only person on this whole fucking planet who'd ever cared about me. Aside from my mom, or so he said, but I didn't remember much of her.

So as much as it hurt to know I'd fucked everything up with Tris... it was just part of the job.

Eventually I accepted that she wasn't coming, and packed up my shit. I headed to my office and spent some time actually working on my *day job* since we weren't allowed to continue the Game for now. Might as well catch up on grading since I no longer had a TA. Dammit.

I had another class in the afternoon, then drove into town to pick up dinner from the Royal Orchid. As much as I tried to tell myself it was just that I loved their food, I quietly hoped I'd run into Tris there. If Grimaldi hadn't already killed her, then they'd come to an agreement. So why *wouldn't* she have returned home? Bram said she was "fine" and my own visit to her bedroom confirmed she wasn't being held captive or punished with torture... so what the fuck was the issue? Why was she still there?

"Pick up for Hank?" a delivery driver asked at the counter while I waited for my food. Coincidence? Surely not. How many Hanks lived in Whispering Willows?

The waitress advised it was almost ready, and to wait two minutes. My order got called before the delivery guy collected Hank's, so I lurked outside the restaurant to wait, pretending to talk on the phone. Then when he exited a minute later with the bag of take-out in hand, I followed.

When the delivery dude approached Tris's building, I sped up before he could press the intercom buzzer. "Are you taking that to unit seventy-one?"

The delivery guy turned to look at me, frowning. "Uh, yeah. Why?"

"Same with this," I held up my own bag. "I'll take them both, if you want."

The guy quirked a brow, then shook his head. "Nah, I'm good." He reached for the intercom, so I acted quickly, throwing an elbow into the side of his head to knock him out while also catching the bag of food before it could hit the ground.

The delivery guy crumpled, though, and I carefully placed both food bags down so I could drag his unconscious form around the corner and into some shadows behind a parked car.

"Sorry, Nacho," I muttered, reading his name badge. "Nothing personal."

Returning to the front door of the building, I retrieved the bags of food and casually waited until another resident exited, slipping my hand into the door to hold it open and allow me access without buzzing Hank and Nelson.

I made my way up to the top floor, glancing briefly at Tris's door when I passed and trying to pretend my chest didn't tighten a little with regret. Then I knocked on Hank and Nelson's door.

"John?" Nelson gave me a suspicious frown, then glanced up and down the corridor. Probably looking for the delivery guy. "What are you doing here?"

I held up the food. "Ran into your delivery guy and offered to bring this up." I smiled in what I hoped was my best, most endearing yet pitiful way.

Nelson scowled. "You can't come in. Hank still thinks you stole the painting and left Ivy for dead." He reached out and snatched the bag from my hand.

"Honey, is that the food? I'll open some wine!" Hank called from inside, and Nelson shot me a hard look as if to say *fuck off*.

I frowned. Shifting forward enough that he couldn't easily close the door. Not without being really rude about it. "You didn't tell him you saw me the other night? About my car accident? Nelson..."

The hurt and accusation banked high in my voice, manipulating him into feeling guilty. It didn't sit well in my gut, but it was better than the alternative. They'd already come so close to ripping off my mask, I needed it firmly back in place.

"What's taking so long, Nels? Is there a problem with—" Hank's question cut short when he came into view and froze dead in his tracks, his eyes locked on me. Then his gaze narrowed with anger. "You! How *dare* you show up here after—"

"Whoa, okay, we're not doing that," Nelson interrupted, stepping between us like he genuinely worried Hank would try and hit me. Yeah, that made me feel like a total shithead, seeing Nelson *defending* me against his partner. "Hank, maybe we should hear John out. I think we *all*, Ivy included, jumped to conclusions."

"What? Since when? Just this morning you *agreed* with me when I said he deserved to get run over by a military tank for what he did to our girl." Hank parked his hands on his hips, his expression a picture of outrage. "And now you wanna *hear him out*? Bullshit, Nelson. I smell some stinky cow crap."

"With a tank?" I muttered, loud enough to be heard. "Kinda harsh."

Nelson cast an exasperated look over his shoulder at me, then refocused on Hank. "Honey bear, let's go inside and talk."

"Why? Who do you think we're disturbing? Ives *still* isn't home... no thanks to this big, handsome bastard." Hank gave a rude gesture in my direction, and I fought the urge to smile. It was a fair reaction, but I needed to win over Nelson and Hank *both* if I had any hope of weaseling my way back into Tris's good graces. Because she was still useful, or that's what I was telling myself. We could make a great team. Right now, I couldn't afford to look at that much closer.

I pressed the advantage and stepped inside their apartment, closing the door behind me.

When Hank shot a death glare my way, I held up the second bag of take-out. "I brought my own dinner."

Nelson nodded quickly. "Yes, good idea, let's have dinner. And wine. So much wine." He bustled past Hank, muttering about wine, and I offered a hopeful smile to the still furious old man staring at me.

"I swear, it's all a big misunderstanding. I would never hurt Tris..." Oh man, that lie tasted like acid and regret. Because I did. And I would again. But I couldn't make myself leave her alone.

Hank rolled his eyes and huffed, throwing up his hands. "Fine. Come on in then. You look like shit, by the way."

Progress. I kept my mouth shut and followed.

"Before you start," Hank snapped when we reached their dining table, "I'm already going to presume you have some *very* credible—and evidence supported—story for where you've been. One that doesn't include moonlighting as an art thief." He shot me another narrow-eyed glare as Nelson joined us with plates and cutlery for three. It didn't shock me that these two gentlemen ate their takeout with proper flatware.

"I do," I confirmed. "Otherwise I wouldn't be here, right?"

Hank was a tough nut to crack, still glaring. "Well, whatever the reason, you hurt our girl. Whether it was because you're secretly a cat burglar or because you got drunk in a ditch somewhere and forgot what day it was, you still hurt her. And we won't forget or forgive that easily."

There was no need to fake the guilt and shame I felt

over that, and I nodded solemnly. "I wouldn't expect anything else."

Hank stared back at me for a long moment, then grunted. "Fine. Sit down then, start talking."

Tris

seventeen

Sin didn't return to his room after storming out, swearing to kill his brother for laying hands on me. If John had done that I'd probably be all hot and bothered about it, but from Sin it just gave me the warm fuzzy of knowing he was on my side. I wasn't here *alone* any more. At least until he left on his next extended work trip, that was.

After waiting for what seemed like ages, I got up and cautiously made my way back to the jade bedroom to change my clothes. The door had already been repaired and the bed was neatly made, but I still shivered when remembering how close Dex had come to killing me. Call me crazy, but I wasn't brave enough to shower in that room. Not until I knew what'd happened to Dex.

So I grabbed my fresh clothes and scurried back to

Sin's room, figuring he wouldn't mind me using his bathroom to freshen up. After all, he seemed totally fine to marry me, so we'd have to share a bathroom at some stage.

That, in itself, blew my fucking mind. How chill he was about the whole crazy idea.

When I'd showered and changed, he still hadn't returned, so I made my way up to my studio in the attic space. It was incredible how quickly that little room had become *mine*. My stomach rumbled as I pulled out my sketch pad and pencils, but I ignored it. No way in hell was I risking running into Dexter in the kitchen or dining room.

Muttering curses under my breath, I tried sketching out as much of the Picasso painting I'd been tasked to replicate as possible. It was totally pointless, though. Fucking cubist bullshit. I needed to put in some serious research before attempting to put pencil to paper on this mess, so it was no real shock that I ended up sketching a realistic pigeon on my page, standing atop a mound of peas.

Le Pigeon aux Petits Pois.

Stupid pigeon with stupid peas. Where the fuck the pigeon was in the original painting, I had no idea. All I could find was a foot. Maybe an eye? That was it. Oh and a small pile of peas. Picasso was one weird fucker, that was for sure.

I tapped my pencil on the sketch I'd just finished. Then I frowned and added a spy camera to the dopey pigeon's head.

A knock on my studio door made me put the drawing down, and I climbed out of my chair where I'd been sitting cross-legged.

"Who is it?" I called out, cautious.

"Your dashing fiancé, Tris darling," Sin drawled in response. "Come to wait on you hand and foot like the queen you are."

Chuckling, I unlocked the door and opened it for him. "Oh, you weren't lying." I eagerly accepted the tray he carried with a cup of coffee and plate of breakfast pastries. "This is something I could get used to."

He closed the door behind himself, then glanced around at my studio space. "This is cozy."

I already had half of an apricot Danish in my mouth, but mumbled *thanks* anyway.

Sin perched his butt on the little seat by the window where I'd been sitting yesterday to sketch. "So... I wanted to talk more about this arrangement my father made with you. Obviously you know what was in it for *him*, and for me too, I guess. But what's in it for *you*, Tris?"

I wrinkled my nose, finishing my mouthful before replying. "You mean aside from staying alive?"

Sin just tipped his head to the side, full of curiosity. "That's surely not enough to agree to marry a man who —as handsome and charming as I am—you really don't know from Joe."

My answering laugh was full of disbelief. "Seriously? I personally think *staying alive* is a pretty strong motivation."

His brow dipped and he shook his head. "Don't get me wrong, I agree. I just think you should get more out of it... He has you working a new forgery for him too, right? Which, in itself, should be enough to forgive your infraction."

I couldn't fight the grin spreading across my lips. "Infraction? You make it sound like spilling red wine on his carpet, not forging and switching a fifty million dollar painting. But if you have ideas, I'm all ears."

Sin shook his head with a laugh. "I can't believe you did that. I mean, I *can*... but damn, Tris. Balls of steel." Then he corrected himself. "Uh, I mean lady-balls. Strong ones. Ovaries of steel."

"More like it," I muttered my approval. "Anyway. What do you have in mind? Also, dare I ask what happened with Dexter?" I indicated the slight swelling on his jaw, the hint of a bruise coming up beneath his stubble.

"Nah, it's handled." He waved a hand dismissively. "He won't bother you again."

I stared at him, not sure I believed that. Dex wasn't likely to be told *no* and obey. Quite the opposite, if my experiences were anything to go by.

"So. I probably can't get you let off the hook entirely," Sin continued, "and to be fair, I wouldn't even if I could because this fixes a lot of problems for me."

I rolled my eyes. "Gee, thanks."

He flashed a grin. "You're welcome. So, I can't—or won't—help you wiggle out of the deal entirely, but I can negotiate on your behalf for other shit. There must be something else you want? The Grimaldis are very wealthy, in case you didn't notice. There's not much off the table in this discussion."

"Except my freedom," I clarified.

He shrugged. "I like you, Tris, but I like me more. And this works for me, so ask me for just about *anything* else and I can likely make it happen. Marriage is just paperwork, and I'll never force you into compromising your morals. But you know that, or you'd have probably cut and run already."

Good point. If Mr. Grimaldi had proposed marriage to Dex, this all would have gone very differently. I'd have escaped that first night, alerted Nelson and Hank, and been on a plane to Timbuktu with a fake name already set up.

Sin was different. He sat there totally at ease as he told me to name my price. His father might be offering my life, but he wanted to make it clear that I could ask for more. And should.

"Okay so... maybe not *total* freedom but can I leave the property?" I arched a brow. Did he really mean what he was saying, or did he think it was more a case of tossing me a credit card? "I'm missing classes at Boles right now, which will be damaging my academic record. And I have my own apartment..."

He pursed his lips, fingertip tapping his chin as he pondered my request. "I don't see why it should be a problem. Classes, I mean. Your apartment will never get approved, not when we're meant to be getting married and, no offense, but you're probably a flight risk so my father will want you where you can be watched."

I expected as much, but it was still disappointing. "Okay but what about Dex? How can you reassure me that I'm *safe* here? Especially if you're gone for these international work trips...?"

"That's a fair concern. I think the easy answer in the short term is that I don't leave again. Dex is a bully and a snake, but he's also a coward. After my chat with him this morning—and the one my father had with him last night—he won't show his face around here for a while. Not until the bruises fade, anyway. Vain bastard." He chuckled, rubbing the bruise on his jaw. "Classes, we can sort out though. When is your next one?"

I glanced at the time on my useless phone. "Technically now. But I have another one on Thursday at eight in the morning, Art History."

"With the professor you were dating?" Sin seemed genuinely interested and not in a jealous possessive way. It was more... friendly interest. Like I was chatting with Katinka. Still, the mention of John made my stomach swoop in a way that I hated. Part of me really hoped he *was* long gone from Whispering Willows. Part of me didn't.

I screwed up my nose. "Yes. But he won't be there." No way was he that bold. "I actually have no idea who would have taken over his classes. Maybe Professor Gregson."

Sin nodded thoughtfully. "Okay, so I have two days to sort this out. Leave it with me." He pushed to his feet, stretching like he had a kink in his back. "And Chef Tony said he expects to see you at lunchtime. He was worried."

I smiled, picking up another Danish. "Understood.

So long as there's no risk of running into Dex, I'll be there."

Sin left, telling me he'd see me for lunch later, and I locked the door after him.

This arrangement was unconventional, no question, but it wasn't *bad*.

Sin had kept his word in negotiating more freedom with Mr. Grimaldi on my behalf, eventually presenting me with a compromise that we could all agree on. Which was how I found myself back in my own apartment on Thursday morning. Of course, Sin was right there with me and I only had ten minutes to grab my school supplies and pack a bag of essentials, but something was better than nothing.

To my intense disappointment, neither Nelson nor Hank were home, but I scribbled them a quick note to reassure them of my continued state of aliveness. Then I handed Sin my heavy school satchel with my computer, drawing tablet, and back-up hard drives loaded inside.

"Two minutes," I told him when he reminded me of the time. "I need some personal items that Naomi didn't provide."

He gave a short laugh. "Don't let her hear that, she

prides herself on being exceptionally thorough. What'd she forget?"

I glanced over my shoulder on my way toward my bedroom. "None of your damn business."

It didn't look like anyone had searched the apartment. It was as messy as I left it. That was a win, right? Grabbing a backpack from my closet, I glanced around for the real reason I'd bullshit about wanting *essentials*. When had I last used the bunny? It was before John ditched me…

"Seriously, what are you looking for?" Sin asked as I hunted under my bed, making me startle so hard I smacked my head.

Huffing a frustrated sigh, I gave up. "Nothing. Never mind. Come on, let's go before I end up late. It's bad enough I'm bringing my *fiancé* into class with me."

Sin just shrugged. "You'll hardly even notice I'm there. Besides, it was me or Tennison, and as far as sparkling conversation goes, he's as interesting as a houseplant."

He had a point there. Mr. Grimaldi had been very reluctant to let me leave the manor, expressing his valid concerns that I was a proven flight risk—which answered my question about whether the security guys told on me. I got the feeling his concern wasn't entirely about my arranged marriage to Sin but more about my new forgery task. That goddamn Picasso. I needed to put in some serious work to that... maybe then he'd consider letting me off the hook on the rest.

Probably not until I returned *Poppy Flowers*, though. Which I had no intention of doing, even if I did know my stalling tactics wouldn't last forever. At some stage, I would need to talk with Nelson.

Leaving my apartment, I posted the little note I'd written for him under their door, then walked with Sin back to his car. I was aiming to get to class early, so I could beg some study notes from one of my classmates for the week of lessons I'd missed. I also needed to follow up on my transfer request... not that Mr. Grimaldi was going to give his blessing for me to move cities entirely.

Not until Sin and I were married, and the Picasso forgery had been delivered, of course.

Arriving at campus, I directed Sin to park in the student lot then gave him a lackluster tour on our way to the arts building. We reached the lecture hall ten minutes early, and I gave a small groan when I recognized the blonde girl setting up her computer in the front row.

"Oh, Tris... hi." She blinked at me in surprise. "I thought you quit?"

"Hi Janie," I replied in a cool voice.

Her eyes flicked from me to Sin, then widened as she took him in, her lips parting in surprise and admiration. He had that kind of effect on most women, I was starting to realize.

"Tris, who is your friend?" Janie batted her lashes. Ugh. I moved over to a seat in the second row, dropping my bag beside me. Sin followed me, taking the seat to my left and draping his arm around my shoulders in an unexpected display of affection.

"I'm not her friend," he answered as I pulled my laptop from my bag and placed it on the desktop. "I'm her fiancé."

Well then. I guess he *also* noticed how she was looking at him.

Janie's eyes damn near popped out of her head, and I tried not to cringe. Still... it was part of the agreement with Mr. Grimaldi. If I was allowed to return to school, there was to be *no doubt* about my new relationship status. Which meant playing the part with Sin, and—

"Oh, wow. That's a *ring*." Janie gaped, staring at my hand where the heirloom Grimaldi family engagement ring sat heavy on my ring finger. It was a four-carat oval-cut diamond in a halo setting and sparkled so hard it could blind someone on the moon. She gestured for me to show her, and I tried not to grit my teeth too hard as I extended my hand.

Sin muttered something under his breath too quiet for me to hear, so I turned toward him and leaned closer as I asked him to repeat it.

"Damn, Tris, that's gorgeous," Janie cooed. "You know, it's so silly, I actually thought you were sleeping with Professor Smith, but here you are... engaged to this guy!"

"You're *what*?" A hauntingly familiar voice barked, jerking my attention back toward the doorway.

A cold chill ran down my spine, but shock held me silent even when my lips parted. All I could do was stare in disbelief.

"Honey-cakes, I thought you said Professor Smith no longer taught this class," Sin commented in a low, vaguely threatening tone. He was smart enough to figure out that my relationship with John didn't end amicably and was more than willing to take my side.

I couldn't respond, though. My pulse thumped so hard I could barely even hear myself think. All I knew was that I was *furious*. He was *still* here, and I'd bet my new diamond ring that he was only hanging around for the painting... not for me. After all, I was merely a means to an end for him. He'd basically said as much to my face.

Well, if he thought he'd have any hope in hell of still recovering the original, he was completely delusional.

I'd never let on. John Smith—or whatever his fucking name was—could kiss my soon-to-be-married ass.

With a flash of vindictive hatred, I turned in my seat and planted a kiss right on Sin's lips before he could flinch away. It was like kissing my cousin, absolutely zero chemistry between us, but John didn't need to know that. All he needed to know was that I was *not his*. Not anymore. He made sure of that when he chose the art heist over me.

John

eighteen

She was here. She'd actually turned up for class. It *was* her, wasn't it? The way Janie stood blocked her from view as I lurked outside the lecture hall, watching through the window, but the way my chest tightened and my guts fluttered, I knew it was her.

My phone vibrated in my pocket and I ignored it. It could wait.

Then Janie reached out to take her hand, looking at something... on her finger? No.

I shoved the door open, panicked and desperate to hear what was happening, only for the worst possible thing to reach my ears.

"*Engaged...*" Janie said as she chattered and cooed over the enormous rock on Tristian's finger.

"You're *what*?" I exclaimed, unable to help myself.

Tris snapped her head around, her eyes locking on mine in a way that made my breath catch. Holy fuck she was beautiful... and *mad as hell*, if the fire in her gaze was any indication. I parted my lips to speak, but no words escaped. Then the Grimaldi *dick* beside her said something that made her flinch ever so slightly. Her gaze that'd already seemed mad turned even harder, practically scorching with fury.

I swallowed, ignoring more vibrations from my phone. This was my chance, wasn't it? To try and smooth things over enough that she might still help me? Wait... she was *engaged?* Yep. Big old fucking rock on her finger corroborated that story.

Then she kissed him.

She narrowed her glare at me, then turned and kissed *him*. Him! She should be over here kissing *me* because—

Because nothing. There was absolutely no reason for her to kiss me again, something she'd made very clear by way of her knee in my balls, so therefore I had no reason to feel so fucking shocked and hurt by her kissing another man. Her fiancé, no less.

And yet, before I could fully process my emotions I was across the room, wrenching Tris out of Sin

Grimaldi's slimy hands, and throwing a punch at his jaw.

"John!" Tris screamed, "Stop! What the hell?"

She threw herself in front of me, her expression blazing with stubborn outrage as if to stop me hitting her fucking *fiancé* yet again. Which I wasn't, because that first punch had taken him by surprise and he'd ended up in a tangle of limbs between the seats and I couldn't easily reach the fucker.

"Oh my God," a girl squeaked, jerking my attention back to the fact that we were in class. At Boles University. With students arriving. *Fuck*.

"Class is canceled!" I barked, spinning away from Tris because holy hell I wanted to grab her by the neck and just— "Miss Ives. In my office. Right now." Before I could do anything *more* foolish than punching the Grimaldi heir in his stupidly handsome face, I stormed back out of the lecture theater while trusting she'd do as she was told. For once.

Thankfully my office was only a short walk from the lecture hall, so not many students needed to witness my march of fury, but it meant that when I basically kicked in the office door, I hadn't cooled down. Not even a little bit.

I heard her footsteps on the tiled floor before she

stepped inside and slammed my office door closed. "How *dare* you?" Tris seethed, full of venom.

I whirled around to face her. Big mistake. All my angry words stuck in my throat and I forgot what I wanted to say. All that came out was a pathetic whisper as I asked, "Engaged?"

Her irate glare faltered for a moment, and a flash of pain crossed her beautiful face. "Yes," she hissed, her hands bunching into fists at her sides. "Engaged."

I swallowed hard, trying not to scream. "To him? That was quick work. I've been gone for what? A week?"

Her eyes narrowed. "What the fuck is that supposed to mean?"

My lips parted but no sound came out. Crap. What *was* that supposed to mean? It sure sounded like I was accusing her of cheating when we both knew I had been using her since day one. What was my fucking problem?

"In case you forgot how things ended between us, Professor, *you* left *me*." She took a step forward, her whole demeanor sharpening like a blade. "You seduced me, gained my trust, stole my access codes and passwords—somehow—then *stole* from my employer, and left me to take the fall for it all. Am I forgetting anything?"

I mean... that was a simplified version, sure. It didn't

sound *great* when put like that, but technically I had tried to remove her as a suspect.

"Oh, wait, that's right." She snapped her fingers like she'd just remembered a key detail. "You then broke into my apartment and *fucked me* before disappearing into the night without so much as a goodbye."

"Some might argue that was a goodbye," I murmured. Instantly, I regretted not keeping that thought on the inside as her palm cracked across my already damaged face. "Ow."

"You deserve that and a whole lot more, John-fake-name-Smith," she snarled, her fist balled up like she was thinking of adding to my collection of bruises. "Why are you even here? I told you, the painting is long gone. So *fuck off* out of my life, like you planned to do a week ago."

I gritted my teeth, my skin prickling with how vulnerable she made me feel. "I can't."

"Why the hell not?" she demanded.

Fuck. "Because you're still here," I admitted in a husky whisper. "And I can't... I don't want to leave you."

Her lips parted, her eyes wide with shock. For once, I'd stunned her speechless. But she quickly recovered, shaking her head. "You already did, John. The only reason you're back is because you stole a forgery."

She was technically right, so I couldn't even deny it.

"What if I told you it was all a big misunderstanding?" I suggested, giving a one shoulder shrug. "What if I said I had nothing to do with the theft and I was in a car crash instead?"

Tris scoffed a harsh laugh. "If you think I'm gullible enough to buy that, then you *really* don't know me."

"Good thing I didn't say that, then," I muttered, running a hand over the back of my neck.

She stared at me for a long moment, like she was trying to decide if I was worth fighting with. Like she couldn't make up her mind between slapping me again, or just walking away. I desperately hoped for the first option.

"Toronto," she finally said with a sigh, her shoulders sagging. "The painting is in Toronto. Now you've got no reason to stay."

Panic filled my lungs as she turned to leave, and I darted forward, smacking my hand against the door to stop her from opening it. "Don't do that, Tris," I said with a groan. "Don't act like you don't care."

"I don't," she lied.

"Bullshit."

She inhaled sharply, spinning around to glare up at me. With my hand still pinning the door shut, she was close enough to kiss. "You're right. I *care*. I care that you seduced me, used me, betrayed me, and broke my heart.

I care that you hurt me, John. I *don't* care about *you*. In fact, I'd go so far as to say I actually hate you."

Her words cut through me, but the fire in her eyes made it worthwhile. It was so much better than the blankness of just a moment ago.

"Good," I murmured, fighting the urge to grab her.

Her perfect nose crinkled. "Good?"

I nodded ever so slightly. "I'd rather have your hate than your indifference. Hate is still passion, Tris, whether you like it or not."

Knowing I was damn near at the end of my control, I leaned down to open the door for her. Except before I could turn the handle, her mouth collided with mine. Against instinct, I jerked backwards thinking I'd accidently given in to my urges and she was about to bite my lip off. But she followed, her fingers twisting in the front of my shirt as she dragged me close.

As unexpected as that was, I sure as fuck wasn't going to complain. I finally released my control and scooped her up into my arms, holding her tight as her legs wound around my body and her kisses drugged me senseless. The bruises on my face ached, but I ignored the pain. It was worth the pay off.

My heart pounded so hard in my chest it *hurt*, and I spun us around to lay her down across my desk. This time, we'd finish what we started in the darkness of the

Grimaldi manor. Her skirt already bunched around her waist, like it had a life of its own and wanted this just as desperately as I did. As much as she did, too.

"I still hate you so much I could happily drown you in a vat of acid," she hissed against my kisses when I unbuckled my belt to free my granite hard dick. "This changes nothing,"

Her delicate fingers wrapped around my shaft, pumping me eagerly and I moaned. Fuck that felt good. Tris was everything. I couldn't wait... clumsily I hooked my finger under the crotch of her panties, dragging them to the side as she guided my cock into her sweet pussy.

A deep shudder of pure ecstasy rolled through me as I thrust deeper, swallowing her moans with my kisses. She was so tight, but she bucked her hips, pulling me deeper with her heels digging into my ass.

I gave a groan as I thrust harder and she rewarded me with a breathy gasp as her pussy clenched around me. Fuck, that was perfect.

"Harder," she demanded, her nails digging into the back of my neck. "Fuck me harder, John, make me come."

Shit... when a lady asked so nicely, who was I to say no?

I pushed her back onto the desk further, ignoring the

crash of stationary hitting the floor, then caressed her throat when she arched her neck. "You're delusional, Miss Ives," I told her with a smirk, pumping into her with hard, deliberate strokes that rocked her whole body. Her hooded gaze met mine and her brows dipped the tiniest bit in confusion. "This changes *everything*."

Not giving her a chance to disagree—denial was cute but not right now—I increased my pace and started pounding her cunt. She gave a little scream, her perfect lips parted as her fingernails gauged my forearms. Those were the kinds of scars I had no problem carrying, so I bit my lower lip and tried really hard not to finish early.

She wasn't making it easy. Her sexy little sounds, the way her back arched and her long fingers gripped my arms... utter perfection. She was exactly where she belonged... and so was I. We both just needed to admit it.

Her body quaked and shook, and I just *knew* she was close. Which gave me a smug jolt of satisfaction since Tris was usually the kind of girl who *needed* clit stimulation to come. She'd been locked up in Grimaldi's house without her vibrator, though, and my girl had a crazy high sex drive. Maybe she was just that worked up? Maybe my dick was just that great.

My office door opened and I gave a feral growl of anger, expecting to find Dean Lawrence standing there in a rage. It was worse, though. It was him. The fiancé.

"Oh, *shit*," he exclaimed.

Tris sat up with a strangled noise, but not to push me away. Nope, she just reached out, snatched off her shoe, and threw it at the Grimaldi dick. "Get the fuck out, Sin!" she snarled. The office door slammed shut again almost immediately, and she gave me a hard glare. "Did I tell you to stop?"

I grinned, and grabbed her by the neck to kiss her. Then renewed my efforts to make her come on my dick. Her sexy sounds turned more urgent as I hitched her thighs higher, filling her in a different way, and I could feel how close she was to release. So long as no one else interrupted, she'd be mine in mere moments.

"Holy shit," she moaned, tipping her head back and bracing her hands on my desk. "Yes, don't stop. Yes, John... *oh!*"

Her inner walls clenched, holding me tight as she climaxed. The way her back arched, her tits pushing forward like she wanted me to suck them, nearly made me lose it. Nearly. I wasn't ready to let this end though... because once we were done, she would try acting like she hated me again.

Did I deserve her hatred? Fuck yes. But that didn't mean I was going to just accept it and let her move on.

The way she was gasping and moaning through her orgasm did me in, though. Before I could even formulate a complete thought, I was coming inside her with the most intense, toe-curling detonation. So intense that the whole fucking building seemed to shake.

Then it *really* shook, hard enough that my bookcase behind the desk started to fall and I had to act quick to save Tris. I scooped her up off the desk and staggered backwards as the whole bookcase crashed down where her head had just been.

"What the fuck?" she gasped, echoing my thoughts.

No question, that sex had rocked my world. But last I checked, that was only a metaphor, not a reality. The campus fire alarm started shrieking, and I carefully placed Tris back on her feet while groaning at the loss of her heat wrapped around my dick.

Thank *fuck* I'd made her come already, because my gut said someone'd just detonated an explosive on campus.

Tris

nineteen

The fire alarm sounded so loud it nearly deafened me, and I flinched. The office door flew open an instant later and Sin burst through—again—with a small cut on his forehead from where my heel must have cut him. At least I had good aim...

"Tris!" he shouted, barely audible over the alarm. "Are you okay?" He totally ignored John as he cupped my face and scanned me for injuries. Aside from the slick mess of John's cum inside my panties, I was just fine.

"We need to evacuate," John said, leaning close to be heard and making my pussy spasm again. His voice was rough and low, still soaked in desire. It made me weak.

Between the two of them, they hurried me out of the office and through the hall where dozens of students were making a swift bee-line for the exits. Before we made it outside, the sprinklers kicked in and I snorted a laugh. The timing of it... at least I'd managed to finish before disaster struck. I'd have been *real* pissed if this had happened *before*.

"Did I miss the joke?" Sin asked with an arched brow, glancing between me and John.

John wasn't paying attention, though. One of his hands rested on the small of my back as we waited for the exit door to clear of panicked students, but his other was scrolling messages on his phone at top speed. The scowl on his face said he wasn't pleased by whatever he was reading.

Then I put the pieces together.

"What's going on?" I demanded, stopping dead in my tracks. Fuck the sprinkler water, it was *just water*. But my instincts told me that whatever had just shaken the building so hard I nearly ended up as the meat in a desk–bookshelf sandwich, was connected to his shady alter ego.

Fuck, that didn't make sense. *This* was his alter ego, wasn't it? Or was this just a disguise? Christ, John was giving me a complex.

"You fucker!" I gasped. "My door was *never* unlocked! You broke in!" I knew it. I *fucking knew it.*

He glanced up from his phone, arching one brow. Then he just shrugged. The fucking man *shrugged* like it was no big deal to gaslight me into thinking I was shit at locking doors.

My jaw dropped in outrage, but Sin gave me a firm shove to get me moving again. The exit doors had cleared and we needed to get outside. That had felt a whole lot like an explosion, so part of the building might be on fire. If it spread... yeah, we were better off outside.

"You wanna tell me what that was all about?" Sin asked quietly as we stepped out into the sunlight. "I thought you were done with him?"

I scowled, crossing my arms over my soaking shirt. "I am."

"Didn't look like it..." His gaze wasn't accusing or judgmental, just concerned.

Fuck, he said his father had eyes everywhere. Had I messed shit up already? My stomach churned and my cheeks turned cool as the blood drained out. "Shit, Sin, I shouldn't have—"

He gave a quiet laugh. "You probably *shouldn't* have, but don't stress. I waited outside and pretended like you were just being berated for missing so many classes. We're good. But that probably shouldn't happen again."

"Agreed!" I practically shouted. It shouldn't have happened in the first fucking place. I was just *so angry* and then he was right there in my face and I stopped thinking.

Glancing around, I spotted the big lying asshole himself a short distance away, his phone to his ear and his expression creased with fury. Whoever he was speaking with had not given him good news, and I wanted to know what the hell it had to do with whatever just happened inside.

The explosion, I meant. Not the other thing that happened.

John saw me approaching and tried to gesture for me to give him a minute, but clearly he'd forgotten that we were *not* on friendly terms. I gave less than zero shits about his privacy right now, and I wanted answers.

"Who was that?" I asked suspiciously when he quickly ended the call.

He scowled. "None of your business, Tristian."

"Bullshit," I challenged, parking my hands on my hips. His gaze immediately dropped to my wet shirt, clinging to my skin like paint, and my stupid nipples hardened. Traitors.

John ran his tongue across his lower lip and I nearly

forgot what we were talking about. What was wrong with me?

"John... you know something," I growled, trying to keep myself focused. "What was that?" I gestured to the building we'd just evacuated from.

A sly grin touched his lips, but before he could try and deflect onto the unplanned, unexpected fuck on his desk, I punched him. Not *hard*, and nowhere near enough to hurt, just a little nudge in the chest to tell him I meant business. Sin didn't intervene, so I had to assume he was confident I could hold my own if necessary. I could feel him at my back, though.

"You're rough today, Tris," John commented with that infuriating grin still in place. "I'm not complaining, though."

"John," I snapped, my hands in tight fists. "What is going *on*?"

He shrugged. "I have no idea. But it looks like Marla wants to take an evacuation head count. We should join her." He tried to move past me in the direction of the main body of evacuated, somewhat soggy students gathered on the grass. I grabbed his arm, stopping him.

"Tell me what is going on. Are we in danger?" I tried to appeal to his protective side, pushing aside my anger in favor of fear.

It was the right tact, because his own mask faltered

and his shoulders sagged with defeat. "Tris... I can't tell you," he finally muttered, rubbing the bridge of his nose. "It's not worth knowing. You should get out of here, though. Go home with your fake fiancé and I'll handle this mess. Please."

The sincerity of his voice almost convinced me, but at no point had John Smith proven himself to be *trustworthy,* so I stubbornly shook my head. "Sorry, John, I've run straight out of faith in your word. If you won't tell me, I'll have to find out for myself. Coming, Sin?"

I spun on my bare foot—since my shoes were in John's office somewhere—and started back toward the front steps of the building we'd just exited. John stopped me with a tight grip around my upper arm before I even made it three steps, jerking me back against him in a way that took the breath from my lungs.

"Sinister, give me a moment to speak with your *fiancée,*" John snapped at Sin, who'd stepped closer to likely try and save me.

I thought surely he would say no, but at my nod, Sin gave a frustrated sigh. "Fine, but just be aware there could be eyes on us. Don't repeat that scene from the office."

Damn it, now I was thinking about fucking John

again, and without even meaning to I butted my ass against him a little more suggestively than the situation warranted. John noticed, too, his grip on my arm tightening and a low groan rolling out of his throat. He waited until Sin retreated over to the group of evacuated students—and poor Marla trying to take some kind of attendance list—before speaking.

"Tris, I get that you don't trust me and that's well deserved, but right now you need to *listen*. This is bigger than just you and me and a stupid Van Gogh painting. Maybe you don't trust my word, but for the love of fuck, trust your instincts." His voice was low and pleading, his breath hot on my neck as I frowned toward the building we'd just exited.

"Does this have something to do with your bruises?" I asked, despite how badly I wanted to yell at him that I couldn't believe a single thing out of his mouth. I *hated* feeling played, and every interaction with him reminded me that that's what I was to him. A game.

Reminded of all the hurt he'd caused me, I tried to jerk free of his grip, but he reeled me back in again. "Yes," he hissed. "It does. Please, Tris, go home with what's-his-face. I'll come to see you later tonight and tell you... something."

"Something?" I repeated, turning to squint at him.

"It's better than nothing," he muttered back, but

his attention had shifted to the firefighter striding across the lawn toward the building. Their truck had just pulled up and the rest of the crew was still grabbing equipment out but this guy— "Shit," John whispered.

"Shit, what?" I asked, looking from the firefighter to John and back again. It was standard procedure, wasn't it? When the fire alarm goes off, the fire department comes in. "John! Why shit? What shit?"

I sounded like some kind of kid's picture book gone wrong. *Why shit, what shit, where shit, who shit? Red shit, blue shit, oh shit—*

"Go with Sinister," John ordered, giving me a shove in my future husband's direction. "Now."

I tripped over my own feet when he released me, and I gave an involuntary cry when my knees hit the dirt. Great, now my knees were dirty to add to my barefoot status. Oh yeah, and I was still wearing cum-soaked panties.

John must have heard me fall, because he was right there helping me up again. Like the gentleman he *wasn't*.

"John, tell me what the fuck is going on," I demanded, holding onto his forearm hard enough I was probably drawing blood. I didn't dare break eye contact with him, or he'd be taking off after the random firefighter again, who'd disappeared into the building already.

His expression creased with frustration as he stared back at me. "I *can't* tell you."

That hurt more than it should have. "You mean you *won't*. There's no gun to your head or gag in your mouth. You *can* tell me; you're choosing not to."

If anything, my words only hardened his resolve. "Not all guns to heads are so literal, Tristian. You should know that." He gave the rock on my ring finger a pointed look, then wrenched free of my grip. "Go home with your fiancé. This doesn't concern you."

My jaw dropped in outrage at his cold attitude, but he didn't even glance over his shoulder once as he stalked back toward the front steps of the campus building. Marla from the dean's office called out to me, but I ignored her. Fuck this bastard for playing with me, using me, then telling me to effectively *sit down and shut up*.

Whatever was going on, it *did* concern me. I was the one caught up in the Van Gogh forgery mess; I was the one now being strong-armed into working for a mobster and marrying his son. None of which would be happening if John hadn't botched the art heist in the first fucking place.

Fueled by anger and indignation, I stormed after

John, determined to pin him down and make him talk. Somehow. I didn't actually have a plan, but with the mess of endorphins and adrenaline inside me, I wasn't really thinking straight.

John paused mid-step halfway to the front door, cocking his head to the side like he was listening or smelling for something... then he surged backward, all but leaping down the entry steps and barreling right into me. He clearly hadn't realized I was following, but just scooped me up and—

Boom.

A massive explosion ripped through the air, and both John and I went flying. Pain lanced through me when we landed, and then... nothing.

John

twenty

Thank fuck Monroe Jones was a loud, mouthy fuck because it was his deep bellow through the echoey halls of Boles University that provided the caution I needed not to enter the building again. Dumb fuck that he was, striding in there dressed as a goddamn firefighter, had actually saved my life this time. His screamed warning, littered with curses, confirmed that the judging panel hadn't been joking in those dozen messages I'd ignored.

The Game had changed. Drastically.

I acted fast, trying to get as far the fuck away as possible, but damn near tripped over Tris in the process. What in the *fuck* was she doing following me? Didn't matter. I scooped her up and ran... but time was up.

The building exploded, throwing me—and Tris—

through the air several paces. I twisted, taking the brunt of the fall on my shoulder, but her head cracked against my chin and I blacked out momentarily. When I came to, my ears were ringing so hard I couldn't hear a damn word as Sin Grimaldi attempted to pry Tris from my grip.

"Fuck off," I growled, but couldn't even hear my own voice. Shit.

Grimaldi dick was trying to tell me something, gesturing urgently until I looked down at the delicate woman cradled against my chest. She was unconscious and her head was bleeding.

Horrified, I released my grip and Sinister gently lifted her into his arms. He cared about her. When the fuck had that happened? She hung limp from his embrace, and I scrambled to my feet to follow when he started walking, carrying her toward the fire truck.

Monroe Jones had just used them as a convenient disguise, but the rest of the crew were probably legitimate. Then again with the shocking development the Game council had announced, anything was possible.

One of the firefighters instructed Sin to place Tris down on the grass—or so I guessed by gestures and his responding actions. Fucking hell, had I burst my eardrums? That would be a problem. Not that it'd matter much if Tris was badly injured. Then I'd have to go hunting down the Game council to make them pay... and that, in itself, would be a suicide mission.

"Is she going to be okay?" I asked, and to my relief I actually heard myself. Faint, but audible. The ringing was fading.

The firefighter glanced up at me, then frowned. "Looks like just a knock to her head, but I'd want the paramedics to check her when they get here. You too, by the look of things. Was anyone else close to the building?"

Grimaldi shook his head, his expression grim. "No, everyone else was over at the evacuation point. Safe from the blast." His accusing glare said the rest. *Why the fuck had we been heading back inside?*

"I can hear the ambulance on its way," the firefighter said. "Stay here, don't move. They'll check you out. I need to help my team."

Ah yes. Because there was a burning wreckage of a university building currently being tended by just four unprepared firefighters only fifty yards away.

I dropped to my knees on the grass beside Tris, gently stroking her hair out of the blood on her forehead. It was just a small split, it seemed, right on her hairline. Probably where her head hit my chin and knocked us both out.

Sinister tapped my arm and I refocused, realizing he must have been trying to talk to me while I was lost in looking at Tris. "Huh?" I squinted at him. Fuck this guy with his caring eyes and strong shoulders. If he wasn't a Grimaldi he'd probably be perfect for Tris.

"What the fuck was that?" he asked slowly and carefully, gesturing to the burning building.

I looked over my shoulder, wincing at a sharp pain in my shoulder. Then looked back at Prince fucking Charming. "I'm no expert, but I'd say it was a bomb."

Grimaldi narrowed his eyes like he was considering shooting me. Actually, it seemed odd that he wasn't carrying a gun. All of Grimaldi's men carried guns at all times. Maybe he just had a bodyguard lurking in a tree somewhere so he never got his own hands dirty.

"No shit," he spat. "Why the *fuck* would someone detonate a bomb in a university building?"

I offered a half-hearted shrug. "Maybe they needed extra time on an assignment. Students do desperate things to get an extension, trust me."

"Funny, real funny. Meanwhile Tris nearly died, but no you go right ahead and make jokes, you insensitive ass. She was right about you." His lip curled in a sneer, and I nearly rose to the bait of asking what Tris had said. Then again, I already knew she had nothing nice to say, and it didn't matter.

Before I had to tell him to get out of my face, Tris stirred on the grass between us.

"What the fuck...?" she mumbled, screwing up her nose as she blinked. "What happened?"

"The building exploded," Sin growled, still glaring daggers at me. "Your professor was just about to explain *why*."

I scratched my chin. "Was I? Oh look, paramedics are here. Tris you need to get checked over. You were unconscious for a couple of minutes. You probably have a concussion. How's your hearing?"

She grimaced, rubbing one of her ears. "Echoey."

I pushed to my feet, gesturing for the paramedics as the first pair climbed out of their ambulance. A few minutes later they had Tris seated in the back of their truck while they gave her a thorough examination and I stepped away to reread my messages.

I'd missed at least a dozen in that time I'd spent with Tris in my office, and still had no regrets. Actually, that wasn't true. I regretted not getting a better heads up of the impending danger so she didn't get hurt... but otherwise I was damn glad I hadn't been distracted by the Game.

Before I could even reread the messages, my phone started ringing again.

"Tink," I growled on answering.

"What the fuck is happening?" she shrieked. "Are you okay? Is Tris?" I'd made the mistake of telling her before the *big* explosion that Tris was with me at Boles. Now she was in full blown panic mode and with good reason, too.

"I guess news travels fast," I replied with an exhausted sigh. "Yeah, we're... alive. Same can't be said for Monroe Jones."

"Jones?" she spluttered. "What the fuck did that dodgy old con man think he was going to do in the Game?"

"Win it, I guess. Even though he's never made it past the first round before. With the new developments..." My head was swimming, my jaw throbbing with pain, so I sat down on the parking lot curb.

"I'm on my way there now," Tink told me, all business. "We can... work it out."

Despite the situation, I gave a short laugh. "You want to team up, Tink? I don't think that's how the Game is played."

"*None of this* is how the Game is played, John. Bombs! Seriously? What the fuck happened to minimizing social impact, huh? I don't know who is making the rules now, but this isn't what I signed up for." She was furious, panicked, but totally right. This wasn't the Game my grandfather had curated for so many years... He'd be rolling in his grave if he saw the burning remains of the university building right now. Let alone if there were casualties aside from Monroe Jones.

"Good point," I agreed with a grunt. "Let me make sure Tris is okay then we can... plot."

"Is she hurt?" Tink demanded, her tone sharpening.

I bit the edge of my lip, looking over to the ambulance where Tris was still being looked at by a paramedic. I'd sat where I could keep her in my line of sight, even though that tall, dark, handsome twat was hovering over her like a mother hen.

Was he gay, maybe? That'd be easier.

"Yeah. She was too close to the fucking building when Monroe's clumsy ass tripped the booby trap. I think she's okay but she took a knock to the head so—"

"Got it," Tink cut me off. "Take care of our girl. I'll wait."

She ended the call and I blew out a long breath as I scrolled back through my messages.

It didn't take long to gather the key facts.

1. The Game objective had changed. It was no longer a single item to be acquired; instead there was a *collection* of valuable items that

had been hidden all around Whispering Willows. Each item represented varying values, and it was a collective total that would declare a winner.
2. More players had been invited to compete. Due to all three of us finalists breaking the rules, the rules had all changed. *All* Game participants were invited to compete again... meaning there were twenty-four—correction, now twenty-three—players.
3. Social impact was no longer a consideration in judging. Where previously, we'd lost "value" on our item if we caused too much of a mess to clean up, now it was a free for all.
4. There would be no forgiveness for rule-breaking in this round. Elimination was for real.

The rules, of course, were not laid out specifically. But killing off the competition was not actually out of the realm of possibility.

Fucking great.

I shot another look over to where the paramedic applied something to the cut on her head. Her *fiancè* had straightened and now had a phone to his ear and his hostile gaze fixed on me. I almost wanted to smirk, but I didn't. Cause this wasn't funny.

When he turned slightly, it made reading his lips impossible. Not that I really wanted to focus on him. My phone buzzed again as Tris started to get up from where she'd been seated and grimaced. The paramedic put a hand on her shoulder and the helicopter-husband-to-be-fucker put his free hand on her other shoulder.

They were both clearly telling her to stay seated.

The best thing I could do for Tris was to walk away. The Game had always been a gambler's paradise—and it had just turned into a hellscape. I could still win it. But it wouldn't be at another cost to her.

And it had almost just cost her her life—*again*.

She glared at me like she could hear what I was thinking. Yeah, I should totally walk away. From her if not the Game. It would be better. For her—I could fucking steal her from the Grimaldis and put her up somewhere far away from them and from me.

That was what I should do.

The fire in her eyes as she stared at me practically threw down a gauntlet. Yeah, I should walk away.

Not a chance in hell would I leave without winning the Game *and* her.

Tris

twenty-one

"I'm *fine*," I snapped at Sin for what seemed like the thousandth time since leaving Boles. We'd had to hang around and answer a few questions for the police, but then I was given the all clear from the paramedics to go home.

I'd glanced around to find John, but he was nowhere to be seen. That *hurt*, way more than my headache or the split in my hairline. Why hadn't he stuck around to... I don't know, make sure I was okay? Talk about a guilty conscience, running away before either Sin or I could pin him down for answers.

We'd just arrived back at RBD's house and Sin was fussing over me, insisting on helping me out of his obnoxiously large truck after we parked in the garage. I glanced across at Dex's Corvette where John and I had fooled around at the party just a few weeks ago. It left a bad taste in my mouth, not only reminding me of how *disappointed* I was at John taking off, but also meant Dex was probably here somewhere.

"Sin, the boss is waiting for you in the library," one of the security goons said as we entered the main house. "Both of you."

I groaned and shook my head. "Do I have to?" I swung my pleading eyes up at my forced fiancé, batting my lashes. "My head hurts and I need to shower." I was *so* dirty and stank of smoke.

He seemed unaffected, just arching a brow back. "What happened to *I'm fine, Sin, stop fussing*?" He placed a hand on the small of my back, guiding me along the corridor with him, past the main staircase. Damn it.

The old guard who'd caught me escaping on my first night was manning the door to the library, and gave my dirty appearance a curious look as he opened the door for us to enter.

"Been climbing down drain pipes again, Miss Ives?" he asked quietly, and I glared. I couldn't reply, because Mr. Grimaldi was already calling out to us from across the room and he sounded *pissed*.

Sin gave me a nudge, and I dragged my bare feet as I crossed the expansive library with him to where his father stood by the fireplace. It wasn't even *that* cold outside, but I guess it was more of an ambiance thing.

"Father, you wanted to see us?" Sin spoke in a cool and careful voice, making me observe him closer. He was different around Mr. Grimaldi. Tense and guarded. "I take it you heard about the incident at Boles?"

"Incident?" Mr. Grimaldi repeated, his voice a harsh bark bordering on a bellow. "Is that what we're calling it when a building *blows up*? An *incident?* Look at Tristian! Look at her face, Sinister! This is not an *incident*, this is an insult, and I won't stand for it."

This was a version of Mr. Grimaldi I didn't know... and he scared me. I shifted closer to Sin without even really meaning to. My arm brushed his and he glanced down, a small frown on his brow. Then he placed a reassuring hand on the small of my back and drew a breath.

"This was not an attack on the family, Father. It was an unfortunate accident and we happened to be in the wrong place at the wrong time. Tris is okay, though. It's just a bump, right Buttercup?"

I wrinkled my nose at the nickname, but at his gentle pinch I nodded. "Yep. Looks a lot worse than it is, sir. You know how head wounds like to bleed dramatically." I instantly cringed, thinking of the men

I'd seen beaten half to death in his ballroom. Yes... he did know.

Mr. Grimaldi nodded, his expression pensive as he looked between the two of us. "You two seem to be getting along well. I admit, I expected a lot more... resistance to this proposal. You wouldn't be playing with me, would you, son?"

Sin gave a gasp, which was a little much in my opinion, but hey, what did I know? "I'm hurt that you'd think that of us. Did you get your sons mixed up?"

To my surprise, Mr. Grimaldi grimaced. "Yes, a little bit. I was just dealing with your brother and..." He flapped his hand dismissively. "Doesn't matter. Tristian, dear, are you sure you're okay?"

I nodded confidently, trying not to wince at the throb in my head. "Yes, sir. I got cleared by the paramedics at the scene. It's a miracle no one else was hurt, except for the one firefighter inside..."

Mr. Grimaldi stared back at me a long moment after I trailed off, waiting for me to say more. When I didn't his brow dipped. "And Professor Smith. I heard he had some injuries from the blast, too?"

My mouth went dry and words evaporated.

Sin tapped a finger on my back, like he was trying to warn me. I didn't *need* warning, though, I wasn't exactly about to go blurting out that I'd fucked my ex on his desk while my forced fiancé guarded the door. Clearly he hadn't been paranoid when he said we were being watched.

"Yes," I said in a weak voice. "I believe so. Things were... chaotic. I didn't see what happened to him."

For a tense moment, I thought he would call me out. Like he somehow knew what'd happened in John's office. But then he just gave a small nod, accepting my answer. "Well, I hope he isn't badly hurt. Not that there will be classes again for a little while, I suppose. The school will need to deal with things..." He trailed off, lost in thought as he looked out the window. It was actually a nice, sunny day out there, and I now realized that the fireplace blazing behind Mr. Grimaldi wasn't casting any heat. It was decorative.

"If that's all, father, Tris is badly in need of a shower," Sin suggested, indicating my bare feet and legs covered with dirt. Not to mention the blood crusted on my face and neck, God knew what in my hair... Yeah, I looked hot.

"Of course, I apologize," the caring old man returned, washing away the fierce mob boss with a simple smile. "I was so worried when I heard you were hurt, Tristian, I had to see you for myself. You're family now, and things like this... will have to be dealt with. Go on and shower. Our nurse is on her way. I'll send her up."

I shook my head. "There's no need, I was already cleared by the paramedics."

He gave me a smile that bordered on condescending. "I'll send her up when she arrives. Do you mind staying for a moment, Sin? I want to talk more about this bomb and why that building."

Sin tapped the small of my back again, silently telling me it was okay to leave, so I quickly retreated out of the library and left them talking. Plotting. Scheming. Whatever, I just wanted to shower and maybe go spend some time in my studio. Take some headache pills too. Whatever I'd hit my head on must have been harder than a damn rock because holy hell.

Knowing that Mr. Grimaldi was sending a nurse up to check on me, I kept my shower quick. She arrived with perfect timing, too, after I was dressed in clean clothes and towel drying my hair. Naomi had moved all my clothing up to Sin's room when it became clear I wasn't returning to the jade bedroom... Fuck getting caught alone by Dex again.

Sin had been a perfect gentleman and slept on the floor.

The nurse was polite and efficient, going through all the routine checks that the paramedics had already done.

She removed the dressing on my cut and replaced it with a fresh one, then scribbled some notes in a small notebook.

"Any other concerns?" she asked, after handing me a couple of headache pills. "Anything else, not related to this head knock?"

I shook my head, curling my fingers around the pills. "Nope, I'm otherwise totally healthy."

She flashed a quick, professional smile. "Are you on birth control?"

I frowned, confused. "Uh... yes. Why is that relevant?"

"Which type?" She was scribbling in her notebook again, ignoring my question.

I almost told her but bit my tongue. "The type that my doctor prescribed and best suited my personal needs. Are we done here? I have somewhere to be."

Not waiting for the nurse to reply, I grabbed my sweatshirt and left the room. My birth control choice had *nothing* to do with my concussion, but I'd bet anything it was all sorts of relevant to my impending marriage into the Grimaldi family. Fuck. That.

Rather than go storming back down to the library to confront Mr. Grimaldi—because he killed people more frequently than I got my car serviced—I took my overflowing bottle of emotions up to the art studio. It had always been my calming place at home, so why not here too?

After letting myself in, I carefully locked the door behind myself then crossed to the stack of fresh canvases. My mood was too big for pencil sketching, I needed to work with color. I'd left a pair of noise-canceling headphones on my workstation when I was working on the goddamn Picasso the day before, so I put those on my head and pressed play on my music.

Intense bass filled my head, and I let myself slip into the creative zone. All my frustration, confusion, worry, fear, it all poured out of me through my paintbrush as I slapped colors onto the canvas without really thinking through the whole piece.

I lost track of the time, switching my brain off and just stepping out of my own head. It was a coping mechanism and always had been: when I got too overwhelmed and didn't know how to fix things, I just... let it all out on paper. Or whatever art medium I was into at the time. Nelson had been thorough in my tuition, making sure I was well versed in *multiple* specialties even if painting was my strongest skill. For him, it was metalwork. Jewelry, blades, trinket boxes... it had all been useful over our years in business.

A knock on the door was what eventually jerked me

back to Earth, and I startled so hard I knocked over my palette of sloppily mixed paint colors.

"Shit," I cursed, peering down at my brand new, probably $500 jeans. Which were now decorated with a mess of purple, pink, and green acrylic paints. "God damn it."

The knock came again, and I grabbed one of my painting rags in frustration. So much for clearing my head.

"Just checking on you," Sin called through the door. "No need to let me in if you're working. Just show me signs of life."

"I'm fine!" I called back, irritated but a little warmed that he cared to check on me. "Just... working on—" I looked at my fresh canvas and grimaced. Not that.

"I'll leave you be," Sin replied, not noticing that I'd cut off mid sentence as I stared at John's face on my canvas. His damaged, badly bruised face that I'd painted without even realizing. Was he that beaten up? Why didn't I remember seeing all those bruises, if they were in fact there?

"Do you want me to send dinner up to you?" Sin called, jerking my attention from the canvas again. His question confused me a moment, because it hadn't even been lunchtime when I came up here. Sure enough, though, it was getting dark outside.

I swallowed hard. It wasn't often I got *that* lost in a painting.

"Yes," I accepted, flooded with guilt and regret. "Please. Thanks."

He murmured a confirmation and I lifted my wet canvas off the easel. That was *not* what I was meant to be doing today… nor was fucking John on his desk, come to think of it. Christ, now he probably had the wrong impression that I might forgive him.

"Not a chance in hell," I muttered, placing the incomplete portrait against the wall. Facing the wall.

With a heavy sigh, I grabbed a fresh canvas and set it up on my easel.

Pigeons and peas. *That* was what I needed to work on. Stupid pigeons and measly peas. No more daydreaming about John, and definitely no more encounters like this morning. It was pigeons, *peas*, and wedding planning.

John

twenty-two

Dealing with the fallout at Boles took longer than I'd have liked, but it gave me a convenient excuse to slip away from Tris. She didn't need me hovering over her like a helicopter—Sinister had that handled—and I sure as shit didn't need her pushing for more answers. Social impact may no longer be a consideration, but I'd bet my new car that telling her would still be a rule break. A big one, with costly consequences.

Too costly.

It was almost dusk when I finally met up with Tink, finding her in a booth at Mary's Diner. As much as I wanted to suggest Royal Orchid, this really wasn't the time to go running into Tris.

"Finally," my petite blonde competitor grumbled

when I slid into the booth opposite her. "You took so long I was running out of menu items to order. I recommend the loaded cheeseburger, by the way. It has peanut butter on it, which is way better than it sounds."

I wrinkled my nose. "It sounds disgusting, but I'm hungry enough to try it out." I ordered the burger from *Maria*—according to the waitress's name tag—and requested a glass of Coke.

"So... Monroe Jones tried to get a head start and got blown to smithereens for his efforts," Tink stated, cutting right to the chase when the waitress left. "I guess he didn't see the follow-up message about booby traps, huh?"

"I can't get past the fact that someone on the judging panel actually used the term *booby traps* in an official message. Surely there's a more technical term for it?" I scratched my very bruised nose thoughtfully. Was there a technical term for it?

Tink squinted at me then pulled out her phone. "Uh, nope, I think that is the technical term. Derives from the Spanish word *bobo* which means *stupid, fool,* or *naïve.* All of which fit the bill for dumbass Monroe Jones."

"Huh." I nodded. "Yes it does. Also, I don't believe Monroe was the only one who jumped the gun. There was an initial smaller blast that sent everyone out of the building in the first place. Which could have *either* been a first, er, booby trap, or it could have been someone trying to break into the basement..." Because the first tip had been about a bracelet planted in the lower level of that particular Boles building.

Why *that* building? Was it just a coincidence that it was in the basement of the art department? Or a casual *fuck you* to put something right under my nose?

"Okay, so that was clearly a warning, to make sure all of us—new players included—understood that they weren't bluffing." Tink tapped her fingernails against the table, frowning at her empty plate. "I need dessert. Sugar will help me think."

She ordered the Splendid Sundae off the menu when the waitress delivered my Coke, while I pulled a bottle of pain meds from my pocket. I shook out two pills into my hand then swallowed them with a mouthful of soda.

"I was going to say, you're looking a little worse for wear..." Tink gave me a scrutinizing look, taking in my various cuts and bruises. I really needed some time off to heal. Putting my pills away, I grabbed the hip flask of vodka out of my jacket and poured a healthy dose into my Coke. "Ah yes, mixing pills and alcohol. That'll help." She snorted a laugh, rolling her eyes.

"Save the judgment for someone who gives a shit, Tink. So... what the fuck do we do, now?" I slouched in the booth seat, struggling to get comfortable.

Eventually I resorted to spreading my legs wide enough that my knees weren't hitting the table top. Then I smirked when I thought how Tris would react to my *manspreading*. She was the sort of woman who'd have something to say, regardless of the fact my legs were just too damn long to sit comfortably.

Tink placed her phone down on the table, meeting my gaze. "We need to make an alliance, obviously."

It was exactly what I'd been thinking, but I was interested in why *she* thought it was a good idea. "Do we? There can only be one winner of the Game in the end."

She shrugged, unbothered. "Sure, in name. But I think between us we can agree on an equitable split of whatever the prize is."

I wet my lips, acting like I was thinking this over for the first time. Like it hadn't been on my mind all damn day since our brief phone call right after the bomb. "I see. But... what's in it for me? I've won the last four Games, so why would I not win this one, too?"

She scoffed a laugh. "You have something to lose this time, John. And you're unfocused. Not to mention the fact that this isn't a Game you've ever even played, let alone won. None of us have. Twenty-four competitors all at once with no consequence for damages or death? It's like the fucking Hunger Games."

I gave a wry smile. "Twenty-three, now. Maybe less, depending if someone else set off the first bomb."

"Good point," she agreed. Then she picked up her phone and tapped into her notes app. When I leaned forward, she tilted her phone so I couldn't read the screen. Probably force of habit more than a deliberate choice to withhold information, but I also hadn't agreed to join forces with her... yet.

I took the bait anyway. "What's the list?"

She quirked a brow. "Are we teaming up?"

The waitress arrived with my burger and Tink's enormous sundae, and we both paused our conversation until we were alone once more. My stomach rumbled with anticipation, and I took a huge bite of my burger, noting the subtle addition of peanut butter mixing with crispy bacon and rich meat patty.

"It's good," I agreed, mildly surprised. Then I shook my head at Tink. "You know that dessert is designed for two people, right?"

She scowled back at me, loading up her spoon. "No it's not."

"Okay sure, that extra spoon must be decorative, then."

Her response was just to stick the enormous spoonful of ice cream and chocolate sauce into her mouth, glaring as she ate. I could see why she and Tris were getting along so well.

"So. This new development from the judges... It's a scavenger hunt. A dangerous, deadly scavenger hunt." As I said it out loud, I realized that was *exactly* what it was. They provided us a hint about what we needed to procure, and we'd only know it was the right item if it was booby trapped.

Weirdly, my grandfather would probably approve of this twist... he loved making scavenger hunts for me as a child. He *wouldn't* approve of the lack of subtlety or subterfuge, though. The mess at Boles would have made him turn in his grave. Christophe—when he was alive—had been affectionately known as the Ghost: totally undetectable to the point of nearly being supernatural.

Tink said nothing, just kept eating her metric fuck-ton of ice cream.

I scowled. "Katinka... you still with me?"

She glanced up from her dessert with a level gaze. "Are we partners, John? Because I can't strategize with you if we're competitors."

Infuriating woman. She and Tris were two peas in a pod. "Yes, Tink, we're partners. Today's demonstration didn't just prove the judges aren't bluffing... it also gave every other Game player the green light to kill their competition."

She paused with her spoon halfway to her mouth, her eyes wide as she stared in realization.

I nodded, confirming what she was clearly just computing. "And if I were in their shoes, I'd be taking out the biggest threats *first*. Meaning—"

"We're fucked," she groaned, dropping her spoon back into the dish. "*Fuck*."

"Yup," I agreed, taking another mouthful of my burger. It really was delicious, even with the peanut butter addition. Weird, but delicious. Silence fell between us for a moment as Tink slouched back, staring at the ceiling.

After a few moments, she sat back up, scowling. "They're gonna try to kill us. Or Igor will, if no one else. Just to clear the playing field so they can scrap it out amongst themselves." I nodded, my mouth full, and she gave a frustrated gesture. "You don't seem worried, John. Why aren't you worried?"

I finished my mouthful, then wiped my hands on the napkin. "Because. The Game primarily favors thieves. It always has. Right?"

She grunted. "Right..."

"So most thieves I know would much rather hide than fight. There are a few who I'd suspect are now back in play who would happily toss a grenade our way, but only a few. The rest will be easily handled...

especially if we work together and watch each other's backs."

Tink picked up her spoon again, digging another scoop of ice cream. "We *are* working together, John." She paused while eating that mouthful, and I sipped my vodka and Coke. "Okay, so what do you propose?"

I nodded, since she'd made her mind up to trust me. And me her, apparently. "For one thing, we need to get a good grip on what sort of booby traps are being used. That means hanging back and letting someone else trigger them."

Tink smirked. "Okay. I like that. What else?"

"Well... after today's demonstration I'd say the judges no longer give a fuck about our cover identities staying intact. So you can probably quit dancing at The Slippery Lips. Especially if we no longer need access to the Grimaldi house." I said it cautiously, because I still *wanted* that access. But I could get in without Tink having to maintain her cover as well. I could keep mine in play and charm my way back into Luther Grimaldi's good graces.

"Nah, I'm good," Tink replied, making me inhale a little of my spiked drink. I coughed, clearing my windpipe, then gave her a baffled stare.

"Huh?"

She shrugged. "I like dancing, and you wouldn't

believe the conversations dancers get to eavesdrop on." She let out a low whistle, then chuckled. "Though I'll *happily* stop fucking Dexter. Not that he's been around much lately... I heard from one of the Grimaldi men that he'd come off second best in a fight with Sin."

"Good," I muttered. "At least he's useful for something."

Tink gave me a sly smile. "Jealous, John?"

I arched a brow. "Jealous of him? Not a chance in hell. Just because she's wearing his ring, doesn't mean she has *any* intention of actually marrying him."

Tink's jaw just about hit the table, and I realized she *also* didn't know about the sham engagement between Sin and Tris. Good. If it actually held water, Tris would have told Tink. Right? They were friends now...

"I'm sorry, *what*?" Her question was a strangled sound of shock that comforted me. This was definitely new information for her.

I sighed. "Small set-back, but nothing I can't handle. Anyway, have you finished that? We can grab your shit now and get you moved in before your shift tonight, if you absolutely must keep your job."

"Moved in? Uh, champ, you need to get both parts of the thought process out loud, not just half of it." She screwed up her nose. "You want me to move in with you?"

I jerked a nod. "Want you to? God no. But if we are watching each other's backs, it would be a bit hard if we lived on opposite sides of town. Besides, I just rented a Hestia safe house. Can't get much better than that."

Tink's lips curled in a wide grin. "Well shit, moneybags, why didn't you lead with that? You can grab this bill then." She checked the time then tucked her phone in her bag. "We have a couple of hours to do some planning. Fuck knows when the judges will release another clue."

She was right about that. Whenever they did, though, we needed to be ready. Not to steal the item, but to observe what happened when someone else did... to gauge how far the judges would take these booby traps. Maybe the bomb today was a mistake?

Time would tell. I paid our bill, smirking at just how big it was, then followed Tink out to my car. It was weird, but having her as a partner felt so much more comfortable than when she was a competitor. Now I just needed to convince her to talk to Tris... and make her see reason with this insane engagement situation.

Tris

twenty-three

As promised, Sin delivered dinner to me in the art studio, but I lost my appetite pretty damn quick when I saw it was roast chicken dinner served with potato gratin and... peas. Then I couldn't get it out of my head that the chicken was actually a pigeon, and I muttered colorful curses at Picasso for ruining dinner.

Eventually, I gave up and took my plates back down to the kitchen, handing them to one of the staff with an excuse that I wasn't feeling well. It was late enough that the house was quiet, but since seeing Dex's car in the garage I was on high alert for him lurking around the house somewhere. Not wanting to risk another attempted rape-slash-murder, I hurried back to the safety of Sin's room where he was already asleep on the floor. Such a gentleman.

I carefully locked the door, then tip-toed through to the bathroom to wash all the paint from my skin and change for bed. For a man I was being blackmailed into marrying, he was actually a very easy person to cohabitate with. Of course the lack of sexual tension helped... a lot.

A couple of painkillers were left with a glass of water beside my toothbrush, and I smiled at how thoughtful that was. I'd largely forgotten about my headache while I was painting, but now it'd returned with a vengeance, so I took the pills and crept back into the bedroom.

Only once I was tucked in under the covers did I realize I hadn't called Nelson. He was probably beside himself with worry, having undoubtedly heard about the explosion at Boles this morning. Guilt churned through me that I hadn't immediately let him know I was okay.

I tried to tell myself that I was just keeping him safe, but in reality my head was all fogged up with John.

"Go to sleep, Buttercup," Sin murmured in the darkness. "Whatever is stressing you out can wait until the morning."

I sighed. "Good point. Night, Sin."

"Night, Tris."

Sleep came surprisingly easy, and when I woke again Sin was gone. He'd left a note for me on the bedside table, though, which made me smile. He was an oddly thoughtful guy, definitely not what he looked like on first impression.

Yawning, I picked up the note, taking it with me as I headed for the bathroom to pee. I flipped it open to read, expecting to see something along the lines of *got hungry, went downstairs for breakfast.* Why? I had no clue, but what else would Sin leave a note for?

Nothing. Because the note wasn't from him at all.

He won't be guarding you forever. I can't wait to get my hands on you again...

A deep chill ran through me, and I dropped the note to the floor. It was the same scribbled handwriting from the first note. The one that said the note writer was *watching* me.

Scared, and fully awake now, I quickly dressed to head downstairs and find Sin. Maybe he could tell me if the note was there before he left or... something. But before I left the room, my crushing guilt reminded me I still needed to call Nelson.

Using my Grimaldi-issued mobile, I dialed his number from memory and nervously paced the room while waiting for him to answer. I had to remember the line wasn't secured, and I would rather cut my own foot off than implicate Nelson as my forgery partner.

"Hello?" he answered the call warily.

"Hi, Nelson, it's Tristian from across the hall." Okay that was probably laying it on a bit thick.

His sharp inhale was the only sign that he'd been worried. "Tristian, dear. Lovely to hear from you. We haven't seen you for a while... is everything okay?"

Nelson was a much better actor than I was, always had been. That was why I made the forgeries and he made the switch, like with *Poppy Flowers* when he'd posed as a caterer and swapped the paintings right under everyone's noses.

"Yes, all okay. I just wanted to check in so you'd know I wasn't in the art building yesterday when it exploded. It occurred to me that since I haven't been home, you might be concerned." I bit my lower lip, holding back the tears that wanted to spill. Nelson didn't need to know that I was there, or that I'd been hurt. It'd only panic him into doing something stupid.

This time his sigh of relief was clear. "That's good to hear, Ivy," he murmured, using my nickname without catching it first. He'd been *really* worried. "Uh, well, I've been taking good care of your plants, but do you know when you'll be back?"

I screwed my eyes shut, rubbing the bridge of my

nose where I could feel a headache building again. "Probably not for a while. I'm working on a new project that could take some time to get right, unfortunately."

Nelson gave a disapproving huff, conveying all his arguments in that one sound. "Well, that sounds interesting. Are you staying with friends?" *Are you in danger?*

I wet my lips, glancing around Sin's bedroom. "One. I think."

"One is better than none," Nelson murmured. "Call me any time, Tristian. Us old people need social interaction to keep our minds sharp, you know?"

I chuckled, feeling hot tears leak from the corners of my eyes. I missed him. "I'll keep that in mind, Nelson. Please send my regards to Hank, and I'll be sure to call again soon. Just to keep that mind sharp."

"Thank you, dear. Take care of yourself." He sniffed as he ended the call, and I crumpled to the edge of the bed like my strings had been cut. It had to be killing him to *do nothing*, but we had built years and years of trust between us, and he had no choice. I'd told him—between the lines—to leave me to handle things. To lay low and *trust me.*

That didn't make it any easier, though. I was so used to leaning on him with *all* my problems, and now I couldn't even speak freely over the phone.

I only gave myself a minute to feel sorry for myself, then I wiped my eyes and left the room in search of breakfast. I recognized one of the guards stationed at the end of the hall and gave him a polite smile and *good morning* on my way past. Since the incident with Dex, I had come to understand the security wasn't there to keep me prisoner. It was to keep me *safe*. For all Mr. Grimaldi's strange methods, he did seem to genuinely care.

As I got to the bottom of the stairs, a familiar voice made me stumble. Panic washed through me, and I frantically searched for somewhere to hide.

"Tris!" Dex called out from along the hall, and I froze in place.

A hot thread of satisfaction coiled through my chest when I saw him limping on a set of crutches, one leg in plaster and his face a mess of bruises. Sin really had come off best in that fight. God *damn*.

"Going somewhere, Tris?" Dex hissed, limping closer.

I straightened my spine, determined not to show my fear. He couldn't attack me. Not here, not in his state. All he could do was threaten and intimidate, and I refused to let him win with that.

"Yes, actually. I was going to breakfast with Sin." I gave a frosty smile then tried to side step around him to escape. He stuck one of his crutches out, though, preventing me from passing.

His bruised face twisted with a sneer. "You think you're safe now that he's here, *sister dear*? You're not. And now you have a lot more to pay for. When I—"

"Tris, baby! There you are," Sin boomed from the doorway to the kitchen, further along the hall. "Come on, Buttercup, I have your coffee ready."

Dex glared daggers, but I gestured for him to let me pass. Was he really going to push the issue with Sin watching? Doubtful.

"He won't always be guarding you," he spat as I moved past him, and I jerked with shock, tripping over my own feet.

Luckily I managed to catch myself on the wall before face planting into the carpet, then I all but *ran* to where Sin waited with an expression of thunder and malice toward his brother.

He wrapped me in a tight, protective embrace, whisking me into the kitchen and out of sight of Dexter, murmuring reassurances into my hair.

"Sorry," I croaked. "He fucking scares me, Sin."

"I know," he replied with a sigh, rubbing my back. "I'm dealing with it. Come on, Tony made you an omelet."

My stomach rumbled. "With lots of cheese?"

"Of course!" the chef called out. "Sit, Tristian, your coffee is underway."

I slid into my usual seat at the breakfast bar, and Sin took the one beside me as he accepted a fresh coffee of his own from one of the staff.

Wetting my lips, I nervously decided to broach the subject of the note.

"So... there was a note beside the bed when I woke up this morning," I said quietly, not wanting to be overheard by anyone else. Who knew which staff were team Dex? "Was it there when you left?"

Sin frowned, shifting in his seat to look at me with concern. "I don't remember seeing anything," he admitted, "but it was still decently dark when I woke up. It's possible... but from who? How? What'd it say?"

I chewed the inside of my cheek, feeling paranoid. "It said something about how you can't watch me all the time, and that they—whoever left the note—wanted to get their hands on me. Or something. I dunno... it's creepy right? Threatening. And then Dex said nearly the exact same thing so... Sin, does Dex have access to your bedroom?"

Sin stared at me, his expression locked and unreadable. Then he inhaled deeply and gave a small nod like he'd just made his mind up about something.

"I'll take care of it. Tony, keep eyes on my future wife for me. I'll be back shortly."

"Yes, sir!" The chef called out, not even pausing in what he was doing on the stovetop.

Sin dropped a kiss to the top of my head, a casually affectionate gesture, then stormed out of the kitchen without another word of explanation. Just that he'd *take care of it*. What did it say about me as a person that I hoped Dex wouldn't survive whatever Sin had in store for him? That I *hoped* he'd die?

"I was just about to experiment on some recipes for the next month's menu," Tony informed me as one of his staff delivered a perfectly smooth flat white on a saucer in front of me. "Would you mind hanging around to taste test?"

Cute. Sin had basically said not to let me leave the kitchen, but Tony was trying to make it fun. I appreciated that, so I accepted his offer. Come to think of it, I needed to find the gym if I was going to keep eating Tony's meals...

John

twenty-four

Tink was surprisingly easy to work with over the days following the bomb at Boles. We spent a lot of that first night—after she got back from work at The Slippery Lips—working out a game plan. Then when the next clue came in at eight o'clock the next morning, we were ready for action.

We made educated guesses on what would fit the clue—and be located within Whispering Willows—then sat back and waited to see what would happen if and when someone less skilled activated the booby traps.

"What do you think it'll be today?" Tink murmured from the passenger seat of my car. It was the fourth stake-out we'd undertaken since the Game changed, and so far none of the booby traps had been the same.

They *had* all been deadly, though. "I'm thinking maybe the statue will be on a pressure plate so when they lift it off, poisonous snakes will drop from the ceiling."

We were parked outside a small art gallery in downtown Whispering Willows where we'd decided today's target must be located. The gallery had been showing an exhibit on mid-century sculpture, and the twelve-inch bronze cast duck fit the clue of the day.

"Maybe," I muttered, because that was hardly any more extreme than the hidden flamethrower that had barbequed one of our competitors yesterday at an estate not far from Grimaldi's house. There seemed to be a mixture of pre-existing and planted objects, which made it harder to work out, but the clues were enough that we weren't the only ones who'd found each piece.

We were also not the only ones smart enough to wait it out until someone else took the heat—literally, in yesterday's case—before lifting the prize from someone's smoking corpse.

"Do you see anyone else hanging around tonight?" I shifted my gaze from the gallery window—where the duck was on display—to the surrounding area. We had been given the clue at eight in the morning—same as every day—but no one had taken a run at it yet. Tink and I surmised that none of them were confident enough to attempt the theft in broad daylight with witnesses and collateral damage.

As I'd pointed out to Tink the other night, *most* thieves were not also killers. Not unless they were pushed into a corner and given no other choice. We weren't assassins or mercenaries... for the most part. Some of us moonlighted, but generally speaking those people were too busy to play the Game.

"Not for the last hour or so," Tink replied, shifting in her seat. "Damn it, now I need to pee."

I rolled my eyes. "Again? I told you not to drink so much water. You're like a child."

"Shut up, *Dad*," she sulked, popping her door open. "I'll be quick."

Tink slipped into the shadows with practiced ease, and I gave a grunt of admiration. After working alongside her for four days, I could see why she'd made it to the final round with me. Igor, on the other hand... not so much.

Movement inside the gallery had me sitting forward in my seat, watching intently to see whether this brave soul would make it out with their *soul* still attached to their body.

The shadowy figure moved slowly, really building the anticipation, but the duck remained in clear line of sight even if I couldn't make out what the person was doing inside the gallery. Right when I thought they were about to make their move, the passenger side door of my car popped open and I nearly smacked my head on the roof with how hard I flinched.

"Seriously?" I hissed to Tink who grinned like a fucking cat as she settled back into her seat. "Couldn't have made a noise to let me know you were there?"

"Sort of defeats the point of being stealthy, doesn't it?" She reached for her bag and pulled out some candy. Tink seriously was a child. "It's a security guard, by the way."

I glanced over at her, confused. "What is?"

"The shadows." She nodded to the gallery. "I took a closer look after popping a squat in the alley."

I tried really hard not to laugh at her terminology, because it only seemed to encourage her to be *more* childish. But it was a good phrase. "Fucking hell. Is anyone going to take a run at this dumb duck?"

"They're all cautious now," she replied with a shrug. "And I don't blame them. Or shit, maybe we interpreted the clue totally wrong and it's not the duck at all?"

I screwed up my face. "Not impossible. But this makes sense... Maybe we need to try for it and find out."

Tink scoffed a laugh. "Be my guest. I'm not volunteering to be snake food tonight, thank you."

"It's probably not snakes," I murmured. "Seems too chaotic. Too many variables."

She just leveled a glare my way. "*Probably* isn't definite enough for me, champ."

I sighed. "Me either."

Silence fell between us for a few moments as we waited for some action, then Tink got restless and started munching on candy again. It was a miracle she didn't have diabetes with her diet.

"So... how's Tris?" she asked, shooting me a knowing smirk. Somehow, she knew what I'd been up to while she was shaking her ass on stage late at night. Visiting Tris while she slept *and* not waking up her guard dog was a continued challenge but always worth the effort.

It reassured me to know it was hard even for me to break in. It meant that anyone less skilled—which was nearly everyone—wouldn't be able to even get past the perimeter fence. Let alone *into* the big wanker's bedroom.

I debated denying it, but... Tink was her friend. She might have insight that I didn't have.

"She's okay," I murmured, full of details.

Tink snorted a laugh. "Have you *spoken* to her? Or just watched her sleep like a total stalker?"

I swallowed, not wanting to answer that. I should

try and visit her during the day, try and talk with her... but I knew full fucking well that she'd be demanding answers that I couldn't provide. So I was being a fucking coward and avoiding her. At least when she was conscious, anyway.

"You're such an idiot. No wonder she's still engaged to Sin." There was an edge to her voice that made me look sharply in her direction.

"What do you know about that, Tink?" I asked accusingly.

She arched a brow, looking like she was about to give me a piece of her mind, but I quickly shushed her when movement inside the gallery pulled my attention.

For a moment we both watched with eager anticipation, waiting for something to happen. Would this thief manage to disable the booby traps? Surely the stupid ones were all dead by now.

"Come on... *snakes*," Tink urged, practically buzzing with excitement. "Dozens of snakes, from a trapdoor in the ceiling."

I cast her a long look from the corner of my eye. "You're a strange person, Tink."

"Thanks!" she replied, grinning.

The thief inside the gallery stepped into view, approaching the duck, and I held my breath with anticipation. Had he already disabled the booby trap? Maybe? That could be what was taking so fucking long...

He reached for the duck, his hesitation clear even from the distance we watched from. Then he confidently grabbed it. Or he tried to.

"Oh shit!" Tink exclaimed on a gasp when a pendulum blade swung out of its hiding place and decapitated the thief. It was crazy surreal to watch with no sound. One minute he was reaching for the duck, the next his blood sprayed across the window and his head dropped from his shoulders.

Wide eyed, Tink turned to look at me. "Uh... should we...?" She tipped her head toward the gallery.

"Not yet," I murmured. "Wait. Remember the bombs on day one?"

She nodded her understanding. A few minutes later, another stealthy figure crept from the shadows and slipped through the front door of the gallery. Poor fool had grown impatient, and was banking on the trap having been fully sprung.

"Oh. Wow." Tink made a gagging sound as more blood sprayed the window, obliterating our view of the interior gallery. "Good call, Professor."

We continued waiting, and a moment later a third thief stepped out into the street with the bronze duck in hand. Then and only then, did I nod to Tink. "Now we can take it. You want the honors this time?"

She grinned, opening her door eagerly. "That was so much cooler than snakes. Back in a sec!"

Full of excitement, she skipped across the street to steal from a thief, just like we'd done each day since teaming up. There was definite merit to this whole not working alone thing. She might be a child, but she had style.

And a point.

Maybe I should take her advice and go see Tris while she was awake. Fuck knew I wanted to see her, wanted to steal her away. But was now really the time?

Tris

twenty-five

Classes at Boles were put on hold for a week, while the administration juggled schedules and classrooms, without the use of their entire arts department. What seemed strange, though, was that everyone seemed to believe it was a gas leak. Not that I'd left the Grimaldi house to interact with anyone, but I had risked using my phone again to call Tink and check in with her when I got extra bored the day before. The rest of my information came from staff and security.

Cohabitating with Sin had fallen into a comfortable rhythm, though. Dex was nowhere to be seen after that morning he'd threatened me, and I worked out that Sin woke before dawn because he liked to go for a run around the grounds. He'd actually asked if I wanted to join him and I nearly laughed so hard I cried. Early mornings and running were not on my list of fun activities—together *or* separately.

Almost a week past the bomb at school, Sin tripped over one of my shoes—he was constantly telling me to put them away—and cursed loud enough that I woke up.

"Sorry," I mumbled, my eyes still shut.

Sin gave a quick exhale. "It's fine, sorry I woke you. Go back to sleep, Buttercup." He exited the room quietly and I rolled over, trying to get comfortable.

It wasn't even light outside, but once I was awake, I was awake. Try as I might, sleep wouldn't come back to me so eventually I groaned and dragged my ass out of bed, stumbling through to the bathroom.

The sight that greeted me in the mirror was like something out of a nightmare, my hair all snarled and rumpled and the bags beneath my eyes heavy enough to carry substantial luggage. I'd been making hopeful progress on the stupid Picasso last night and barely got to bed before midnight.

"You're a fucking catch, Tristian Ives," I muttered to my unappealing reflection. Yellow paint streaked down the side of my face, and I scratched it with my fingernail. Crusted on. Fantastic. That's what I got for not cleaning up before passing out.

Yawning, I stripped out of my pajamas and turned on the shower. Maybe it'd make me feel a small amount more human, although I was pleased that I'd *finally* made progress on the goddamn cursed pigeons.

I needed to get the forgery done *yesterday* so I could deliver on that part of the deal with Mr. Grimaldi. Cubism could seriously kiss my ass.

The steam from the shower filled the bathroom like fog, making me feel hidden and calm as I stepped under the water. I closed my eyes, letting the shower beat down on my face and melt away the streaks of yellow and gray paint.

A cool draft breezed across my legs and my skin pebbled. Weird. I rubbed the water from my eyes. Maybe I left the door open slightly?

I'd barely even formulated that thought when the screen door opened and a large, imposing figure stepped in. A small scream escaped my lungs before a huge hand clapped across my mouth, silencing me.

Harsh, violent memories of Dexter assaulting me shot through me like a lightning bolt and my whole body tensed, ready to fight, but then—

"Shhh, Venus," John's deep voice rumbled in my ear, melting the fear out of my limbs in an instant. "You're not usually awake so early. I couldn't resist joining you."

He kissed my neck, and I leaned back into him,

relishing in his touch. He must have sensed the drop of my guard, because his hand released my mouth and moved to cup one of my breasts instead. I moaned, my nipples hardening under his touch and my hips rocked backward. Fuck, he was naked...

"John," I gasped, letting him pull me close as I braced my hands on the wall to keep my balance. "You shouldn't be here. If you get caught..."

"So don't get me caught, Venus." He kissed my neck, and his hand slipped down between my legs. "I missed you so much this week... all I could think about was my desk, and the way you looked spread out underneath me as you came apart."

I moaned, rocking against him as his fingers pushed inside. It felt so good. Between my work in the studio and sharing a bedroom with Sin, I had barely even touched myself since John last fucked me. I was way overdue.

"I'm mad at you, Casanova," I muttered, then gasped as his thumb found my clit. *So good.* "We have things to discuss. Important things."

"We do," he agreed. Then he spun me around, pressing my back to the wall as he hitched my legs up around his waist, bringing us eye to eye. "Many important things." Then his cock pushed inside me and

I forgot my own name, let alone all the *important things* I needed to discuss with him.

A gasp escaped me as he thrust deep, causing my eyes to roll. I needed this. Even if I was still *furious* at John. I'd take the sex, then pick a fight. Priorities.

"Shhh," he laughed softly when I moaned, "We need to be quiet, Tris, or you'll get me shot before I can get you off."

"Fuck," I gasped, gripping his neck as he pumped into me with determination. "Hurry up, then, because I would quite like to see you shot."

His efforts stilled. "You don't mean that."

I bucked in his grip, trying to get him to keep fucking me. But also, I wasn't going to blow smoke up his ass just to get a good orgasm. "I really do. You're an asshole, a user, and now I can add *coward* to that list. Literally the only thing you're good for right now, is making me come. So do that, then leave."

John's brow furrowed with a deep scowl, and his eyes narrowed in frustration. Knowing what an infuriating prick he was, I wouldn't be at all shocked if he just left me all worked up and disappeared into the shadows again just to piss me off.

"We'll see about that," he growled. Then his mouth crashed into mine and his cock plunged deeper within me. For a few moments our tongues wrestled as he drilled me into the wall, and I quickly forgot why I was so angry... again. He had that effect on me.

My stomach clenched and tightened with heightening pleasure, curls of ecstasy chasing through my pussy with every strike of John's thick shaft. I moaned and gasped against his kisses, trying so fucking hard to remain quiet and failing miserably.

"Tristian," he growled, his kisses shifting to my jaw. "I said, *quiet*." His hand came to wrap around my throat, squeezing gently.

I swallowed back the cries that wanted to escape, arching my back to impale myself harder on his dick. John grunted, his hips working hard as he gave me what I wanted, fucking me brutally hard against the shower wall.

My orgasm built up again quickly, the heat blooming through my core as my muscles clenched hard around him. The hand around my throat tightened again, reminding me to stay quiet as endorphins swarmed my mind, making me forget.

"Come on, Venus," he breathed, his voice husky. "Come for me. Let me feel that exquisite vise of your cunt gripping my cock like we're one." As if he could hear my body crying out, he slipped his free hand between us, those long fingers of his finding my clit while his other hand pinned me to the wall by my throat.

Stars exploded through my head as he flipped my switch, and a silent scream burned through my lungs. John didn't go easy on me, continuing to pound into me in brutal thrusts even as I came with toe-curling intensity.

"...so fucking good," he gasped as I slowly ebbed off my climax. "I can't get enough of you, Tris. You haunt my dreams. I hate that you've started sleeping in clothing."

What?

My head clouded with an overdose of pleasure, and I couldn't be held responsible for my own decisions as I tapped his chest to be let down. He obliged, slipping free of my still-pulsing cunt then grinning as I sank to my knees. A low groan rolled out of him as I wrapped my hand around the base of his cock, guiding his slick length into my mouth while the shower beat down, forgotten, beside us.

"Tris," he moaned, threading his fingers into my soaking wet hair while I sucked his crown. "Venus... *fuck*." He gripped my head, pushing himself further into my mouth and triggering my gag reflex.

I didn't draw back, though, instead swallowing to relax my throat and meet his eager thrusts.

"Oh my God," he whispered, his fingers flexing against my scalp. "Tris, *fuck*..." That was the only warning I got before he exploded in my mouth, his hot load lashing the back of my throat. I swallowed quickly, keeping from choking, then ran my tongue along the length of his shaft as he withdrew.

John kept his grip on my hair, using that hold to lift me to my feet once more.

"Why... did you call me a coward, Venus?" he asked in a breathy whisper, his forehead against mine and his chest heaving. His bruises had faded considerably, but they were still there. His torso was littered with splotches of greens and yellows, too.

I wet my lips, trying to catch my breath. "Why would I not? We nearly get blown up, and you just disappear. Not a word, not a call... nothing. If I didn't know better, I'd think you didn't care about me at all. But you do, I know you do. You're just a fucking coward... hiding from me, so I don't ask for answers."

Regaining a modicum of strength I pushed against his chest, attempting to create enough space to clear my head. He wasn't having it, though, answering my gesture by kissing me breathless. Damn it all to hell, my body responded too, with heat pooling in my belly all over again.

"Maybe I was avoiding you," he admitted between

kisses, his hand slipping between my legs again. "Maybe I didn't want to be forced to lie to you." Oh *fuck*, the way his fingers filled me was pure delirium. I turned to putty, whimpering as he teased the threads of another climax out of me. He left that thought hanging in the air between us, his hand fucking me harder and faster until I shattered all over again.

"John!" I cried out, trying really hard to control my volume. "Enough!"

"Never enough," he growled, biting the bend of my neck like an animal claiming his mate. "And you knew I hadn't abandoned you. I visited... I left notes. Didn't you get them?"

He left... *notes?*

This time when I shoved him away, it was with enough strength that he stumbled backward.

"You!" I exclaimed, shell shocked with disbelief. "*You left those notes?*"

He frowned, clearly confused. "Yes. So you'd know I was checking on you. Who did you think—"

"Out!" I ordered, pushing open the shower door. "Get out, before security hears us and finds you in here." My voice was like pure ice, my anger barely restrained.

John's jaw dropped, his expression perplexed as he retreated out of the shower. "Tris, why are you—"

"Get *out*," I snarled, then punctuated my point by throwing a bar of soap at his head.

He wanted to argue, it was written all over his face. But I'd been loud when I yelled at him, and if I did it again it'd definitely bring security running. He stared at me for a moment, trying to gauge if I was bluffing. I was not.

"You have thirty seconds, John Smith," I hissed, "then all bets are off. Get out, *never return*. Not when I'm in the shower, and definitely not while I'm asleep." I reached for the shower door, slamming it shut to place a physical barrier between us, then I started counting out loud.

Before I even got to *ten*, I knew he was gone.

John

twenty-six

The encounter with Tris played on my mind all damn day. I kept replaying it in my mind, remembering how she'd melted when she realized it was *me*. How her body had responded to my touches like we were merely two halves of a whole, like we shared more than just a physical connection. It was fucking spiritual. There had been no doubt in my mind, we could make it work. Yes, she was mad at me right now for my subterfuge, but that was just one of those things that we'd tell our grandkids about as a funny anecdote.

Then something I said changed everything. Was it when I challenged her about calling me a coward?

She was technically right, I had been avoiding her out of fear of hard questions. But I *couldn't keep lying,* so

I decided avoidance was the lesser of two evils. And she knew I was visiting, right? I hadn't made it a secret... I'd left notes for goodness sake!

"Okay, you're driving me fucking insane," Tink finally announced. We were staking out another game piece. This time it was Rolex Pearlmaster located within a private residence in Oakville Hills. Tink and I had been sitting on a park bench in the little reserve opposite the house, waiting for someone to make a move.

Or rather, she'd been sitting and sipping her fourth coffee while I paced in restless frustration.

"Why?" I asked, frowning.

She rolled her eyes. "Why don't you just tell me what happened? Maybe I can provide some kind of insight?"

I blew out a long breath. Maybe she could. "I went to see Tris this morning," I admitted in a quiet, annoyed voice.

Tink scoffed a laugh. "I know *that*, dumbass. But you've visited her a *lot* this past week. You usually come back in a good mood and jerk one out in the shower. Why the sour face today?"

I paused mid-step and turned to stare at her in horror. "You knew that I—" I gave a shudder of revulsion. "Gross. This must be what it's like to have a sibling."

Tink laughed. "Trust me, champ, I was just as repulsed. So... what happened today?"

I blew out a breath, scrubbing my hand over my face. "Um, she woke up early, so I took your advice about talking to her." Yes, I was definitely going to share the blame with Tink.

"Oh, really?" she seemed genuinely shocked. "Good. That's progress. What did you tell her? I bet she had some hard questions about the bomb last week... and about why you've been avoiding her. What did you say?"

I grimaced. "Uh... well... we didn't talk *that* much."

Tink blinked at me a moment, then barked a sharp laugh. "Oh my God, you fucked her didn't you? I'm amazed she let you, without any answers. Then again, she has been stuck there for two weeks now without her vibrator..."

A deep scowl furrowed my brow. "You think she just used me for sex? It's not like that between us. Besides, how do you know she doesn't have her vibrator?" Surely Tink hadn't found my drawer of Tris contraband...

Tink shrugged. "She told me when I spoke to her yesterday. She's not *actually* a prisoner, John. She has a phone that works. It's just probably being monitored, which isn't an issue for me because as far as Tris is concerned, I know nothing about forgeries and thefts."

She shot me a toothy, smug-as-fuck grin. "I'm just her friend who she can vent to about her crappy taste in men."

Little shit.

I gritted my teeth. "Yes, well. Things were all going great... better than great. Amazing, even. And then all of a sudden she's kicking me out of the shower and threatening to scream."

Tink looked like she was caught halfway between confusion and amusement. Not at all helpful.

She sipped her coffee thoughtfully, then shrugged. "Have you considered whether you might be a shit lay?"

I scoffed. "That isn't it."

Tink rolled her eyes. "It never is." Her sarcasm was way too thick for comfort, but I wasn't going to debate my bedroom skills with her. "Okay so you must have said or done something that pissed her off. How mad are we talking? Like just a little offended, or...?"

I sighed, sinking my butt down to the bench seat beside her. "She threw a block of soap at my head."

Tink bit her lip, doing a crappy job of holding back laughter. "Okay. So. Pretty mad, then. Did you try anything new? Finger in the ass maybe? That can sometimes be alarming if it's unexpected."

Somehow, I thought Tris might actually be into that. Ideas for another day.

"No, it wasn't... she said something about how I'd been avoiding her and how I'd disappeared since the bomb at Boles. Obviously she knows it's because I don't want to have to answer questions that could get her dragged into the Game."

Tink startled. "She knows about the Game?"

"No. That's the problem. She still thinks this was about a *single* art theft and that I'm only trying to recover the stupid Van Gogh. But still... calling me a *coward* for avoiding her questions was a bit much." I was still sulking about that. This whole thing with Tris was new for me. I didn't have *relationships* with women... I had convenient liaisons that served a purpose. Feelings were never involved when they were just a means to an end. That's what Tris started out as. When had it changed? When had I started caring about what she thought of me as a person?

Tink hummed a sound, reminding me that she was here. "How'd you react to that? When she called you a coward?"

I frowned. "I told her that she was wrong. Just because I was avoiding talking to her didn't mean I'd abandoned her entirely. She knew I was around, keeping her safe."

Tink tipped her head to the side. "She did? Are you sure?"

"Yes, of course. I've been leaving her notes when I visit in the night so she would know I'd checked in on her. I'm not totally clueless, Tink. It would be creepy if I didn't let her know I was there." I rolled my eyes, already having predicted that outcome if I'd just been sneaking in and out without telling her.

Tink shifted in her seat to face me more directly. "What did the notes say?"

"Huh? What does it matter?"

"It *matters*," she insisted. "What did they say?"

I shrugged. "Just... reassuring her that I was watching. You know, that she wouldn't be a prisoner for much longer."

Tink squinted at me hard. "Is that what you said, though? That she wouldn't be a prisoner?"

I scratched my head, thinking about what I wrote. "Uh I think so? Or something about Sin Grimaldi not guarding her forever."

Tink's lips twitched with laughter, then when I continued frowning my confusion she busted up into full blown giggles. "Oh my God, you're so dumb, John. How have you become *so good* at thieving when you're *so fucking myopic*?"

"What the hell does that mean? I was trying to be reassuring that I would save her!" I protested, but she laughed even harder, actually sliding off the park bench in her overwhelming mirth. The fuck was wrong with her? "Women are fucking strange, you know that?"

Whatever she tried to say back was lost under peals of laughter, and tears streamed from her eyes as she lay on the grass chortling like some kind of... something.

Frustrated and embarrassed, I rose to my feet once more. "This is stupid. We must have the wrong house. No one has even tried to break in." Usually we spotted at least one other thief surveilling the location, but we'd been watching for hours and had seen no one. "Maybe we should just grab it ourselves."

That sobered Tink up pretty fast and she scrambled to her feet to follow me. "Uh, big man, I know you're all butt hurt about Tris tossing you out on your naked ass this morning, but killing yourself won't make her take you back."

I huffed a short exhale. "I'm not going to kill myself," I muttered, checking both ways for cars before crossing the street. "I just want to take a closer look. That's all. For all we know, we totally read the clue wrong and the game piece has already been collected."

"Okay but we know it hasn't," she argued, "because they haven't sent a points tally out."

Good point. Each time we turned in an item, the judges sent out a points tally. Names were all encoded, but we both knew it was Tink and me at the top of the board, thanks to our patience in letting others lose their heads. Literally, as last night's mission proved.

"Okay so, we can just get a better look," I replied, unlatching the gate and letting myself into the front yard. "Maybe we've been checking the wrong room. Or, maybe this isn't the right mark after all. Only one way to find out..."

We'd planted a camera inside the house earlier in the day, and that was how we'd been watching and waiting, but surely there would have been *some* kind of action by now.

"John... come on, you're being reckless and a reckless thief is—"

"A dead one, I know. But I need to go and see Tris again, apparently, and explain myself. So I can't be stuck here all damn night waiting for something to happen!" I was annoyed now, letting my emotions get the better of me. "Besides, now that we know there are booby traps, we can work around them. Right? Or are you *not* as good as I thought you were?"

Her response was to punch me in the spleen while slipping past to take the lead. "I'll show you, big arrogant fool. Maybe just stand back and take notes, hmm?"

I raised my hands in surrender, letting her pick the lock on the side door—where we'd entered hours ago to plant the camera then re-locked it—and disabled the house alarm system. The owners were out of town, something we'd noticed as a trend. Despite the casual disregard for Game players' lives, the judges *were* trying to minimize collateral damage. Aside from the cuts and bruises Tris and I took on that first day, there hadn't been any other casualties to innocent bystanders—not that I was innocent.

In fact, there hadn't even been much reported on about the players' deaths either. Every scene was scrubbed clean by morning... as much as possible. Which led me to think *someone* still gave a fuck about keeping our secrets.

"Ta da," Tink announced just a few minutes later when she lifted aside the painting of a pig concealing a safe beneath.

"Okay, now crack it without tripping a booby trap," I challenged, glancing around the room for any clues. Our camera was where we'd left it, so I slipped it into my pocket.

Tink stood in front of the safe for a long moment, silently inspecting it. "I can't work it out," she finally announced.

I smirked. "First time cracking a Barska?"

She rolled her eyes so hard I worried they'd become disconnected from her head. "Ha ha, funny guy. I mean,

I can't work out where the trap is. I don't see *anything* out of the ordinary with the lock mechanisms."

As much as I wanted to stand back and be all *you said you could do it*, I didn't actually want Tink dead. I liked her, in an annoying bratty sister sort of way. So I sighed and nudged her aside to take a look myself.

It took a few minutes using my microscopic thin access camera, inspecting the inside of the combination lock *carefully* so as not to trigger anything before it could be found. But then I gave a hum of satisfaction.

"Found it," I murmured, keeping the tiny trigger wire in my sights. "Hand me two needle knives?"

Tink silently did as I asked, and I worked with total concentration to disable the booby trap without triggering it. Sweat beaded on the back of my neck. Cracking safes usually weren't a life or death matter, but I pretended it was just an alarm.

A moment later, I tugged the trigger wire free of the lock and handed it to Tink. Then, because I couldn't let her run the risk in case I'd fucked it up, I made quick work of cracking the combination itself.

I breathed a sigh of relief when it clicked unlocked, and I cautiously opened the door whilst checking for secondary triggers in all the hinges.

"Alright, show off," Tink said with a nervous laugh. "Nice one."

She reached inside the safe to grab the watch and I saw the secondary trap just a split second too late.

"Tink, no!" I shouted, but she'd already lifted the watch from the tiny pressure plate mounted in the safe. A jet of liquid squirted from a hidden nozzle in the frame of the safe but sailed harmlessly over Tink's five-foot-one head.

Where it landed, the carpet sizzled and burned, melting a hole not just through the carpet but through the underlying floor boards, too.

"Holy shit," Tink squeaked, staring down at the damage caused by what had to be some seriously hardcore acid. "That could have been my face!"

My heart thumped frantically in my chest as I grabbed my pint-sized partner and checked her over for acid burns. "That was too close," I finally admitted.

If she'd been even two inches taller... it didn't bear thinking about. We needed to be more careful.

Tris

twenty-seven

All my progress with *Le Pigeon aux Petits Pois* went right to shit the moment I stepped foot back into my studio after John's surprise visit to my shower. No, scratch that, it went to shit the *second* he decided to join me in the bathroom; I just didn't realize it until I tried to paint.

Suddenly all my carefully placed yellow and white squares turned to shit, and my straight lines became curves. I tried everything to get back in the zone, but before I even knew what I was doing, I'd swapped canvases back to the one of John.

"*Fuck!*" I yelled, glancing at the time and realizing I'd just lost nearly two hours while perfecting the exact shade of his eyes, and capturing the way the light reflected on his iris. "No, no, no, get out of my *head!*"

Very deliberately I took the fucking painting and placed it back against the wall, grabbing for my working *Pigeons* canvas once more. Then grimaced when I realized what a fucking mess I'd made of it and decided to start over.

I *should* trash the John image entirely... but selfishly I felt like it was one of my best, so I didn't have the heart to ruin it. Especially after the first one I painted of him then destroyed with a big purple dick and balls across the whole thing.

Sin joined me for lunch, but I was in a shitty mood and made for crappy company, so it was no great shock when he disappeared quickly to deal with whatever he did for work, leaving me to return to my studio and beat my head against the wall some more.

Eventually, I admitted defeat for the day and scuffed my feet the whole way back down to Sin's bedroom to change out of my paint-splattered clothes. Before I got there, though, I almost ran into Mr. Grimaldi coming up the stairs.

"Tristian, dear, you look exhausted!" he exclaimed, patting my arm when I wobbled. "Are you feeling okay? Did you recover from your head injury?"

"Yes, sir, it was just a small bump. All healed up, thank you." I offered a polite smile, attempting to sidestep around him. He didn't seem in any hurry to move on, though, and it'd be rude if I just walked away. Dammit.

He nodded to my painting shirt. "Been working on our little project?"

"I have, yes." If I kept my answers short and sweet, surely he'd continue on.

"And how is it going?" he prompted.

Fucking awful. "Um... good?" I didn't even sound slightly convincing, but Mr. Grimaldi didn't look annoyed. He just gave me a sympathetic nod.

"You'll get there, Tristian. You're an exceptionally gifted artist. Take your time and trust in your natural talent." He patted my arm again as he moved past me. "I believe in you, my dear. You just need to believe in yourself."

He left me standing there at the top of the stairs, flabbergasted. Here was a mob boss who just two weeks ago handed me a gun and told me to shoot a man or be shot... and he'd just given me so much sincere encouragement that I had tears in my eyes. What the fuck was wrong with me?

By the time I made it back to Sin's bedroom, I was sniffling like a little girl because for a moment there I could see Mr. Grimaldi as a father-figure, rather than the literal threat hanging over my head.

"Hey, Buttercup, what's wrong?" Sin asked, stepping

out of the bathroom with a towel around his waist. He didn't hesitate in coming to comfort me, either. What was it with this family?

"N-nothing," I whined. "Your dad just said some really nice stuff and it got me all... upset."

He tipped his head to the side, seeming to repeat that inside his head. "Uh... you want to dissect that a little more or are we leaving it at that very loaded and confusing statement?"

"I don't think I could, even if I tried," I admitted, heading for the wardrobe to grab clean clothes. I grabbed some for Sin, too, tossing them out to him. "I just didn't expect him to be so supportive. I thought... I dunno. He basically put a gun to my head to lock me into this deal, you know? He literally made me kill a guy, then casually added this marriage deal on as an afterthought, and then—"

"Whoa, Tris, hold up. My father made you kill someone? When did that happen?" Sin quickly pulled on his sweats without flashing me any dick—which I appreciated—then gestured for me to sit on the edge of the bed.

I shrugged, running a hand through my messy hair. "Uh, when he found out I switched the painting for my forgery. It was a whole *him or me* thing, where I chose me. You know, because I like breathing. Then it was a heavy implication that he now had me on camera shooting a guy so... don't go trying anything dumb. Standard mob boss shit, right?"

Sin blew out a long, frustrated sigh, scrubbing a tattooed hand over his face. "Yeah. Pretty much. I just thought he was different with you. Shit, Tris, I'm sorry. So what'd he say to make you cry just now?"

I groaned, dropping my head to my hands. "I'm struggling on this forgery he wants done. Like *really* struggling. To the point where I genuinely don't think I can do it, and then I have to ask what the fuck happens to me if I can't deliver? Does he keep me around as your indentured bride? Or is that not a good enough penance for stealing from him and therefore I become fish food? But then he was all kind and supportive and said he *believed in me* and all this other nice stuff and it just..." I trailed off with a frustrated sound, tugging at my own hair.

Sin hummed a thoughtful sound, sitting back on his heels in front of me. "How come this forgery is so much harder than the others you've done? Surely forging a Van Gogh held just as much pressure?"

I sniffed, wiping my eyes with the heel of my hand. "The difference is, I usually have the original to study under a microscope. I have a whole system where I photograph it in sections to capture all the fine details then project that photograph onto my new canvas as like... a guide. That doesn't work when all I have as reference is fucking Google images. So now I have to rely heavily on my own artistic talent and when I tell you I loathe cubism—and all Picassos—I really mean I *loathe* it."

"Ah," he murmured. "Right. I know what you need." He pushed back to his feet and disappeared into the wardrobe. He muttered to himself as he flicked through the racks of clothing—almost entirely untouched since Naomi delivered it all—then popped back out holding a dress. "Get changed, Buttercup. We're going out."

I caught the dress he tossed me, then frowned my confusion. "Um... what?"

He tugged me up and gave me a shove in the direction of the bathroom. "You heard me. Do something with this mess—" He gestured to my tangled hair. "—then we're heading out. You're stressed out, exhausted, and scared. You need to clear your head, and that can't be done inside this house. So we'll get some cocktails and see if that soothes your artistic muse into cooperating."

My mouth opened and closed a couple of times, but I couldn't think of any reason *not* to go along with this plan. Would it help my failed forgery? Probably not. But it would be nice to get out of the Grimaldi house, for sure. Maybe I could even see if Katinka was free to hang out. So I did as I was told and got myself changed into Sin's selected dress, then fixed my hair and makeup because I really did look like a bedraggled mess.

An hour later we pulled up in front of Red's, a sexy nightclub in downtown Whispering Willows that had only opened a few months ago. There was a line of sparkling party-goers already waiting to get in, but Sin tossed his keys to the valet and swept straight past the tattoo-covered security with just a nod.

"Perks of being a Grimaldi, huh?" I muttered as we made our way inside the club.

Sin just shot me a knowing smirk and led the way over to the bar. "What's your drink of choice, Tris?"

"Uh... alcohol," I replied with a grin. "I'm not fussy, just get me whatever you're having."

He shrugged. "Alright. Tequila shots it is."

"Um, wait, maybe I'll start slower. A Tommy's Margarita would be perfect." Because I'd skipped dinner and straight tequila on an empty stomach sounded like a recipe for disaster.

Sin laughed but ordered my drink along with one for himself. We waited while the bartender mixed them up, and I let my gaze scan the busy room. "This place is popular. I've never been here before!"

"It sure is. I probably spend a little *too* much time

here, but that's because I'd rather not hang around at The Slippery Lips because for one thing, Dex likes to hang out there. And for another, the name is just fucking awful." He handed his credit card over to pay for our drinks, then slid one my way. "Cheers."

I tapped my glass against his, then took a sip of the citrusy cocktail. It was well-balanced, and I immediately took another sip. Yum. Sin gestured for me to follow as he led the way over to some vacant seats, and I smiled as I bobbed to the music, following along happily.

Just as Sin sat down, though, my roaming gaze snagged on a couple sitting a few tables away, laughing as they chatted with the cocktail waitress delivering them fresh drinks. My smile dropped, and I stared intently. What... was happening? Were they on a date?

"Tris?" Sin asked, waving his hand to pull my attention. "You okay? You look like you've just seen—" He broke off as he followed my line of sight. "Ah. Your ex."

"And my friend," I added in a croak. Then I shook my head. Why was I getting bent out of shape when John and I weren't *dating*? If he wanted to go out with Tink... that was their business, right? But surely there was a rule about not dating your friend's ex. If there wasn't, there should be.

"Do you want to leave?" Sin asked, glancing from me to them, and back again. They hadn't even seen me, but why would they? They were too busy telling jokes to the waitress.

I shook my head. "No." But I did want answers. So I gulped my margarita in a few huge swallows then placed my empty glass down on the table. "I'll just say hello."

Before Sin could stop me, I marched my emotional ass right over, and when the waitress left, I took her place with my hands on my hips and an accusing glare set across my face.

John paled instantly, his smile evaporating. "Tris!"

Katinka choked on her drink, coughing dramatically even as her panicked gaze met mine. Pure guilt etched all over her face, and that was almost worse than my unfounded assumptions. She knew she was doing the wrong thing by me, and yet she was doing it anyway. No wonder I didn't have any friends.

I flicked a look at John's pained expression. *Or lovers.*

JOHN

twenty-eight

Well, *fuck*. The way Tris glared made it pretty damn obvious what she was thinking, and she had *not* reached the correct conclusions. Not that I could really blame her... it did look a hell of a lot like Tink and I were out on a date, and since Tris knew nothing of the Game or even that Tink was a thief, it was a logical conclusion, even if it was incorrect.

"It's not what it looks like," I blurted out, then instantly cringed. Every other woman I interacted with, every other *person*, I could turn on the charm like a damn light switch. I used to pride myself on how effortlessly I could manipulate and influence others, but since meeting Tris, I was back to being a clueless child once more. A fumbling idiot, severely lacking in any degree of game.

Tink elbowed me. Hard. "Seriously? That's the line you're going with? Make it sound *more* suspicious, why don't you?" Rolling her eyes, she turned her focus back to the enraged beauty standing before us. "Tris, maybe you should sit down. We can try to explain some things."

I grunted at that. "No, we can't." Because if we told her about the Game, she'd be required to put up collateral to ensure she followed the rules of secrecy.

"Not *helping*," Tink growled with gritted teeth. She gave an exasperated sigh and motioned for Tris to join us. "John and I were celebrating something. We're *not* on a date. If you come sit, I'm sure we can explain it somehow."

"Alone, though," I added, scowling at Sin Grimaldi. "I'm not telling your fake fiancé shit." Because he was still a Grimaldi, and despite the fact they hadn't *physically* hurt Tris, they were blackmailing her into marrying. So they weren't the *good guys* no matter how Sin tried to play it. I could break the rules for *Tris*, I could trust her... maybe. But him? No way.

"Whatever bullshit lies you want to spin, you can do it with Sin beside me or not at all," Tris replied, finally breaking her silence. She hadn't said a single word since turning up in front of our table, but her thoughts had been crystal clear across her face.

Tink gave me a hard look, and I shook my head. "We need to talk to *you*, Tris. Not him. Tell him to go wait at the bar or something." I indicated the bar well out of earshot of us. Actually, with how loud the music was, the next table over would be far enough.

Tris scowled even deeper. "He's not a dog. I'll spare you the trouble of fabricating a story for this," she waved her hand between Tink and me, "and leave you to it." Her parting glance was pure betrayal as she shook her head, then took Sin's hand as she walked away from us. From *me*.

"John!" Tink squeaked, her expression pure panic. "Do something! She thinks we're fucking!"

Good. Maybe she'd be jealous enough to admit she cared. Fuck, no. Not good. Tris was as stubborn as they came, and if she genuinely thought I was screwing around... "*Damn it.*"

"Exactly!" Tink agreed, whacking me with the back of her hand. "Fix it. She's my only friend and *you're* in love with her, so this needs to get straightened out. Now. Go."

Nodding my agreement, I stood and climbed over the low couch to follow in the direction Tris had just left with Sin. Tink hurried after me, clearly not trusting me to work it out on my own, and with fair reason too. She *was* Tris's friend, so her seeing us on what seemed to be a date must have been a double blow.

After the whole near miss with acid, Tink and I had been riding an adrenaline high and decided to go out to celebrate. Bad move.

It took me a few moments of searching the room before deciding they'd probably left the club entirely. I headed out the front door with Tink on my heels and spotted Tris just a short way along the street. Hard to miss her with Sin fucking Grimaldi by her side like a six-foot-three shadow. At least he was shorter than me. That was something.

I approached quickly, determined to steal her away from her bodyguard and make her listen to at least part of the truth. Just enough that she knew I wasn't fucking her friend behind her back. But as I approached, I saw she was talking to Hank and Nelson, who were all dressed up like they were on a night out.

"Oh good, we're all here," Nelson announced, locking eyes with me and not looking pleased. "John, how unexpected."

"Nelson," I replied, dipping my head in greeting. "Hank."

"John," Hank replied, narrowing his eyes like he could *smell* my bad decisions.

"Katinka," Tink spoke up, announcing herself. "We met briefly. I'm friends with Tris."

To that, Tris gave a scoff of disagreement. Ouch.

"I remember," Nelson replied with a polite smile, then frowned up at Sin. "And you are...?"

"This is Sin," Tris hurried to answer, not even once looking over her shoulder at me. "Maybe we could go somewhere and catch up? I'd love to introduce you properly." She took *his* arm, leaning into him like they were a real couple.

Hank gasped, staring at them. "Is that an engagement ring?" he asked in a shocked breath.

Tink nudged me with her elbow. "Is that Bram? Tris's neighbor?" She pointed across the road where a man was walking toward the corner. Was it Bram, the useless fuck mercenary? Probably. He was still being paid to keep Tris alive, even though she didn't seem to be in any physical danger at the Grimaldi house.

A tense pause fell over the whole group of us, then Nelson nodded slowly. "Yes, I think I'd like to catch up, Miss Ives. Would you and your... *Sin* like to join us for a glass of wine? We were on our way to Frank's."

"Is that okay?" Tris asked Sin, still totally ignoring me. That was fine, I could wait. I wasn't going anywhere.

Sin glanced my way, though, his gaze full of

warning like he really wanted to pick a fight but knew it wouldn't go down well. "Of course, Buttercup. I'd love to. Shall we?" He gestured for the four of them to continue along the street—past me and Tink—then stopped me from following with a hand on my chest. "I'll catch up, Tris love. Just need a quick word with your professor."

I ground my teeth together, trying really hard not to start a fight with this dick right here in the street. For one thing, Tris was not in the mood to take my side. For another, he was still a Grimaldi and they had eyes everywhere.

He watched *my* girl walk away with her chosen family, waiting until they were a good distance from us before his gaze snapped back to mine. "Listen, John, I don't know what—"

"Don't touch me," I snapped, shoving his hand away from my chest harder than necessary. "That's exactly the problem, Grimaldi, you *don't know,* and I am not inclined to fill you in. Stop fucking pretending that this thing with Tris is real for you when we both know it's not."

His answering smile was too fucking confident. I expected him to be shaken or confused at least, but he was just... relaxed. Totally unruffled. "Here's what's going to happen, John. I'm going to go and join Tris for a glass of wine with her dear friends because they must have all sorts of questions about how our whirlwind romance came about. I'm going to lie and tell them everything they want to hear to feel confident that Tris is not, in fact, being forced into anything she doesn't want to do. Because she isn't. *You* are going to take my brother's whore and fuck off." He flicked a derisive glance Tink's way, then effectively dismissed her.

Fury and frustration swelled my chest. "Why the hell would I do that?"

Sin smiled again. "Because you know just as well as I do how much she misses those old men. *She* needs this. So you can put your big dick ego away and take the night to form whatever bullshit excuse you were going to offer her to explain this."

He gave me a shove, then brushed past to catch up with Tris without giving me any opportunity to argue further. Massive twat.

"Um, what now?" Tink asked, chewing the edge of her lip. "Are you going to do what he said?"

I shot her an incredulous look. "Are you fucking high? Of course not. But I also have to tread carefully because Tris is already pissed enough at *both* of us, so *if* I go starting fights with stupid Sin and she'll undoubtedly take his side. No... I need to distract him." I'd been putting in some research, because I would be an idiot not to, so I knew the one thing that would pull his attention away from Tris. Even if it was only brief.

"You should go home," I suggested to Tink. "Let me deal with this for now. I have an idea."

Indecision crossed her face, but she shook her head and threw her hands up. "*Sure.* Fuck, you *can't* make things any worse at this stage. Surely."

With that vote of confidence, she stalked away, leaving me alone in the middle of the sidewalk. I started slowly in the direction of the wine bar that Nelson mentioned, Frank's, while scrolling through my contacts. It took me a moment to find the one I was looking for, then I hit dial.

The PI answered quickly, and I only had a moment to reconsider my choices. This was a cruel game, even though I didn't particularly like Sin Grimaldi. But... if this was what it took for him to leave Tris for even a few minutes, then so be it.

"Send him a picture," I told my long-time business acquaintance. "Something with no location clues, and nothing to betray where she is. Just enough to distract him."

"You got it," my contact replied. "That one do?"

I glanced at my phone to check the image he'd just sent through. It was of a woman of maybe thirty years old, her honey blonde curls falling around her face as she slept. The photo was taken by long-range telephoto lens, not from inside her bedroom, but I scanned the background to check there were no convenient newspapers or coffee cups that might clue Sin in to her whereabouts.

"Yeah, that'll do," I agreed. "Send it off."

I ended the call then took up position in the shadows opposite Frank's wine bar. All my research told me that *this* woman was Sin Grimaldi's Achilles' heel. I was about to find out if that was true.

Tris
twenty-nine

Running into Hank and Nelson outside the club had hit me so hard I nearly fell over. I missed them *so* much, and seeing them was like ripping the scab off a wound I'd been carefully avoiding for two weeks. I'd staggered and Sin had caught my arm, steadying me.

Of course fucking John followed. I expected nothing less. But when presented with the opportunity to reconnect with Nelson and Hank, even for just a few minutes, John and his drama could damn well wait. I barely even glanced at him and Tink when I brushed past, the sting of betrayal too hot and raw to deal with just yet. All I wanted to do was sit down with a glass of wine and reassure my favorite two old men that I was fine.

Frank's Wine Bar was only two blocks away, and I commended myself for not looking back even once. I didn't want to know if John was following... but more than that, I didn't want to know if he *wasn't*. As mad as I was, I still wanted him to put up some kind of fight. To show he cared.

When we stepped inside and found a table, I let my gaze drift to the door. Any moment now, he'd come bursting in all full of indignation about whatever Sin had stayed back to say. But Sin joined us alone, and I tried to pretend I wasn't disappointed.

"So, Ivy, are we... uh..." Nelson trailed off when Hank kicked him unsubtly under the table. "I mean to say, I hope you've been well... Tristian?"

Sin glanced my way with a lopsided smile, draping his arm over the back of my chair. "You can speak freely, Buttercup. I'm not my father." He gave me a long look, and a small amount of tension eased within my chest.

Wetting my lips, I shifted my attention back to Nelson. "I've been better, old man."

His polite, hopeful expression creased into concern. "Talk to me, Ivy, what's going on? You're engaged?"

I sighed, glancing down at the enormous rock on my ring finger. "Yep. Sin is Mr. Grimaldi's son." I gave Hank and Nelson both a pointed look. Nelson winced, sitting back in his seat and motioning for Hank to pass him the wine list.

"We should celebrate," he muttered, flicking through the pages. Then he nodded and gestured for the waiter. "A bottle of the Penfolds Grange Hermitage, the 1971 please. My little girl's fiancé is paying."

I chuckled, despite myself, and caught Sin's good-natured smile from the corner of my eye. "Good choice. So, um, aside from my new relationship status... I'm otherwise fine. Just a little restricted in my movements outside the Grimaldi house."

"Ah, good. Here I was thinking you were avoiding us on purpose," Hank said with a gentle smile. There was an element of truth to that comment, though, and it struck me in the heart.

"I would never," I whispered, trying really hard not to be offended. "Until the terms of my arrangement have been completed, I need to... you know..."

"Behave," Sin murmured, filling in the gap. I frowned at his choice of word, but I guessed it applied. I would have gone more with *play along*, or *comply*, but it was all much of a muchness.

The sommelier brought our wine out and I bit my cheek, waiting patiently through all the pomp and ceremony of opening an expensive bottle of red, *then* waiting for him to decant and produce crystal goblets.

Sin's phone beeped in his pocket, and he tugged it out to check.

Whatever the message was, he stiffened up and just about knocked the table over when he stood abruptly.

"What's happened?" I asked, alarmed. Had something else blown up? I knew Mr. Grimaldi was *pissed* about the explosion at Boles, and I'd overheard multiple conversations where he was demanding answers from his goons about it. I couldn't think what else could have made Sin so upset.

He glanced down at me, his phone still in hand, and his eyes showed straight-up panic and *urgency*. "Nothing," he lied without even trying to make it convincing. "I need to make a phone call. It's time sensitive. Do you... are you okay if I just step outside? It's a bit loud in here." He glanced back at his phone again, and it was obvious that whoever had messaged now had his *full* attention.

"Of course, we're fine here," I agreed, "we have a whole bottle of Grange to enjoy, after all."

Sin frowned, hesitating. Then he raked his fingers through his hair. "I'll be just outside, and one of my father's guys is sitting at table eight." He indicated to a suited guy sipping a white wine and reading a newspaper across the wine bar. How in the *fuck* did he get a bodyguard in here so quickly? Or was it just a coincidence?

Whatever Sin had on his mind, it was important enough that he didn't even wait for my reply before hurrying out of Frank's with a frown marring his brow.

"What was that all about?" Hank asked with an edge of gossipy interest in his voice.

I smiled back at him. "No clue. But it's nice to get a moment alone with you two... sort of." I glanced across the bar to the Grimaldi guy. For all appearances, he wasn't paying us any attention at all. But Sin wouldn't have pointed him out if he was just here on his night off, would he?

Nelson glanced over then shrugged. "Well out of ear shot, but who knows how long that important phone call will keep your *fiancé* busy, so you'd best give us the abridged version, dear. Hit the key points. What happened after Luther's man picked you up that day?"

I combed my fingers through my hair, trying to quickly sum things up in my head. "Um, okay, so I got hauled into RBD's, and it was sort of useless denying the forgery at that point. He already knew the one stolen was *not* the original, and it didn't take a genius to put two and two together to label me a thief."

Hank gave a startled noise, and I looked at him in confusion. "Uh... has Nels not filled you in already?"

He shot a scathing glare at his partner, shaking his head. "Only the vaguest of details, Ivy dear. And he let me *assume* that Grimaldi never owned the original. But he did, didn't he? You two stole it?"

Nelson cringed, looking decidedly uncomfortable. "Listen, you didn't specifically ask, so I didn't technically lie to you."

"Well, this is awkward," I murmured, raising my glass to take a sip of the expensive wine. Yes, I knew that Hank was being kept in the dark during our *Poppy Flowers* project, but I sort of figured Nelson would have told him by now.

Nelson huffed, his lips pursed as he reached for his own wine. "We can disagree later, Hank. Right now we need to hear from Ivy about what happened at RBD's."

Hank scowled and folded his arms, visibly pissed off, but gestured for me to continue nonetheless.

"So..." I cast my mind back, then wrinkled my nose when it came to the whole *shooting a guy to save my own life* part. They didn't need to know that. "Uh, long story short, RBD decided I was more use to him alive than dead so he has tasked me with a new forgery, and arranged my engagement to Sin—who is not actually interested in me, I might add—and in exchange I get to keep my head attached to my shoulders."

Both old men stared at me a while then Hank threw

his hands up in frustration. "If you two had *told me* that you were forging a fucking Van Gogh, then maybe we could have avoided this whole damn mess. Why don't you just give Luther the painting's location and ask him to release you from the engagement at least?"

I clicked my tongue, trying not to exchange a loaded look at Nelson. "I can't do that."

"Can't? Or won't?" Hank snapped the question, practically steaming with indignation. "Who'd you sell it to? It can't have been one of my contacts, or I'd already have heard all about it. Please tell me you didn't send it to The Styx House."

I quickly shook my head, not willing to let him think *that* badly of us. The Styx House was not the kind of place I would *ever* visit willingly. I was more than happy letting Hank broker all our sales, keeping Nelson and me well out of the transactions. I'd never undercut him with *that* auction house.

"What does Luther want you to forge for him, Ivy?" Nelson asked, smoothly changing the subject to save me needing to evade Hank's accusation.

I took a bigger sip of my wine before answering. "*Le Pigeon aux Petits Pois.*"

Hank's jaw dropped and Nelson must have inhaled the sip of wine he was taking, because he coughed and spluttered, his face turning beet red while he tried to catch his breath. I sighed, handing him my napkin while he got his breathing back to normal. Then he shot me a panicked look, eyes wide and cheeks flushed.

"But you're awful at cubism, Ivy."

I rolled my eyes. "Thank you so much for the vote of confidence, old man. I have it handled." I most assuredly did not, but I wasn't going to make it his problem. When he continued staring at me like I'd said I was growing a tail, I put my wine down. "I'm going to pee."

The second I walked away from the table, they broke into hushed, angry conversation and I groaned to myself. I really had assumed Hank knew everything by now, and it made me all anxious that I'd caused trouble between them. Nelson *really* should have told him, though. That was on him.

Before I reached the ladies room, someone grabbed my arm and dragged me into a supply closet. I gave a small scream, wrenching myself away before my brain fully recognized who'd just snatched me into privacy.

"Dammit, John!" I hissed, letting the fight ebb away and leaning against the closed door. Just because I knew what he was like, I fumbled around and found the light switch before he could go seducing me with those deep drugging kisses in the dark. "What the *fuck* are you doing in here?" *And why am I so relieved to see you?*

"You didn't seriously think I was going to let Sin Grimaldi, biggest douche in Whispering Willows, tell me what to do? Fuck that guy, I needed to talk to you myself. Figured it was safer away from Hank and Nelson so we didn't cause a scene." He offered a sheepish look, tucking his hands in his back pockets. It was such an awkward gesture it almost seemed like he was doing it to prevent himself touching me.

Probably for the best. I would have to shove him away on principle, and I didn't want to do that.

I swallowed, trying to keep my thoughts straight and not be swayed by his magnetic energy. "You were out with Katinka. Weren't you inside me a little over twelve hours ago? Seems a bit rude to be on a date with my only friend so soon." I tried to keep my words light and carefree, but I was *hurting* inside. It'd been a double blow.

"We weren't on a *date*, Tris. No more than you and Grimaldi were." He arched a brow, challenging me.

Guilt and anxiety tripped through me. I'd never really believed John was buying my thing with Sin, especially when I kept letting him fuck me... but I could see how I might be jumping to conclusions with Tink. Maybe. "If you weren't on a date, what were you doing? I didn't know you two were friends."

John tipped his head to the side, his gaze steady and

unguarded. "We live together. She had a... life or death scare earlier this evening so we decided to go for a few drinks to celebrate the whole *life* outcome of that."

I parted my lips to respond but... that was a valid excuse, so snapped my mouth shut again. Then I frowned. "What kind of *life or death* situation? Something at the club? Was it De—"

"No, not at the club. And she's fine." That was it. No further explanation.

Fuck off. "She's like you, isn't she?" I murmured in disbelief. "She's a fucking thief, just like you."

John said nothing. He didn't even blink.

They *lived* together? Of course, she was like him. I was so, so stupid not to see it sooner.

"Tell me I'm wrong, John. Tell me that I wasn't only played by the man I lo— *liked*, but also by the only woman I'd considered a friend, my first in fucking years? *Tell me I'm wrong!*" I practically shouted that plea at him, tears already burning at the backs of my eyes, but still he said nothing.

My inhale shuddered through my lungs, my whole body going ice cold with the awful truth of it all. I reached for the door handle, determined to put space between us, but John stopped me with his palm against the door.

"Don't do that, Venus," he whispered, his voice

rough with all the secrets he was holding. "Let me try to explain."

"Can you?" I scoffed a bitter laugh. "Can you *actually* explain everything to me, John? No bullshit, no lies, just the truth no matter what I ask?"

His silence told me the answer to that, much clearer than any words ever could. This time when I tried to open the door, I wrenched it hard, forcing him to either back off or hold me against my will. For once, he chose wisely, letting me step out of the closet.

"I need this to stop, John." I didn't trust myself to look at him as I said it, needing him to believe me beyond shadow of doubt. "I need you to let me get over you and move on with my life."

He exhaled heavily, the sheer regret and defeat evident in just that breath. "Venus…"

I shook my head and walked away, returning to join Hank and Nelson with a pasted-on smile. I simply wasn't strong enough to do anything more. It was a palpable relief when Sin returned a moment later, even if he was a million miles away inside his head.

John

thirty

The hurt and betrayal in Tris's face as she connected the dots on what I was carefully *not* saying fucking killed me. It gutted me even more when I couldn't offer her any quick reassurances. No pretty lies would roll off my tongue, and I was bound in my silence by my oaths to the Game. So I said nothing and let her walk away like a goddamn fool.

I watched from the shadows as the Grimaldi gremlin returned, but not even the troubled, distracted look on his face could cheer me up. What did messing with him matter when my girl was so broken right now?

Reluctantly, I slipped back out through the kitchen of Frank's Wine Bar, hanging my head low as I made my way home. I couldn't seem to *stop* fucking things up with her, but I also couldn't lie. Not any more. There was a whole mental block in place, where every time I *tried* to soothe Tris with pretty fallacies and convenient half truths, I just froze. The words wouldn't pass my lips.

At this point, my silence was worse than any fabrication, but what other choice did I have?

I couldn't face Tink. She would expect me to have fixed everything, and all I'd done was make it worse. I should have just pretended we were on a date. That would have been a softer blow than Tris finding out her friend was also deceiving her.

"Out for a stroll, son?" A shadow detached from a tree to my left, and I stifled a groan.

"Every time I think you'll do me a favor and just die of a heart attack, you disappoint me. You're drastically out-classed in the Game now, Igor, so why are you still hanging around?" I didn't stop walking, because I'd hate for him to get the impression I was interested in chatting.

He followed me anyway, like the bottom-feeding eel he was. "You're right, son. I'd be wasting my time trying to steal the Game pieces myself. Much better off waiting for someone else to do it, then steal from them when the danger is over, eh? Oh wait. Was that your plan? I guess the apple doesn't fall far from the tree."

I stifled the need to scream at him to back off. Or to strangle him. Or just to push him out into the road if a bus conveniently passed by. That last one was very tempting.

"Igor... I'm not in the mood for your shit. Not tonight." I glanced back at him and grunted a satisfied sound at how messed up his face still was. "Or would you like me to freshen up that pretty purple eyeshadow, hmm?"

My father's smile slipped to a scowl, and I turned my back on him once more.

"I'm not going anywhere, Ivan," he called after me, always needing the last word. "That legacy is rightfully mine, and you know it."

I extended my middle finger but didn't otherwise reply. Talking to Igor was nothing more than a waste of my oxygen. Because he wasn't above following me like a bad smell, I took the scenic route home, making triple sure I didn't have a tail by the time I climbed into my Cobra. Facing Tink and admitting I'd *really* fucked up wasn't an option, and the urge to see Tris again was so strong my skin was itching.

It was an inevitability that I drove over to my vantage point near the Grimaldi manor and parked to wait for my girl to get home. With him. Gremlin.

I bided my time, waiting until all the lights were

turned out, ignoring Tink's messages all the while. Around two in the morning—my favorite time to visit Tris—I picked my way silently through the gardens, following my carefully mapped route to avoid all security.

My access point wasn't anywhere near as pedestrian as Sinister's bedroom window. How utterly predictable that would be. Instead, I circled around the far side of the manor, climbing into the garage roof, then up onto the awning of the second floor... a little shimmy along the side of the house, precisely timed to evade the spotlight, cameras, and physical security guards, and then I was silently raising the sash window of an unused guest bedroom.

I climbed through, then just as quietly lowered the window back into position, not leaving any sign of my entry in case security happened to look up. They rarely did, but every now and then...

"You took your time." The voice came from the shadows and I nearly jumped out of my damn skin.

Pulse racing, I steeled my spine to hide how much of a fright the slick dickhead just gave me. "Had to be sure everyone was asleep," I replied, casual as *fuck*, like I'd expected him. Because clearly he'd expected *me*. "Or most everyone. Shouldn't you be snoring and sleep talking on your bedroom floor at this time, Grimaldi?"

"I normally would be," he admitted, flicking on the bedroom light and making me cringe at the sudden brightness. "But I had a *feeling* my wife's stalker would try and pay a visit tonight. Looks like I was right."

He was trying to get a rise out of me, and it was working. Anger burned hot in my chest and my fists tightened at my sides. "She's not your wife."

His lips curved in a smug smile. "Not yet, maybe. But she will be... sooner than you might think."

The effort it took not to give him the satisfaction of a reaction nearly put me into cardiac arrest. Somehow I managed to pull off nonchalant though. "Hmm, we'll see. Tris doesn't take well to being forced into anything she doesn't want to do. I wouldn't go counting my chickens just yet, friend."

He folded his arms over his chest, oozing confidence. "Who says she doesn't want to? We've been spending so much time together lately, getting to know one another... it won't be long until she's totally on board with becoming Mrs. Grimaldi. I can offer *so much.* Can you seriously compete?"

I shook my head, counting to five in my head to keep my cool. "I'm surprised you're so eager to see this little farce through. Did you remember to send a wedding invitation to *her*?"

Sin's face clouded with anger and frustration, and

he took two steps closer like he wanted to kill me with his bare hands. "I don't know how you got that photo, or who sent it to me, but you're playing with fire now."

I smiled, clasping my hands. "Oh good, I packed marshmallows."

Sin's eye twitched, and it warmed me inside. Fuck this guy, playing nice and approachable to my girl's face but plotting to seduce her? He really was his father's son.

"These little visits will stop, effective immediately," he snapped, puffing up his chest a bit. I wonder if he felt short against me? I hoped so. "Your creepy little notes are terrifying Tris, and it's *my* job to take care of her now. I understand that you're having a hard time accepting defeat, but it's done. She's *mine* now, and this arrangement suits me well. I can't have you fucking it all up, John. Leave her alone. She has nothing to do with your Game."

I inhaled sharply, alarm stiffening my spine. What the fuck did he know about the Game? How? Or was I reading too much into that statement and he just meant a generic relationship game?

Regardless, I needed to tread carefully. "I fail to see why I should give a fuck about ruining your plans, Sinister. If Tris wants me to stop visiting, she can tell me herself." Of course, she *sort of* had when she threw a block of soap at my head, but I was confident she didn't really mean that.

"Because if she doesn't fulfill her end of the deal with my father, she will be shot. It's that fucking simple, John. You want her alive? I can make that happen, but alive *and* yours? Not an option." He paused, staring at me hard for a long moment while he seemed to let that information sink in. "Unless... you have something better to offer me?"

This sly motherfucker. He wanted what I'd found... what he'd failed to locate for more than two years. Why the fuck he thought I was in a position to need his help, though, I wasn't sure. Then again, he didn't know who I was. Not really. Sure, he might have figured out I was a thief, but not that I was *Hermes*.

I knew the value of the information I held, so I just smiled and tipped my head. "Interesting. I'll be sure to take that under advisement. For now, I'll let you get some sleep... You look like you need it. Tell my Venus that I'll see her in class on Monday. She still has grades to maintain, after all." Tugging the window open, I left the same way I'd arrived.

The light stayed on in that room for a while, then flicked off right as I reached my car. I wondered how long it'd taken him to work out how I was getting in. Each night when he failed to find me, was he growing more and more enraged? That thought gave me a chuckle as I drove away. But then as soon as the amusement faded, I was back to being irritated and frustrated that I hadn't seen Tris.

Sin was proving to be a problem, and I had to grudgingly admit I'd underestimated *him*.

I needed to remove him from the equation entirely. Maybe I would give him the information he wanted... although he really should be careful what he wished for in that regard. It'd definitely remove him from Whispering Willows, though. And Tris would be totally forgotten the moment he got what he wanted.

Then again, for all his selfish reasons, he was currently the best protection for Tris. He was standing between her and his father, and that was something I couldn't personally do while the Game was running. So... as much as I wanted to get rid of him, he was also helping by being here.

It was something to ponder on, at very least. For now, though, I needed to confess my mistakes to Tink. She was going to kill me.

Tris
thirty-one

As soon as I woke the morning after Frank's Wine Bar, I looked for a note. When I found nothing, my heart sank so low I ended up crawling back into bed and throwing a pity party. Eventually Sin came to check on me, and I pretended I was hungover from all the wine I'd consumed with Hank and Nelson. A poor attempt to drown my sorrows.

All Saturday, I pretended that I was sick. Chef Tony made me soups, and Sin delivered them on trays while I binge-watched Netflix in his bed and faked a cough whenever someone walked past the room. Guilt drove me out of bed on Sunday morning, though. My pity party for one shouldn't be causing more work for everyone else, so I forced my sad ass into the shower then headed for my painting studio.

Despite the revelations from John and Katinka, it'd been such a joy to spend time with Nelson and Hank. They'd had a damn good laugh about me working on a Picasso, but before they'd left for the night Nelson gave me some really sound advice about how to tackle it.

Dana from the kitchen delivered a tray of breakfast and coffee outside my studio only five minutes after I got settled, which made my skin prickle with paranoia. I hadn't told anyone where I was going, but I'd passed some of the Grimaldi men on route, so someone must have been reporting on my whereabouts.

Still, I was hungry and never said no to coffee, so I took the tray inside to place beside my workstation. I was working with oil paints today, so I'd opened a window to keep the turpentine fumes moving. As high up as my attic studio was, I doubted there was any security threat in having it cracked.

Taking a sip from my coffee, I turned my headphones on and selected some music to get me in the right headspace for creating. Emlyn's version of "Glimpse of Us" poured through my headphones, and instead of running from all the hurt John had caused lately, I embraced it. I let it pour out through my paintbrush, but only in the subtlest of ways. Something Nelson had said about Picasso's work had struck a nerve. That there was so much more passion and emotion in the cubist pieces than might be obvious to the naked eye.

He'd suggested I was approaching the work too analytically and stifling the art. So I was trying it his way and letting my instincts guide the brush.

It was surprising, but it worked. When I paused for a break to finish my breakfast—more than an hour after I started it—I was shocked at how well my forgery was coming along. Was it perfect? No. But without the original, no one *else* could possibly pinpoint my errors with accuracy. Half the work on a convincing forgery was in the work I did *after* the painting itself was done. The work done to believably age the piece. That was what set mine apart from others, and that would be what sold this one as the original.

Or, that was the hope I clung to.

"That looks really good," Katinka said.

"Thanks," I replied, absentmindedly. Then jerked with shock. "What the—? How? You can't *be* here!"

My pixie-like fake friend tipped her head to the open window with a lopsided grin. "Well then maybe you shouldn't have left the window open, babe. It's basically an invitation, especially when you've been ignoring my calls all weekend. What was I supposed to do, just give you space?" She scoffed, shaking her head.

"I don't think so. Is this what Grimaldi has you working on? It's... very yellow."

"It's a Picasso," I snapped, defensive of my work. "It's meant to be yellow."

Katinka wrinkled her nose. "I know that, silly. I just think your work on *Poppy Flowers* was way nicer. Flowers are such a better image than... pigeons and peas. Where even are the pigeons in this?"

"That's what I said," I muttered, tossing my paint brushes into the jar of turps and grabbing a rag to clean my hands. "You can't be here. Aside from the fact that it's a massive breach of security, which you already know, I *don't want you here*. Which you *also* already know. So just... shimmy back down the drainpipe or something. Go play your dumb fake friendship games with someone else."

She heaved a sigh, making no move to exit. She and John were more alike than I'd realized.

"Look. John told me that you worked out I'm more than just an excellent stripper and fucking incredible seductress. I wanted a chance to explain because I know you've gone right ahead and assumed the worst." She parked her hands on her hips, giving me a hard look that said she wasn't leaving unless I tossed her out the window myself. Or called for security.

I gritted my teeth, really thinking about those

options. "I assume you want to try and spin some bullshit that convinces me I jumped to conclusions and you're *not* an art thief just like him? Maybe mess with my head a little more, like when you pretended my door was unlocked, hmm?"

She winced, confirming my guess. It was never unlocked; she'd picked it. "God no, why would I try to deny it? You *guessed*... which means no rules were broken in you knowing the truth. No one told you, so no one is at fault. This is great! I've been wracking my brain trying to think of a way to drop hints without actually making you think I was crazy. Or hitting on your man, which I'm one hundred percent *not*, for the record."

Confusion rendered me speechless for a moment. There was a lot to unpack there—about *rules*?—but all I could grab onto was the trivial shit. "But you *do* live together?"

Katinka wrinkled her nose. "Yes, but not romantically. We have separate rooms. Things are dangerous right now so we're keeping an eye on one another to avoid... um... problems."

She was picking her words carefully, and she'd already told me I needed to draw my own conclusions. "Problems of the life or death kind? That's what John mentioned the other night. That you'd had a life or death situation and were celebrating the *life* outcome."

Katinka started laughing at that, snorting a little as she tried to contain it. "Yes, that's... yes. Fuck he's a doofus. Oh my *God* he told me about the serial killer notes he's been leaving you! Can we please talk about that when we're good again? Because it sounded awful but maybe it wasn't so creepy on your end?"

I bit the edge of my lip, fighting the urge to slip back into friendship with her so easily. She was so confident we could, though. She said *when* we're good, not *if*.

"They were in scribbled block capitals on ripped paper," I muttered, folding my arms under my breasts. "I thought they were from Dex."

She gave a strangled sound, turning red as she tried to contain her laughter at John's expense. "Okay. We can circle back to that dumpster fire. Let's clear the air between us first. Yes, I hid some rather important facts about my professional career, but that's it. And technically, didn't you also do the same?"

My jaw dropped. "What? No! I never lied to you about—" I cut off as Katinka slid her gaze to the half-finished Picasso forgery on my easel. My cheeks heated. "Ah. Well. I can maybe see where you're coming from."

"Look. I need you to know, I never used you." She locked eyes with me, her gaze confident and sincere. "I didn't befriend you for any ulterior motives. I just *liked* talking to you, without any side benefit. Actually, that would have been against the rules anyway since you were someone else's mark."

My mood soured. "John's."

Katinka grimaced, shrugging. "Anyway. My point being, you weren't *mine*. I just wanted to be your friend, and I'm selfishly glad you worked out some stuff because now we don't have to pretend not to know the things we know. You know?"

I did know. Sort of. It wasn't like I'd been totally upfront with her about my forgeries or my little side hustle with Nelson, so could I really be *that* upset that she never mentioned she was fucking Dex because of—

"Oh ew, Dex was your mark?" I gagged. "Were you and John working together to steal the Van Gogh or something?"

She chuckled. "Yeah, look. He seemed like an easy pick when this started, but now I really wish I'd gone for Sin instead. Not that I would have gotten far with him."

I sighed in exhaustion, sinking down to my painting stool. "I need more, Katinka. You need to explain more."

"Tink," she said quietly. "You can call me Tink. Katinka *is* my name, but only on legal shit. And I can't. Like... there are rules and I'm already *so* close to breaking them, but like... if you could just work it all out on your own then I think that's okay? I don't actually know. I've never been in this position before. Maybe I've already fucked it all up."

I stared at her for a moment, trying to make sense of her chaos. Then I shook my head slowly. "If you can't tell me, then I think you need to leave."

Her stricken expression almost made me change my mind. "Tris... I promise, I never tried to use you. Ever. You're basically my only friend, so knowing you feel betrayed has me all cut up inside. I want to make things better. How do I do that?"

"You *tell me what the fuck is going on!*" I cracked, shouting at her then immediately clamping a hand over my mouth as I looked to the door. How close was the nearest security guy? Close enough to hear that? Maybe he'd think I was just yelling at my work. But, my point stood. "Tink, you either explain *everything*, or you can leave. I get it, I also hid things from you, but right now I'm having an extremely hard time trusting anyone, and knowing that you and John are hiding some big *thing* with all these *rules*... Christ, this isn't a fucking game!"

"Yes!" She brightened up. "Yes, it is! That's..." She nodded encouragingly. "That's what it is."

I squinted hard. "It's... a game?"

She nodded again, eagerly.

"Stealing *Poppy Flowers*... was part of the game? You weren't working together, you were competing against each other?" I said it slowly, piecing it together as I spoke, and Tink kept nodding with that big grin on her face. "Does this have something to do with the bomb at Boles last week?"

"Yes," she confirmed. "But before you think the worst, it had nothing to do with me *or* John. I wasn't even on campus and he was, um, busy? With you, I think? And missed the warning messages."

Oh great. John was busy nailing me on his desk and nearly got us both blown up.

"I see," I murmured, feeling sick with anxiety and disappointment. "Is it still going, this... game? Are you still looking for *Poppy Flowers*?"

"Still going, yes. *Poppy Flowers*, no. The um, target shifted after the whole forgery, FBI incident. It's legit nothing to do with you *or* the Grimaldis anymore, I promise." She smiled reassuringly, but I still felt like I wanted to vomit.

Shaking my head, I tried to make sense of it all. It was a lot, but also it made so much sense. "I don't believe you, Tink. I want to, but... if it had nothing to do with me, why is John still pursuing me to the point of stalker behavior and totally incapable of taking no for an answer? Unless there is still a game to be won... it doesn't add up."

Tink gave me a puzzled look, crouching down to

take my hand in hers. "Babe. It does add up, you're just deliberately missing the point. If there's no *other* reason for him to be chasing you like a dog in heat, doesn't that sort of give you the answer? He's totally in love with you, Tris. And at this stage, it's kind of detrimental to *everyone's* safety."

My jaw dropped, and words dried up. John was... *no.* He wasn't *in love, he just* hated being told no. He was the kind of guy who couldn't take the ego blow and needed to always have women falling at his feet.

A sharp knock on the studio door almost saw me fall off my stool, and I frantically gestured for Tink to leave out the window once more.

"Tristian, just checking you're okay? I thought I heard... something." The guard's muffled voice sounded familiar, and I realized it was Bram. I let out a small breath of relief but still shooed Tink faster nonetheless.

"Yep, yeah, all good! Sorry, I was, um, I sometimes talk to my work when it's not cooperating. Sorry." I scrubbed a hand over my face, adrenaline coursing so hard through me that my fingers trembled. When I turned back to the window, though, Tink was gone. Like a thief in the night.

John

thirty-two

Tink was not happy with me and made no secret of that fact. She barely spoke to me all weekend, and we missed the Saturday game piece entirely because we couldn't agree over what it was. She thought it was a horse; I thought it was a car. Because I was *trying* to make amends, we went with her instinct so we were staking out the Willows Thoroughbred Stables when an explosion went off in the luxury car dealership across town.

Turned out, I was right. To add salt to the wound, Igor got the points.

Tink disappeared early Sunday morning, and when she returned her whole mood had shifted. She was no longer angry and frustrated at me, she was... squirrely. Almost seemed guilty about something. Somehow she managed to evade my questions, though, so I focused on preparing for the classes at Boles that were restarting on Monday.

Nervous energy kept me thoroughly distracted during that first class back, waiting for Tris to show up—with or without Sin, I didn't care. She didn't, and a sour feeling of dread settled within me for the rest of the class. By the afternoon, I'd checked in with her other professors and none of them had seen her either. Eventually I checked in at the dean's office.

"Oh, honey, your face is looking so much better," Marla cooed as she bustled out from behind her desk to pat my cheek. "Those bruises are healing up well. You poor thing."

"I'm quite fine, Marla, I assure you. I came to ask about a student absence, if I may? My TA, Tristian Ives. She was hurt in the incident, and she hasn't turned up today. Do you know if she's okay?" I didn't need to feign concern. I was genuinely worried. Had something come of my chat with Sin? Had he locked her up?

Marla hummed a thoughtful sound, perching her glasses on her nose as she returned behind her desk, looking for something. "Ah yes, here. She applied to defer her courses for the remainder of the semester, and Dean Lawrence approved it already. The sweet girl must be so traumatized after that awful gas leak. I heard she took a nasty bump to the head."

What? No... Tris didn't get traumatized.

"She called?" I asked, puzzled. Maybe if it came from Sin and not actually Tris, then it was a sign that she was being manipulated. That she needed me to save her.

Marla nodded. "Yes, dear. I had a message from her on the voicemail when I arrived this morning and emailed over the paperwork. Looks like Dean Lawrence signed off on it a couple of hours ago."

"Oh. I see." I couldn't help the disappointment in my voice.

Marla gave me a gentle smile. "It was a very scary thing, what we all went through. I admit, even I was nervous returning to work today! I'm sure Miss Ives will be fine with some more time to process everything."

My answering smile was tight, but I thanked her and left. Tris wasn't *processing* or even remotely traumatized. She was tough as nails, and this deferral of her classes reeked of Grimaldi control tactics. I desperately wanted to visit her and ask for myself, but after my run in with Sin I'd been hesitant to return. He had a mean streak, one that he hid well, but I had concerns for Tris's well-being if I continued to push him.

When I got home, Tink was cooking dinner but glanced over at me with a guilty expression.

"Okay, what happened?" I snapped. "You've been slinking around with your tail between your legs since you got back yesterday. What did you do that put *that* look on your face?"

Her eyes narrowed and stubborn irritation flashed. "Nothing. Fuck you. I didn't cook enough for two, so make your own." She tipped her entire frying pan of beef stir-fry into one bowl—enough to feed a family of four—then stabbed a baby corn spear with her fork like she was daring me to challenge her.

"Tink..." I groaned, dropping my ass onto one of the kitchen stools. "I'm too tired to fight with you. We missed another game piece today, because we aren't on the same page anymore. This stuff with Tris—"

"I fucked up!" she blurted out, slamming her fork down. "I fucked up, okay? And... I'm sorry. Can we move on now?"

My lips parted in surprise. "Whoa, wait, *you* fucked up? I thought I was the one who fucked up. What did *you* do, Tink?"

She cringed hard, her face crumpling. "I went to see her."

Alarm rippled through me. "Her. Tris? You went to

see Tris? When? Yesterday? What did you say? What did *she* say?"

Tink puffed out her cheeks, looking to the ceiling as she considered her words carefully. "I... broke into her art studio because she wasn't returning any of my calls and I needed her to know that I was never using her because she wasn't *my* mark."

The implication, of course, being that she was mine. Which she already knew, but still... "Dammit, Tink. What else?"

"I thought... if she *guessed* everything, then she could know about the Game without being told about the Game. Then there wouldn't be any more secrets and we could all make amends and shit. Right?" Her pleading expression told me there was more to this story, and I slowly shook my head.

"Wrong," I replied. "That's not how the rules work, Tink. It was okay for her to guess you're a thief like me, but when it comes to the Game..."

She threw her hands up. "Well I know that *now*! Like I said, I fucked up and I'm sorry. But also, the judges know that Tris knows so I'm pretty sure they have ears within the Grimaldi house. Um, just FYI."

I groaned at the implication of that. "They will want collateral from her."

"I have it handled," Tink snapped, stabbing another

vegetable from her huge bowl. "And I feel bad enough about it, but she's not exactly going to go running her mouth to anyone about the Game, right? So... no harm done."

No harm done. I bet Tris would disagree if she found out. "What did you offer as her collateral, Tink?"

My petite partner in crime just glared. "It doesn't matter, I have it sorted. Judges accepted, and Tris never *needs* to know, so long as she doesn't break the rules."

"She doesn't *know* the rules, Tink!" I was having a hard time keeping my temper, but *shit*.

She shrugged helplessly. "Well... there's no reason why we can't tell her now. When you think about it, I sort of did you a favor. You should thank me."

I parted my lips to tell her where she could shove my thanks, but a hard knock on the door interrupted us. I shot Tink a hard glare to say we were far from done with this conversation, then went to check who it was.

Peering through the peep-hole, I almost questioned whether my eyes were playing tricks on me. Then I swung the door open quickly. "Tris... you're here."

"Yeah, I am. Can I come in?" She didn't look happy, but she was *here,* so I wouldn't question things further than that. I stepped aside, gesturing for her to come inside, then closed and locked the door behind her.

"Tris! Hi!" Tink called from the kitchen, startled. "Uh... how did you know where we lived?"

Good question.

"Sin drove me over," she replied, her voice flat and emotionless. How the fuck did Sin know where we were? What did he do to my Venus?

Tink cast me a long look and I shrugged. "Um, where is he now?" she asked Tris, glancing to the door like she expected him to come storming through it. I also wanted to know, but was trying to contain the wild jealousy where Tris was concerned. Particularly right now, when she wasn't herself. I locked my jaw shut and folded my arms.

"He's waiting in the car," Tris replied. "I asked for privacy so I could... deal with things here."

Well shit, that didn't sound good. Tink must have agreed, because she hastily put her bowl back on the kitchen counter and wiped her hands on a tea towel. "You know what? This seems private. I'm going to just leave you two to... um... talk." She practically tripped over her own feet with how fast she grabbed her coat and shoes, then took off like her tail was on fire.

"She's... uncomfortable with confrontation," I offered in Tink's wake. "And it definitely seems like you have *things* to say." I didn't have the heart to say exactly what I meant, that she seemed like she was here to end things between us. For good.

Not acceptable on any level to me. But if she wanted to throw down that gauntlet then I needed to be ready to pick it up.

She wet her lips, glancing around the living room. "This is... classy. Much bigger than the cottage at Boles. Why'd you move?"

I quirked a brow at her small talk. Was she reconsidering?

"I was concerned there might be surveillance," I answered truthfully.

She sucked a breath in alarm. "From who?"

I hesitated, but then reminded myself about Tink's fuck up. If she'd fronted up Tris's collateral, then she was all in. "My father, Igor," I answered. "He seemed to be one step ahead of me, and I discovered a tracker under my skin. Cameras didn't seem out of the realm of possibility."

She stared at me for a moment, then blinked in stunned disbelief. "Your father? He's also *playing*?"

I inclined my head. "Yes. And he is a cheat."

Tris nodded to herself, taking that information in. She raked her fingers through her hair with obvious exasperation, "Right. Have I met him? Is working at the Royal Orchid or something?"

"No, you haven't. Or not that I'm aware of. He's working for Luther Grimaldi but in his gaming rooms. I can't see why your paths ever would have crossed." And I intended to make sure it stayed that way.

She was silent for a long pause, and I made no attempt to fill the air with empty words. She had something on her mind, and I needed to let her get it out.

"The whole thing with *Poppy Flowers*," she said quietly, her gaze on the floor. "You used me to get to the painting, because I had access."

I nodded. "Yes. I leveraged my own interests to get the position at Boles. Initially I thought Bailey was working for Grimaldi, but then I discovered it was you... and by that stage I was already in way over my head."

Her brow dipped in a scowl. "What is that supposed to mean?"

"I think you know what it means, Venus." For some reason, I needed her to draw the correct conclusions. Like hearing me *say it* would just be more empty words from a con man but if she could trust in her own feelings... take a leap of faith...

She gritted her teeth hard enough that her jaw clicked, and her hands balled into fists at her sides. "You used me, John. You deliberately set out with the intention of earning my trust, of making me fall for you, then used that position to steal the painting and then just... left. You walked away from us, John, because the painting was more important to you than I ever was. Don't try implying that your feelings for me were ever sincere or strong."

Guilt and regret churned inside me, and I wet my lips. "Yes. That's all true."

She inhaled in surprise, like she'd expected me to deny it. I couldn't fucking lie to her though. I just couldn't do it. And those were the facts. "I used you. I earned your trust and plied you for information that revealed your passcodes, then walked away when I had what I wanted." If anything, me repeating it all, admitting to it all, made her flinch like I'd tossed acid. "I can't change the past, Tris, but I'm here *now*. I can freely admit, I totally screwed things up with you, and I didn't realize what I had until it was gone."

She swallowed, her gaze not meeting mine. "You're back, but not for me. You're still here for 'the game,' aren't you?"

I wet my lips, choosing my words carefully. "The Game is still on, yes. Would I have returned to Whispering Willows if it'd ended with *Poppy Flowers*? I honestly don't know."

"What *do* you know, John? Because right now I'm having a hard time understanding why you won't leave me alone. I don't have anything to give you. Tink said no one is looking for *Poppy Flowers* anymore, and I have nothing else of value. I don't even have access to Mr. Grimaldi's gallery anymore so I am *useless* to this... game."

I frowned, taking a step closer. Logically I knew I was trying to keep my distance to let her speak her mind, but everything about her posture and tone was screaming how hurt she was. How insecure and confused, and all I wanted to do was hold her.

"Tris... I won't even start on how much value you hold in just being you, because that's beside the point. I can't leave you alone because you literally consume my thoughts day and night. From the moment I left town with that cursed forgery, *all* I could think about was how badly I regretted my choices. How much I missed *you*. How guilty I felt for deceiving you. So I tried to convince myself it was better to stay away, that you wouldn't want to see me anyway." I paused for breath, my feet carrying me closer without conscious intention. "Then I watched you fall down a drainpipe and I knew..."

"You knew what?" she whispered, sounding so utterly defeated that I wanted to die. "That I was still an easy mark? That I was stupid enough to still be of use? That I could—"

"That I was in love with you," I snapped, cutting her self-deprecation off before it could go any further. "I knew *then* that I was totally in love with you and would do just about *anything* to gain your forgiveness. No matter how long it takes."

Her jaw dropped and I cupped her cheek, tilting her face up until she met my eyes.

"I will *do* anything, Tris. I don't know how to fix it, but I'm not going to stop trying." Searching her eyes, I looked for anything—just a spark of acknowledgment that I hadn't fucked this up beyond all repair.

"I *don't* love you, John," she replied, her voice a hoarse murmur.

Pain lanced through me at that statement, but the way she looked at me, the intensity of her gaze, told a different story. It bared the lie for what it was.

"Bullshit," I said softly, dipping my head until my lips brushed across hers. "You *feel* our connection just as much as I do. Let me prove it to you."

She didn't even make me wait a second before closing the gap between us. The physical bond between us sizzled to life. It was always there, always burning. *Thank fuck.*

And right now, she was burning for me. I would happily die in that fire.

Tris
thirty-three

After Katinka—Tink—dropped all her information in my lap then disappeared almost literally before my eyes, I spent the rest of the day locked away with my thoughts. She'd given me so much, about thieving games and rules and... John. She seemed to think he was in love with me, but I couldn't accept that. I couldn't move past the knowledge he'd used me, and probably still was.

The idea of returning to class, after *everything*, nearly had me hyperventilating, so I'd called and pleaded to take the rest of semester off, citing residual trauma. They didn't need to know my trauma was over a shitty breakup, rather than the bomb blast.

Unfortunately, my presence within the house during the day gave Naomi an open invitation to talk *wedding plans...* leaving me with a pounding headache and overwhelming sense of dread. I liked Sin; he was a good friend. But the idea of actually going through with marrying him? It terrified me.

Part of me was scared he was putting on an act right now.

Come the end of the day, I was desperate to see John and hash things out. I knew he lived with Tink, but not *where* that was. It couldn't be at his staff cottage on campus—that only had one bedroom, and Tink had been firm that they had their own rooms. Sin found me pacing back and forth in his room, and when he gave me a long look, I just blurted it out. I needed to see John, but I had no idea where he was.

To my surprise, though... Sin knew where they lived.

When I asked *how* he knew, he laughed and told me that I *didn't want to know that*, which only added to my growing suspicion that his amiable nice guy act was just that. An act.

I went to see John under the guise of ending things. Sin made it pretty clear that was the *only* reason he was willing to take me *and* let me come inside without him.

The insanity of the last few weeks between *Poppy Flowers*, Dexter's assaults, John's sudden appearance in my life, and the detonation that was John stealing the painting kept having catastrophic ripples.

That didn't take into account the actual explosions on campus, or RBD's decision to have me marry Sin. Oh, and the fact that I was now officially a murderer myself.

Good times.

I was losing my mind. But Tink's guilty confession about the gaslighting and her *heavily* dropped hints, just muddied the colors all the way around.

She said John loved me. That was why he was back. It was why he wasn't going away. Did I want that to be true? Fuck if I knew.

But I *needed* it. I needed him, and I needed him to prove that the thing between us was *real* and not just convenience. So when he spoke those heartfelt words... when I tried to push back and claim I *didn't* love him... I got what I needed.

I closed that infuriating gap he'd left between our mouths, kissing him with the full force of that electric magnetism that kept him on my mind every waking moment.

He was my personal Stendhal syndrome. Everything about him provoked an intense physical and mental reaction. Whether he was insulting my painting in the hall or challenging me in the classroom, John Smith, or whatever the fuck his name was, had invaded every part of me—my life and my soul.

Talking to him turned me on. Kissing him was my

drug of choice. But when he gripped my hips and lifted me up, I sank into him. We had on too many damn clothes, but he was already shedding mine, and when he turned to sit down, I had his cock in my hand and I guided him home.

The lack of prep made it a challenge, cause goddamn was he hung, but I wanted every ounce of that burning stretch. I needed to feel him everywhere. They say the syndrome hits when you encounter something so overwhelmingly beautiful it leaves you in tears or in passion.

John left me in fucking both. I gasped against his mouth as he fisted my hair. He didn't allow even a millimeter of space as his tongue plunged against mine. His shirt was rough against my nipples, and I didn't want the fabric—I wanted him.

When he refused to let up on the kiss, I bit down on his lip and he reared his head back. I pushed up on my knees, pulling him so far out that only the tip was inside of me.

"What the fuck, Venus?"

"Off," I demanded as I yanked at his shirt. He grumbled, the low growl vibrating all the way through me until my cunt seemed to spasm. He was so much better than any vibrator I'd ever owned.

His shirt went flying then he dragged me back to

him with one hand on my hip and the other on my nape. I devoured his mouth like the starving woman I was. I needed this, craved the connection. With almost no urging at all, I began to rock against his lap.

The hot flesh of his chest scraping against my nipples was another turn on, and then John squeezed my ass as he sucked on my tongue. He was turning me inside out. The pressure of his thumb against my anus wasn't even enough to startle me out of this wild haze.

I wanted everything he could give me and the press of his digit against the tight ring burned, the pain edged the pleasure, and I came with a scream. He swallowed the sound, increasing his pace so that he kept me rocking onto him as I came.

Too much.

Not enough.

I dug my fingers into his shoulders as he began to ease his thumb in and out and then he was fucking me with his tongue, his fingers, and his fantastic cock.

"Yes," I whimpered, needing more. Wanting it. I was shaking and sweating, but John seemed to get it. Thank fuck he got it. I went from riding him to flat on my back with my ankles over his shoulders as he pistoned into me with such force the sofa moved.

Or maybe it was an earthquake.

Who cared? I didn't.

We blew up the fucking sofa.

I was going to feel him for days, and when his pace stuttered and he flicked my clit, I came again. His shout muffled against my mouth as I clung to him. We were still shaking, clinging together, and the only thing I could think of was one word.

More.

I needed John. I needed more with him.

I needed everything.

Fuck me, I did love him no matter what I wanted to tell myself.

Reluctantly, I peeled myself out of John's sweaty embrace and stood up. Then I grimaced. "Bathroom?"

"Through there," he pointed to a short corridor off the living room. "Second door on the left."

I grabbed my clothes in a bundle and made my way down there, peeing and cleaning up before getting dressed once more.

Fuck, sex with John was so goddamn messy. The best kind of mess. If it weren't also sticky and uncomfortable, I'd leave that cum right where it was. But I could still feel him, like his dick was imprinted inside my pussy where it belonged.

A hickey on my throat registered, as did the fingerprints on my hips. Sin wasn't going to be happy.

Sorry, buddy. Join the club. Maybe if there had never

been a John this whole relationship thing could work. Better friends than enemies, yeah?

I used some water to damp down my hair then finger-combed it before I got dressed. What I needed to do was walk out there, tell John I was leaving and go out to Sin's car.

It would be safer for John if the Grimaldis weren't looking in his direction. He didn't need *Poppy Flowers* anymore, and they weren't going to let me go. As long as he was Whispering Willows, I'd be a threat to him.

So yeah, I should go.

The door opened behind me with a knock, and John stared at me from the open doorway. His bare chest was still decorated with sweat and marks from my nails. His jeans weren't even buttoned all the way up.

"I don't know what you're thinking about right now, Venus, but I want to make sure you know the absolute truth right now."

Licking my lips, I held his gaze in the mirror before I turned slowly. "That is?"

"You and me?" He reached out with one hand, tracing gentle fingers over my cheek to my hair where he loosened a wisp from the corner of my eye and then smoothed it back to the rest. "We're inevitable. We're the goal post. We're together. I don't care about whose ring that is or what that fucking gremlin says you're doing—we're together. We're going to be together...and when I leave, you're going with me."

My heart fisted in my chest.

"Tell me you believe me, Tris," John said. "Tell me, because I need to hear it."

John

thirty-four

The game piece was in plain fucking view this time. Not locked away in a secured house or in a vault, this time it was in the middle of the memorial park on the north side of Whispering Willows.

"It's right there," I snapped at Tink, gesturing to the decorative stone archway framing the main path to the lake. "I clocked it weeks ago when I went for a run through here. The gem on the inside of the arch is a real ruby."

"How come no one has stolen it before now?" Tink asked, puzzled. "Not as a part of the Game, but just out of greed?"

I shrugged. "I don't know, and I don't fucking care. Let's just grab it and be done with this."

Angry, frustrated, and impatient, I started toward the arch, but Tink grabbed my arm with a sound of alarm. "Whoa, big man, what's the hurry? We just going headlong into a death trap now? What happened to our careful plans of letting someone else trigger all the traps?"

I ground my teeth so hard they creaked. "We don't need to, Tink. Between the two of us, we're good enough to handle booby traps without letting other people die. Come on, it's an easy one."

Her eyes widened with disbelief. "Is that a joke? Have we already forgotten the *acid*, John? I nearly lost my face!"

That gave me a small pause. "But you didn't. And we will be more careful this time."

"Is that what this is?" She gestured in frustration. "John, Hermes, buddy, you're in a fucking *foul* mood and have been since Tris left last night. Whatever went down between you two... push it aside. It's not worth losing our heads over. Literally."

Her reminder of how things were left with Tris had me angry and impatient all over again. "I don't want to talk about her."

Tink's brows shot up. "I didn't ask you to. But I also don't want you getting us killed because she broke up with you, when we both know you had that coming for weeks."

"She *didn't* break up with me," I snarled, my skin hot with anxious dread. "Not yet, anyway."

Tink's lips rounded in surprise. "Oh. I thought... she seemed like that's what—"

"I know," I cut her off, scrubbing a hand over my face. "She... maybe that was why she came over but we ended up sleeping together."

"Oh! Well... that's good. Isn't it? Did you tell her that you're in love with her?"

"Yes," I growled, still stinging from how we left things. But she felt the same for me, I was *sure* of it. She just...

Tink gave me a narrow eyed look. "And she said...?"

I threw my hands up. "She fucked me, then *left*. With him. She went back to the Grimaldi house with *him*."

Tink winced. "Oh. I see. That's not good."

Frustration rumbled through my chest. "Thank you so much. Very encouraging. So, can we just grab this fucking ruby so I can go and stalk the love of my life again?"

Tink's expression softened, and she patted my cheek. "Aw, honey. The love of your life? Okay, we need to fix this. Let's... get this damn ruby and then strategize. We better be careful, though. I just spotted someone on the far side of the lake who seems suspicious."

Unsurprising, since there were ten or so competitors still alive and in the Game. We couldn't be the only ones who worked out this clue; we just had to be the smartest. Tink started toward the arch and I hurried to overtake her.

"I'll do it," I told her in a firm voice. "After the acid incident, it's my turn to take the risk."

She huffed a laugh. "No arguments here. I'll just help look for traps."

As much of a hurry as I was in, we didn't cut corners. We searched the area meticulously, ignoring the several spectators we gained—thieves, not public thanks to the *Park Closed Due To Renovations* sign over the main gate. Eventually, Tink and I evaded the path-wide trapdoor which would have seen us fall into a pit of razor-sharp spikes, *and* disabled the spider-silk-thin tripwire that would have seen us stabbed right through by a spear embedded in the arch wall.

"What is this, fucking Indiana Jones?" Tink muttered, inspecting the spear we'd removed—just in case—and wrinkling her nose. "Someone on the judging panel is a hardcore Indi fan. I'll put money on it. Or maybe Lara Croft."

"Probably," I murmured, eyeing up the ruby in

question. It was above my head height, which maybe helped with people failing to recognize it as an authentic stone. "My grandfather was a huge Indiana Jones fan. Had the hat and whip used in the first movie mounted in his house."

"The *actual* ones from the movie?" Tink squeaked, then laughed. "Of course he did. He was a fucking legend. Did you get to inherit that?"

I nodded, my focus still on the ruby. "Yes. He was a hoarder. It'll take me years to rehome half the shit he collected over his lifetime."

"So cool," Tink murmured. "Is the story about the S.S. Minden true? Your grandfather found the wreck and all the long lost treasures on board?"

My lips tilted in a smile. It was one of my favorite stories from when I was a child. Christophe hadn't just been a thief; he was a *treasure hunter*. Sometimes the treasures he hunted happened to belong to other people, and his being a thief was just a byproduct of that. He'd often tell me stories of the S.S. Minden, a Nazi ship that sank off the coast of Iceland in 1939 whilst fully loaded with some of the most coveted pieces stolen as the war ramped up. How he and his best friend had grown obsessed with searching for the wreck and eventually... found it.

That was my grandfather's legacy. The Valenshek

Legacy. That was what was on the line in this Game. The treasures of the S.S. Minden and Christophe's proudest achievement.

"The stone has been here a long time," I thought out loud. "I wonder who placed it. And why."

There were plenty of other "gems" decorating the piece, all varying colors which cast pretty lights through the archway when the sun hit them, but they were all glass. All except the one ruby about the size of a quail's egg a foot above my head.

"Speculate on the story later, Hermes," Tink prompted. "Just pry that fucker out and let's run before someone snatches it off us."

Her phone rang, and she glanced down at the screen, instantly distracted. I smiled. "Someone important, Katinka? Do you need to take that?"

She glared up at me, then nodded. "Actually yes. Grab the stone, Lurch. I'll be by the ducks." She answered the call, bringing it to her ear as she walked away for privacy. Did Tink have a secret lover that she hadn't told me about?

Chuckling about how I could now give her a taste of her own medicine—after all her *advice* around Tris—I pulled out my pretty blue butterfly knife. It was a gift from Constance, my best buyer, and wicked sharp and strong. Her late husband had made them as a hobby, apparently.

It only took a moment to get the tip of the knife under the edge of the stone and pry it out. The ruby popped free... way easier than it should have.

"Oh shit," I breathed, right as a trap door opened in the center of the arch overhead. I braced myself, and choked back a scream as a dozen scaley danger noodles fell from their trap, the muscular ropes of hell-nope striking my head and shoulders as gravity did its thing.

I clamped my jaw shut, staying silent and dead still, hoping against all hope that they'd ignore me completely and slither away. Many of them did, poor terrified animals that they were, but three seemed less inclined to leave. One was an enormous green and black python, which I *thought* was a non-venomous variety, but the other two were most definitely venomous. God damn it.

Tink was one hundred percent to be blamed for this. Someone on the judging panel must have heard her and thought it'd be funny to include snakes. Fucking *snakes*!

She must have finished her phone call because she was wandering back toward me from the lake, her focus on me, not on the fucking snake-infested grass she was walking across. Crap.

I glanced at the two lingering vipers who seemed

pretty pissed at being so rudely dropped from a height... then back to Tink. I couldn't see where the rest of the snakes were, but she was stomping along without a care in the world. Almost guaranteed, she was going to step on one and get bitten by something deadly.

Fuck.

"Tink, be careful!" I shouted, trying to leap *over* the snakes wriggling across the path between me and Tink. Sharp pain struck my leg, just above my ankle, and I frantically kicked to dislodge the legless demon from my calf. The bastard got its fangs stuck in my jeans, so it took another kick to get it off but then all the snakes were scared enough they disappeared fast.

"Oh shit," I moaned as pure agony ripped up my leg from the bite. The *highly venomous* bite.

Tink came running as I collapsed onto the path. "Fuck! Was that what I think it was?"

"I hate you," I groaned, clasping my leg in excruciating pain. "This is all your fault."

"Okay, yes, I can see how this seems like more than a coincidence," she admitted with a lopsided grin. "Who'd guess, huh? Snakes! Did you get the stone though?"

I moaned but held out the ruby for her to take—and keep safe—then went back to writhing in pain on the ground.

"Nice," Tink enthused, inspecting the stone for a moment before tucking it into her bra. "Lucky for you, Hermes, old friend, I came prepared for snakes." She unzipped her ridiculous fanny pack that she wore on every stake out, and hunted within it for a moment before pulling out a little roll of slim vials no bigger than perfume samples.

"The fuck, Tink?" I gasped. "Is that what I think?"

She grinned. "If you think it's antivenom for snake bites, then yes! Do you know what kind of snake it was or should I jab you with all of these and hope for the best?"

The pain in my leg was making me a little delirious because for a moment I thought the Grim Reaper was approaching behind Tink, and I gave a startled shout. As it turned out, when I blinked my vision clear... I'd have preferred the Grim Reaper.

"Snakes, huh?" Igor gave a dramatic shudder despite the gun he held to Tink's head. "Disgusting. Better you than me, son."

Tink rolled her eyes. "Igor. Of *course* you'd be here with the snakes. How utterly fitting."

"No need to be unkind, Tink," my father chided. "This is purely business. The ruby, please. I'll be collecting the points for this one, thank you."

My little partner's face hardened and I had no

doubts she'd rather call Igor's bluff than hand over our prize so easily... but she didn't know him like I did. The only reason I wasn't dead already was because he wanted to *beat me*, and he couldn't do that if I was dead. There were no such restrictions keeping Tink alive.

"Give it to him," I grunted, my jaw locked against the waves of agony swarming my body. "Tink, give it to him."

She scowled at me, incredulous and confused. But when I repeated myself a third time, she slowly reached into her bra to retrieve the stone.

"No funny business, Tink," Igor warned.

She scoffed, withdrawing the ruby from her hiding place. "Unlike you, some of us are too honorable to try *funny business*. Here. Take it and fuck off."

Igor snatched the ruby from her hand and made a show of inspecting it against the light. When he was satisfied we hadn't duped him, he backed away slowly. "Always lovely working with you, son. Let's do it again soon... if you recover from that nasty bite, of course." He walked away laughing like a fucking clown, and I glared at Tink.

"Antivenom, Tink. Inland taipan... I think."

"You think? Or you know? Because if you're right, we only have minutes to get you the—"

"Just *do it*!" I shouted, my back arching from pain.

"Based on how I currently feel, it's an educated guess." Sweat poured from my brow, and my vision was starting to blacken.

Tink muttered to herself about dumb fucks trying to jump over angry snakes, but a moment later she injected me with the antivenom then patted my cheek aggressively. "Still with me, John?"

I groaned and mustered up a nod.

"Good. It'll take ten minutes or so for that antivenom to start working, but then we need to get you to a hospital. Depending how much the sneaky snake delivered, you may need further doses. I'm gonna help you stand up, alright?" She crouched down, arranging my arm over her shoulders then heaved me up to my feet.

For a little woman, Tink was impressively strong. Thank fuck she was on my team.

Tris

thirty-five

After everything with John—his confession of loving me and all the intense emotion it stirred up—I wanted to talk with Sin straight away. I wanted to somehow find a way out of my deal with Mr. Grimaldi, and that was something only he could help me do. If he *told* his father about the mystery woman, the one who put such a distracted look on his face the past few days, then maybe…

His head seemed a million miles away when I got back in the car, though, until he gave me a long look as we drove away.

"You stink of sex, Tris." It was delivered in a harsh, judgmental snap that made me reconsider everything.

Words failed me, and I just curled into myself. "I'm tired, Sin," I confessed in a soft voice. "Can we talk in the morning?" Seeing as it was already late, that wasn't such an unreasonable request.

He grunted, his sour mood evident. "So much for ending things."

I bit my tongue, deciding to bide my time instead. Starting this conversation with him now, when he was already moody, seemed like a recipe for disaster. I'd seen what happened when his brother got mad. And his father for that matter. I needed to tread lightly.

The only reason I'd decided to leave John, to return with Sin, was because there was still a lot on the line with the Grimaldis. Nelson's safety, for starters. Not to mention the fact that I still hadn't given back the Van Gogh. I could imagine that if I just up and left, ran away from my consequences, then the ones I cared about would suffer instead.

John wasn't going anywhere. He made that crystal clear. So I hoped, seriously hoped, he would be patient and trust me to work things out with the Grimaldis myself.

The next morning, Sin was gone early—as per usual—and I used the time to continue working on my Picasso replica. Nelson's advice had helped a lot, but when I grew stuck on the lettering which Picasso incorporated, I risked a call.

I kept it vague and professional—technical

discussions between two artists and nothing more—but just hearing his voice helped to ground me. He was more of a parent to me than my genetic donors ever had been, and this extended absence was longer than we'd ever spent apart in the last eleven years.

I'd barely hung up the phone when a rapid, firm knock hit the door to the studio. "Tris," Sin called, not wasting any time on mystery. "Let me in." That was definitely *not* a request.

Dropping my phone onto my work bench, I made my way over to the door and opened it a crack. "Hey, what's up?"

"We need to talk about what happened last night," he informed me in a clipped voice, his brow drawn. "Can I come in? Please?" That *please* was added as an afterthought and a grudging one at that.

It scared me.

"Um, I was just finishing up for the day," I said, wiping my hands on the front of my paint splattered shirt. "I'll just clean my brushes and we can talk downstairs in your bedroom? I'll only be a few minutes."

His expression darkened further. "In *our* bedroom."

I nodded. "Yes, that's what I said. In your bedroom. I won't be long." Quickly closing the door between us, I let out a silent breath, listening for the sound of his footsteps retreating. I'd made so much progress on *Le Pigeon aux Petits Pois* in the last few days, I didn't want negative energy fucking up my creative space.

I'd already started cleaning my brushes while I'd chatted with Nelson, so there wasn't much left to do. Better to get this chat with Sin over with, anyway.

Pulling up my metaphorical big girl panties, I locked up my studio and made my way back down to Sin's bedroom. Inside, he was pacing the carpet beneath the window, speaking on his phone with clipped, angry tones. When he saw me, though, he quickly ended the call and slipped his phone back into his pocket.

"Everything okay?" I asked, placing my keys—for the studio and bedroom—down on the bedside table along with my phone.

Sin jerked a nod, his expression troubled. "Yes, fine. Just... work."

I folded my arms around myself, nodding. "Okay. So..."

"So we should have talked last night, but I wanted to give you some time to process things," he started, jumping right into what seemed like a speech he'd been thinking about in advance. "Will you come and sit with me?" He indicated the small window seat.

A trickle of unease ran down my spine, but I quickly convinced myself I was just feeling guilty about letting him down. He needed this marriage arrangement to get his father off his back, but... it couldn't be with me.

"Sure," I agreed with a faint smile, crossing the room and sitting down where he indicated. He sat beside me, close enough that our knees touched and I tried not to shift away obviously. "Sin, I—"

"What happened last night, Buttercup? You said you wanted to break things off with John... that he was starting to scare you with his notes and how you wanted him to back off and leave you to move on. With me. What changed?" Sin's gaze felt heavy as he stared into my face, searching for answers.

John changed. He said everything I needed to hear, and made me face up to how I really felt for him.

"Sin... this arrangement between us... I can't go through with it."

"Cold feet are normal," he said without a trace of irony.

"This isn't cold feet," I told him. "I love John. He loves me. I thought—when I thought this was the only way to save my life and that he'd betrayed me—you know that doesn't matter."

"No," Sin said slowly. "He doesn't matter."

"That's not what I said." I was trying not to snap, but Sin wasn't listening.

"It's what I said. The professor isn't any good for

you. Clearly, all he needs is a little access to manipulate you..."

"Sin, please," I said. "Listen to me. I can't marry you just to get your dad off my back. I know that was his arrangement and I owe him for the painting. Neither of us asked for this, so surely we can come up with something else that he wants."

Rather than agree with me, Sin stared at me with an enigmatic look on his face. "Such as?"

"I don't know," I said, tugging at my hair before staring around his room. "Forgeries for the rest of his life? Something quantifiable that will pay him back for the hassle and the—I don't know insult?"

"What did the professor say to you, Buttercup?"

Everything. "Nothing that would interest you," I answered instead. "Even if I wasn't in love with John, you don't love me, Sin, and I don't love you."

"Marriages have been built on far less. The professor is just using you. He used you before, and he's using you now."

Oh my God. I shoved up from the window seat. "It's not like that."

"I wish I could believe you," he said, in the kindest of tones. It was *almost* patronizing.

Almost.

"It doesn't matter if you believe *me*," I said. "I believe John."

"I don't." It was that simple, or so his tone suggested. Clasping his hands together, Sin leaned forward, elbows on his knees as he studied me. "Buttercup—Tristian, listen to me. Men like the professor? They get to where they are in the world because they know how to tell people what they want to hear. They know how to manipulate, cajole, and even bully in just the right amounts to get what they want."

"The only thing John wants is *me*." I believed him. I needed to hear that from him and it had been there in every single nuance of his expression—and if it hadn't been, the fact he bumbled every damn lie to me since he got back would have given it away. "I don't know how else to convince you."

Sin rose. "Tris, you and I—we make a good match. My father is many things, but he's not a fool. He sees great potential in you and I have to admit…"

When he didn't finish the statement, I took a couple of steps forward. "You have to admit?"

"He's not wrong—most of the time. I can admit that. You're beautiful, you're intelligent, and you're talented. Even more…you're a survivor."

"What does that have to do with anything?" I was

FORGERY

so confused. "Because this doesn't mean marrying is the thing to do. This doesn't work for me."

"But it could," Sin said, his tone infinitely gentle as he reached out to brush two fingers down my cheek. "You just have to get the professor out of your head. It's been a lot the last few weeks. He took the painting and abandoned you to my father's mercies."

I closed my eyes. I knew all this, but I also knew that he'd come back.

"My father could have killed you," Sin reminded me. "You stole from him and you haven't given *Poppy Flowers* back."

I swallowed as Sin narrowed the distance, the concern in his voice echoing in his expression.

"Betraying my father? Never a good plan. Not for me. Not for Dex. And certainly not for you. He's offered you this olive branch because he likes you—the last thing I want is for something else to happen to you because the professor is a selfish, vainglorious bastard of a man who used you like his personal whore on his mission to steal something that doesn't belong to him."

I flinched, both from the warning and the description. Sin made it sound so real... "You don't know John."

"And neither," Sin said in an almost soft, regretful voice, "do you." He leaned forward to press a kiss to my forehead. "I'm sorry, Buttercup. I truly am. But this man has your number and he's going to get you killed."

"Sin..."

"I know, you believe him." He sounded almost sorry. "I wish you didn't, but I accept that you do. But here's the thing, Tristian. You're my fiancée, and you're going to be my wife. I protect what is mine. You need time, and I'll make sure you have it."

What? I stared at him. "What does that mean?"

"Exactly what I said." He smiled, then pressed another kiss to my forehead. "Why don't you take a bath and relax. I'll bring you some wine, and you can have a quiet evening. No one will bother you."

"Sin.."

But he was already walking away and I turned, tracking his exit.

"It'll work out," he assured me. "You'll see." Then he was out of the room, and the door locked automatically. It always did.

Then a second lock sounded and I frowned.

A second—there was another deadbolt on the door.

A second one. On the outside.

Shock rocked through me as I hurried over to the door. My key didn't fit the second lock.

Son of a bitch.

He'd just locked me inside.

JOHN

thirty-six

As far as patients went, I was an awful one. I knew it, Tink knew it, the hospital knew it... but if they'd just let me go then I could stop making everyone's life hell. Unfortunately due to the type of snake that'd bitten me, they admitted me overnight for IV fluids and more antivenom.

The following morning, I made enough of a nuisance of myself that the nurses discharged me earlier than they'd intended. When Tink arrived, I was already dressed and sitting on the edge of the bed to put my shoes on.

She raised a brow but didn't try to push the issue. Smart.

"How are you feeling?" she queried as we walked—

or she walked and I limped—out of the hospital. I'd refused a wheelchair because my God, if Igor saw that...

I glanced over at Tink. "I feel like I got bitten by a fucking taipan, but I'm insanely grateful you had antivenom. Why?"

She cocked her head. "Why are you grateful?"

My gaze flattened. "Why did you have antivenom, Tink? It's not the usual supplies we'd take for a job. I thought you used that bag for lockpicks and laser mirrors, not antivenom for deadly snakes."

"Yes, maybe. But look how useful it turned out. Aren't you glad I have a small fascination with snakes now, hmm?" She grinned, proud as fuck of herself. Crazy little thing.

She opened her car door for me, and I lowered myself into the passenger seat with a small groan. My leg *hurt* despite the painkillers I'd been given this morning. Apparently that pain, along with my pounding headache, was likely to hang around for another couple of days.

"Let's talk about today's treasure clue," I said, peering up at the moody clouds overhead.

Tink sighed. "Let's not. I can handle today's score, and you are in *no* condition to be of use. Besides, I need to get the points for yesterday's... fumble."

The way she said that was edged in accusation and I

shifted in my seat to glare at her. "There was no *fumble*, Tink. If you didn't give Igor the ruby, he'd have killed you."

She rolled her eyes, pulling into the parking space outside our shared Hestia house. "He's all bark and no bite. He was just taking advantage because you needed antivenom or you'd have died."

Tink climbed out of the car before I could reply, and I followed a touch slower with my new limp. She probably wasn't wrong about me being useless today. We were so far in the lead, we could skip one game piece and still win... unless it was something of significant value.

"You're wrong," I told her when we got inside. "He absolutely would have killed you, then he'd have given me the antivenom himself because he doesn't actually want me dead. Not until he can *win* and rub my face in it."

"So you let him take the ruby to save me?" She headed for the kitchen, shooting me a long look over her shoulder. "I didn't realize you cared, Hermes."

I huffed, lowering myself onto the sofa to take weight off my leg. "Yeah well, you grow on a person, Tink. Like moss. Or mold."

"Awww, I love you too, you big grump! I'm making you coffee. Elevate that leg and chill for a bit."

I grunted but did what I was told. That was a solid sign of how shit I felt. "Have you heard from Tris?"

Tink didn't respond for a moment, then emerged from the kitchen with two coffees in hand. She headed over to where I'd just rearranged myself on the sofa with my leg propped up on pillows, and handed me one.

"Um, no. I haven't. But I spoke with one of the security guards at Grimaldi's house and he mentioned she's... fine." There was an odd pause before she said *fine* which raised the hair on the back of my neck.

"The fuck does that mean, Tink? She's *fine*? What aren't you telling me?"

Tink sighed, sitting down herself and sipping her coffee. "It means she's fine, John. She's, you know, just busy with... *schmedding schmanning.*" She mumbled over those last two words and I frowned.

"She's busy with what? I couldn't quite... did you say *wedding planning*?" I started out of my seat in alarm, but Tink flapped her hand at me to stay where I was.

"Calm down, John, you need to rest and recover. Yes, that's what I said, but I'm sure it doesn't mean anything. Right? Like, she was engaged last week too; this isn't a new development." She shrugged, sipping her coffee.

I rumbled with frustration and anxiety. "I need to go and see her. I need to ask why she is still going along with this bullshit deal with Grimaldi. I could keep her safe."

Tink wrinkled her nose. "Could you, though? You just spent a night in hospital because you tried to *jump over* a deadly snake."

I glowered. "To save you, *Medusa*. I only got bitten because you were about to step on a murder rope in the grass."

She snorted a laugh. "Okay, but my point remains. While you're in the Game, you can't protect her. Not the way she would need to be protected... and what about Nelson?"

"What *about* Nelson?" I asked, confused and *frustrated*. Then realization dawned. "She's not protecting herself. She's protecting Nelson. Fucking hell... well, it doesn't have to be like this. I have resources. I could arrange protection."

Tink tilted her head. "Like the amateur mercenary you hired to keep an eye on Tris? He's not very good. You know that, right?"

I groaned, running a hand over my face. My headache was pounding. "Yeah I know. But he was all they could send on short notice, and now it's too awkward to fire him. Maybe I could get him to—"

"Just *leave her be* until you're in a better position to do something. Seriously. She's not being hurt, I don't believe Sin would ever be inappropriate with her, and they're not exactly going to rush down to the courthouse tomorrow to tie the knot. You have time. Just be patient."

"Be *patient?*" Yes, it came out a growl as I stared at Tink.

"Yes, be patient, *Hermes.* There's no way you've achieved this level of success and notoriety by rushing headlong into everything. Aren't you the one always cautioning me?"

I kept staring at her.

"John..."

"What?"

"Tris is *fine.*"

"If she marries him..." The whole idea made me sick. I told her I loved her. I saw it in her eyes. She believed me. This was...

"You know, divorce exists," Tink informed me. "It's not like she's going to jail for the rest of her life or a *grave.*"

I glared at her.

Rising, Tink fixed me with a look. "You're going to *rest* and heal. That's what the doctors said and what the nurse said and what I *say.*"

"Uh huh." Like she could stop me if I decided otherwise.

"Look, Sin is—" She spread her hands. "You know, I don't know who he is. He's not like Dexter. That's a good thing. But he also knows right where we are and he hasn't come after us. So maybe—just *maybe*—we finish the Game. Get this done, then get Tris."

"Just like that?" I raised my brows, disliking every single word coming out of her mouth.

"Well, yeah, unless you have a better idea that doesn't involve throwing everything over and just going on the run for the rest of your lives. I'm sure Tris won't mind at all if Nelson is already dead."

"*What?*" Where did she come up with these ideas?

"Easy. If you two take off, Grimaldi's going to go after everyone close to her. Nelson. Hank. Me."

I rolled my eyes on the last.

"What? We're *friends*, remember? She's *my* friend, John. Not my fuckbuddy turned soulmate or whatever it is the two of you have going on—by the way, I found the wet spot on the sofa. I'm never sitting on it again." She bounced from topic to topic like a sugared-up teenager.

I stretched my leg and winced at the pain. I could handle that. The ache was a bitch and the headache sucked, but I could handle all of that if... "Go see her."

"What?"

"I need to know she's okay. Go see her."

"You want me to just go and see her?" Tink tilted her

head from side to side like she was having some imaginary argument with herself. Honestly, I could believe it. "I am her bestie and she is wedding planning...think she'd ask me to be her maid of honor?"

My jaw dropped as I sat forward, and I ignored the pain lancing through me to stare at her. "Are you fucking with me right now?"

She paused, her gaze darting from side to side. "No?"

"Her *maid of honor?*"

"What?" She looked almost insulted. "Don't you think I'd make a great maid of honor? I could throw her the best bachelorette party ever." She sniffed. "Then help her be the best runaway bride ever..."

I groaned and rubbed a hand over my face. "You're not helping."

"I am... you just can't see it yet. Pain fucks with perception. That's why you'll stay here and I'll go and see her, just like you asked, and make sure your Tris-woobie is fine and dandy. Then if she makes me maid of honor, well, I guess I can take over the wedding planning. It's brilliant, really."

Could you want to hug and throttle someone in the same breath?

"We're good, right?" Tink said. "Yeah, do you need help getting to bed?"

I glared at her and she threw up her hands.

"You're such a grumplestiltskin. Fine, I'm going. Stay there and be a good boy."

I didn't even have the energy to flip her off before she hurried out. Leaning back, I stared up at the ceiling and scowled. Nothing about this job, this *Game,* had gone the way it was supposed to.

Nothing.

Now I was stuck here and...

The next thought I had was Tink shaking my shoulder and I glared up at her bleary-eyed. "What the fuck?" I demanded. "Aren't you supposed to be going to see Tris?"

"I did go see her..." Tink was incensed. "Jesus, John, I went last night. You've been sleeping like a fucking log since I left." Her teeth tugged on her lip nervously and her eyes couldn't stay still.

"What happened?"

"She's fine. But it just turned eight AM..." She didn't bother to explain further, just thrust the phone in front of me with today's clue.

Instantly, I knew what the game piece was.

Poppy Flowers.

Fuck.

Me.

Tris

thirty-seven

After Sin locked me in the fucking bedroom for the remainder of that day, he'd eventually returned and been exceptionally apologetic about the whole thing. He explained that he was under a lot of stress with work, and that his mind was elsewhere… all the excuses. None of them repaired the damage he'd done to the trust between us.

Despite some of my questionable choices lately, I wasn't stupid. So when Sin asked if I forgave him for locking me in his bedroom, I lied through my teeth and told him what he wanted to hear. All the while, planning my escape. I barely slept, lying awake and playing out all the possible scenarios in my head. Could I come to a mutually beneficial arrangement with Mr.

Grimaldi? Could I convince Hank and Nelson to go on the run with me?

During dinner the next night, Sin had another *very urgent* phone call and disappeared. Security had been watching me a lot closer all day, but no one stopped me when I mentioned being tired and retired to bed early.

When the lock clicked shortly after I changed into pajamas, I braced myself for another uncomfortable interaction with Sin. To my surprise, though—especially given only Sin and I had the key—it was not my forced fiancé. It was Tink.

To my embarrassment, I'd burst out crying.

She proved her friendship, not asking for information. She just assured me that Sin wouldn't be back for a few days and climbed into bed with me, wrapping me in a tight hug.

I told her enough to assure her I was in no immediate danger, but then I'd fallen asleep while she patted my hair and told me meaningless stories of a pet snake she used to have. His name had been Ssssam after she read it in a book and found it funny.

Tink—the fucking empathetic queen that she was—stayed all night, leaving in the morning after I'd showered, dressed, and *promised* I would be totally fine.

Her reassurance that Sin would be gone for several days *minimum* was the opportunity I needed to approach Mr. Grimaldi with my plan. My flimsy, hopeful plan. I had to try that first, before endangering everyone I loved by fleeing.

After breakfast, I went to his office, but it was closed up and locked. I hadn't factored *finding* him into my plan.

"Um, hello, sorry." I waved awkwardly at one of the security guys hanging out near the main staircase. "Hi, I'm Tris. Um. Tristian."

He leveled a flat stare at me. "I'm aware who you are, Miss Ives. Is there a problem?"

"No, sorry. Um, I wanted to talk with Mr. Grimaldi. Do you know if he has any time today?" I nervously twisted my fingers, glancing along the corridor like Sin would appear at any second. Or Dex.

The security guy shrugged. "Check with Naomi. She runs his schedule." He checked his watch for the time. "She should be arriving in about an hour, but you can call her. Her phone is on twenty-four seven."

Shit. I hoped she got well paid for that. "No, that's fine, I can wait. Thank you."

"Alright, I'll tell her to come find you if I see her." The guy gave me a small nod, and I smiled my response, heading up the stairs. Without being able to negotiate terms of my penance with Mr. Grimaldi, I figured I may as well continue working on my pigeons and peas.

Maybe if I could prove my worth as a forger, he'd be more open to my offer.

Naomi stopped by to see me during lunch and scheduled an appointment into Mr. Grimaldi's diary for seven that evening. Right before lasagne-night dinner. Nerves had me distracted for the rest of the day, and all my painting progress halted. Eventually I gave up, showered, then headed down to Mr. Grimaldi's office a whole twenty minutes too early for our scheduled meeting time.

Before I even passed the Greek statue, I heard the raised voices.

My footsteps faltered, and I paused, listening.

"...fucking *find him*!" Mr. Grimaldi shouted at someone, his voice like that of an enraged demon. "Find that two-faced, lying, thieving fake professor and bring him here to me. I want *answers,* and he's the one who will provide them. One way or another."

My skin went icy, and all the air backed up in my lungs. He was talking about John. He somehow knew John was a thief. How? Had Sin done something?

Someone replied to Mr. Grimaldi, their voice too quiet to be heard properly, but whatever they asked made the mob boss pause for a moment.

"Her too," he snapped after a tense silence. "They're both involved in this *Game, so* they can both provide useful information. Then they can fucking well pay for the insult in blood."

Me? Was he talking about me?

I shrank into an open doorway near the steps to Mr. Grimaldi's office, not wanting to be caught eavesdropping.

"...believe they live together..." one of Mr. Grimaldi's men was saying, and I sucked a sharp inhale. They meant Tink. Fuck. I had to warn them, John and Tink both. I needed to use my phone and fuck the consequences. They needed to know they were marked targets.

"Good. Send out a team and grab them both. I don't care if you have to shed a little blood in transit, so long as they're alive enough to answer questions when they get here." Mr. Grimaldi's voice was pure ice. Judge, jury, executioner.

I was woman enough to admit I was fucking terrified. The people he brought back here didn't survive. Sometimes—no, so far I was the only one I knew who had, and the clock was practically ticking down on me.

"What about Miss Ives, sir? Did you decide about..." The end of his sentence muffled and I bit my cheek to keep from groaning in frustration. Decide about *what*?

I was close enough to hear Mr. Grimaldi's frustrated

sigh. "I'll handle her. She's coming in to see me in fifteen minutes. I will... impress on her the precarious nature of her existence here. If she will return the Van Gogh tonight before one of those filthy thieves gets their hands on it, then maybe we can find an amicable agreement and keep the wedding on track."

One of those filthy... what? Everything inside of me just froze. Thieves. Game. Van Gogh.

They said it wasn't part of their stupid game anymore.

They *promised.*

"What if she can't get it back? Our network has suggested it got sold to a buyer in Toronto recently." That was someone else talking. No idea who. Not that it mattered.

My heart slammed so loudly it had to be audible. Even my breaths seemed to echo abnormally in the silence. Breaths I could barely suck in. They said *Poppy Flowers* wasn't part of the Game anymore.

Goddammit.

"I don't believe that. It wouldn't be included in this stealing game if it wasn't still in Whispering Willows. She *will* give it to me, or..." Mr. Grimaldi trailed off, and I swallowed hard. "We'll soon see. Go and dispatch the team to collect the professor and my son's whore. I'll deal with Tristian myself."

Panicked and terrified, I stumbled out of my hiding place, scurrying back along the corridor as fast as I possibly could. So fast that I wasn't looking where I was going and when I turned a corner I ran straight into a man's chest.

"Whoa, Tris, you okay?"

Thank fuck. Thank *fuck*, it was Bram. My new, sort of, neighbor. He was a good guy, right? He'd saved me when Dex tried to rape me. I had to take a chance.

"Bram, I'm in trouble," I told him in a frantic whisper. "I need to leave. Now. Can you get me out?"

He studied my face, confusion and concern etched across his features, then he nodded firmly. "Of course. Come on, this way. I was just finishing for the day, anyway."

"We need to hurry," I whispered with a whine as he grabbed my hand, leading the way through the manor and down a hallway I didn't recognize. "They'll know I'm missing soon."

Bram shot me a reassuring smile. "I've got you, Tris. We'll get out."

He picked up the pace, and I jogged to keep up. His swipe card unlocked the door at the end of the hall, and it opened out onto what seemed like a staff parking lot. Weird, since I'd never parked out there. I used to have my own spot on the other side of the house, closest to the gallery.

"Passenger seat or trunk?" Bram asked as he clicked the key fob to unlock his nondescript silver sedan.

"Trunk," I answered without hesitation. "They aren't looking for me just yet, but no way will they let you just drive out with me sitting there in plain view."

"Got it," he murmured, helping me into the small space, then covering me with a dark blanket. "You good? Where am I taking you?"

Fuck. Where was I going? To warn John and Tink?

No. Fuck them. Both of them *swore* to me that I had nothing to do with their Game. They both made a fucking point of telling me in no uncertain terms that *Poppy Flowers* wasn't involved anymore. They lied. *Again.* Both of them. They were on their own...

"Back to my apartment," I decided, going against my gut and heart. "I need to see Nelson." And retrieve the Van Gogh that was well-hidden within my loft. If I gave the cursed painting back, then this whole thing could *maybe* be put behind us.

"Done," Bram confirmed, closing the trunk gently then climbing into his seat. The engine rumbled alive, and it didn't escape my attention that I was placing a whole shit load of faith in a man I really didn't know.

Something I'd been doing a lot lately, and so far not with good results.

Bram *seemed* like a good guy... but so did John. And Sin. He could take me anywhere and no one would ever know. I might just disappear without a trace, and in a year's time my body might wash up on some distant shore. If he even left a whole body. What if he was an axe murderer? Surely there wouldn't be much left if one was murdered with an axe?

My theories and paranoia got worse with every passing moment until I was almost hyperventilating. When the car stopped, the short pause between Bram getting out and opening the trunk almost gave me cardiac arrest.

He just offered me his hand to help me out, totally oblivious to my panic, and I quickly recognized where we were. The back alleyway behind our apartment building.

"Thank fuck for that," I murmured with a shaky laugh. "For a moment there I started wondering if I'd just trusted a serial killer."

He shot me a grin. "Nah, only when I'm well paid for it. Killing is a messy business. Want to tell me what happened back at Grimaldi's manor?"

I shook my head as we entered the building through

the fire escape door. "Not really. I just need to talk to Nelson. Thank you for the lift. I really appreciate it."

"Of course, any time." He pressed the elevator call button and gave me a long look from the side of his eye. "Nelson will be glad to see you, I'm sure. I hope he and Hank are doing better?"

I frowned. "How do you mean?"

"They were having a pretty heated argument the other night, I could hear it from downstairs. Someone definitely threw a plate at one stage." Bram shrugged, giving a lopsided smile. "I've had spats like that with exes. Make-up sex is always worth it."

He must have just realized he was talking about my elderly surrogate parents and gave a grimace. Same, though. Not a mental picture I *ever* needed.

"That doesn't sound like them," I murmured, stepping into the elevator when the doors opened. "They never fight. I mean, sure, they disagree like any couple, but I could count the number of real *fights* they've ever had on one hand. They're life-companion goals."

Bram laughed. "They're still human, Tris. Anyway, this is me. Are you going to be okay?"

The elevator had just stopped on the sixth floor, where he lived, and I quickly shook my head. "No, I'm totally fine from here. Nelson will know what to do. He's my Yoda."

Bram smiled warmly. "I can see that. Very wise. Come knock on my door if you need *anything,* okay? No matter what time. I'm not due back at work until the morning."

"Thank you," I told him sincerely as the doors started to close again. It only took another moment to reach my floor, and I took a deep breath as I stepped out into the hall. I was *home.*

My nose twitched, though, and I sneezed. What was that smell? It was like... smoke? Gunpowder? And... something else. Something I desperately didn't want to name.

Hank and Nelson's door was closed but *mine* was open.

"Fuck," I breathed, dread washing through me so hard I nearly staggered. Had I not hidden *Poppy Flowers* as well as I thought? Had someone else from the Game found it already?

Unable to stop myself despite the danger, I approached my apartment and pushed the door open further with my fingertip. It swung silently into the room ,and I instantly realized how strong that smoky, gunpowder smell was. How strong that metallic, meaty smell was.

I covered my mouth and nose with my sleeve, stepping further into my home. My safe place.

Not anymore.

The side wall of my studio—the wall where I had hung a personal painting of deep crimson tulips—was gone. Destroyed. In its absence, my hidden gallery of stolen greats had been exposed, and I'd bet without even turning on the lights that *Poppy Flowers* was gone.

"Tris," a choked, hoarse voice echoed through the open space, and I jerked like I'd been shot.

When I located the source of the voice, I nearly tripped over my feet in my hurry to get across the room. John knelt on the floor at the foot of my bed, his expression cold and shuttered. His hands and forearms were dark and wet, and in front of him...

"Nelson!" I screamed, collapsing to the floor beside my mentor. "Nelson! It's me, I'm here! What *happened*?" I shrieked the question at John, deep racking sobs already shaking my rib-cage. Nelson was laying in a puddle of blood, his chest a mess of wounds. He wasn't dead, though. Not yet. No... he couldn't be. Nelson was an immortal; he'd never die. Right?

"Venus," John choked out, spreading his blood-stained hands helplessly. "I'm so sorry. I never wanted this—"

"Ivy..." a weak voice sighed out of my favorite

person, and I leaned down closer to his face. He was still alive. He could be saved.

A bloodied butterfly knife lay on the carpet beside him. Was that the weapon used on him? It had to be. That was the logical connection. Someone stabbed him. My Nelson. Why?

"I'm here," I sobbed. "I'm here. Don't leave me, Nelson. Please, *please don't leave me.*"

"Tris..." John tried again, but my sole focus was on Nelson.

"Stay with me, Nelson," I begged, stroking his weathered cheek as agony ripped through my chest. "Fight it, old man. We have too much to live for. You can't leave me here alone. You promised. You swore to me, I'd never be alone again."

My whole body trembled, my skin freezing with shock. I was bleeding inside, my heart ripped to shreds as the only man who'd ever loved me unconditionally gasped for breath on my bedroom floor.

"Ivy..." his weak voice tried again, and I choked back my sobs in an attempt to hear him better. "Don't... trust..."

That was it. He ended that word on an exhale and didn't inhale again.

A scream of loss rattled through me as I sobbed over Nelson's lifeless body, a pain like I'd never known flaying me from the inside. Then a warm hand touched my back and I startled like I'd been electrocuted.

"You," I breathed with pure fury. In a flash, my grief morphed into venomous rage. "*What the fuck did you do*?!" I bellowed the accusation at John, and he just shook his head slowly.

"I'm sorry," he croaked again. "Tris... it was an accident. Nelson was never meant to get hurt."

If that wasn't a confession, I didn't know what was.

I saw red and grabbed the knife from the floor.

Rage and grief consumed me utterly, and they would be to blame for what happened next.

To Be Continued in *Restoration*

Please note: there is no current release date for Restoration. After massively overcommitting myself this first half of 2023, I need to give myself some breathing room and spend some time with my crotchgoblins.
When the manuscript is closer to completion, the release date will be updated.
I hope you will stick with me, and wait for the conclusion of John and Tris's tangled tale.

also by tate james

Madison Kate

#1 HATE

#2 LIAR

#3 FAKE

#4 KATE

#4.5 VAULT (to be read after Hades series)

Hades

#1 7th Circle

#2 Anarchy

#3 Club 22

#4 Timber

The Guild

#1 Honey Trap

#2 Dead Drop

#3 Kill Order

Valenshek Legacy

#1 Heist

#2 Forgery

#3 Restoration

Boys of Bellerose

#1 Poison Roses

#2 Dirty Truths

#3 Shattered Dreams

#4 Beautiful Thorns

The Royal Trials

#1 Imposter

#2 Seeker

#3 Heir

Kit Davenport

#1 The Vixen's Lead

#2 The Dragon's Wing

#3 The Tiger's Ambush

#4 The Viper's Nest

#5 The Crow's Murder

#6 The Alpha's Pack

Novella: The Hellhound's Legion

Box Set: Kit Davenport: The Complete Series

Dark Legacy

#1 Broken Wings

#2 Broken Trust

#3 Broken Legacy

#4 Dylan (standalone)

Royals of Arbon Academy

#1 Princess Ballot

#2 Playboy Princes

#3 Poison Throne

Hijinks Harem

#1 Elements of Mischief

#2 Elements of Ruin

#3 Elements of Desire

The Wild Hunt Motorcycle Club

#1 Dark Glitter

#2 Cruel Glamour (TBC)

#3 Torn Gossamer (TBC)

Foxfire Burning

#1 The Nine

#2 The Tail Game (TBC)

#3 TBC (TBC)

Undercover Sinners

#1 Altered By Fire

#2 Altered by Lead

#3 Altered by Pain (TBC)

Printed in Great Britain
by Amazon